VIRGINIE

VIRGINIE
her two lives

by JOHN HAWKES

CHATTO & WINDUS
THE HOGARTH PRESS
LONDON

Published in 1983 by
Chatto & Windus
The Hogarth Press
40 William IV Street
London WC2N 4DF

Parts of this book appeared originally, in
somewhat different form, in *Antaeus*, *Conjunctions*,
The Massachusetts Review and *Occident*.

British Library Cataloguing in Publication Data

Hawkes, John
Virginie, her two lives.
I. Title
813'.54[F]   PS3558.A82
ISBN 0-7011-3908-0

Printed in Great Britain by
Redwood Burn Ltd
Trowbridge, Wiltshire

Dearest Sophie
for you

My subject was, from the start, that wisp of shell-pink space shared equally, I am convinced, by the pornographic narrative (in color photographs) and the love lyric, from the troubadours, say, to the present. Thus parody, archaic tones, and an overall comic flavor were inevitable, as were sources and influences.

One episode departs from *Vive La Mariée,* by P. Quentin, and two others from Georges Bataille's *L'histoire de l'oeil.* The adaptations from the French are mine, and include the debate poem of Gaucelm Faidit, Tristran L'Hermite's seventeenth-century map of love, "Royaume d'Amour," and two of the *Chansons de Toile,* thought by some to date back to the earliest troubadours.

French though it purports to be, and conceived though it was in a reverie about de Sade, nonetheless this book contains its English-language borrowings, notably from Charlotte Brontë. Finally, 1740 was the year of de Sade's birth.

J.H.
Venasque, France

Birth was the death of her
SAMUEL BECKETT

beauty is paradox
HEIDE ZIEGLER

HER POEM

Michel

André, I will share three games of love
with you and Philippe. You may have
your choices, which you must defend.
I shall be satisfied with what remains,
then prove it superior to yours.

Three lovers love equally a lady.
When all three are in her company
she plays her games.
To one she looks with loving eye;
the hand of the next she squeezes;
as for the last, beneath the table
she presses her foot to his, speaking
with the three of them agreeably.

Now, André, by which of her games
does one of her lovers
know himself to be the lady's love?

André

Michel, I do not hesitate.
The lady's friend on whom her eye delights
is the one she loves.
The look of love comes from the heart
and cannot be shown forth but by the eye.
Holding hands is sweet
but without significance,
while the lady who presses her foot
to her lover's foot beneath the table

is teasing.
Let me be looked at lovingly
by my lady.

Philippe

I am well satisfied with your choice, André,
since you leave me foot and hand,
and hand I wanted most of all
before you spoke.
If the lady's eye looks at one lover
it looks at a crowd.
No one believes a lady's glance,
despite the look in her eye.
As for the foot, a nudging foot
nudges the nearest and in mere play,
hence is no sign of love.
But the hand! The pressure of the
ungloved hand tells all,
for its touch is deliberate
and both are bare.
I would know my lady's love
by her gentle hand.

Michel

My thanks to you, gracious Philippe,
for it was the foot I wanted.
The eye speaks not of love
but conquers friends for the lady,
and everyone has held her hand.
But foot to foot in secrecy,
shared privately,
denying the knowledge of what
everyone would know,
and preventing the amusement

it would provide:
there is love!

André

Our lady has looked into my eyes
with love!

Philippe

She has held my hand!

Michel

She has touched her little foot to mine
beneath the table!

The Lady

Trust neither eye nor foot nor hand.
I love a fourth,
who each day receives my letter.

HER JOURNALS

[1945] Maman's muteness; our household grows

Mine is an impossible story. My journal burns. My body burns. Child with no past, child forever denied her passing time, her maturation, her future realm of womanhood which justifies all our course of indentured innocence and is the golden glow that rewards the mere light of the female's purest youth: thus I lie asleep, awake, unmoving beneath Bocage on my little bed, bed from which I shall never arise, fixed as I am forever in the very center of my flaming nest, the true child poised once and for all, for a mere moment, in the throes of love while yet and always ignorant of that mysterious adult she too must have been destined to become. But I do not speak, I do not write, in all my naked silence and nearly smothered as I am between the pure rumpled surface of my small bed and the great bare body of Bocage, who lies asprawl my bed and me its occupant, now my writhing is imaginary and yet consumes the stationary body of this miniature female person.

My small hand is impressed in the thick pure flesh above Bocage's heart like a fish in stone, while my other hand is crushed and lost in the glory of his massive ribs. Thus he is heaviness itself while I am weightless; thus his great body gives solidity to the sounds of his passion, while my own small breaths of sweetness are mine alone and toneless. Thus I am as impossible a child as the story I tell, and on the stone floor beside my bed my discarded night frock burns, and the scattered copybooks of my journal burn, and in the arms of Bocage, to me, to me, comes the world of fire in all its forms: bright hearths, the briefest coals in the eyes of the kitten in my night of fire, and the sparks, the burning tongues above the forests, the very bees on fire, the ashes lofted brightly into the black heavens, the cities collapsing in meteors of light. . . .

All is aflame. I do not exist. I am only Virginie, and melting.

Outside these fiery windows, in the dark street below, five women huddle together to console each other, to despair, to cry out in helplessness to Bocage and me. Apart from them stand three stricken, half-naked men. Madame Pidou ignores her husband and Lulu and Monsieur Moreau, while Minouche with both arms binds her trembling and fatherless Déodat tight to her bosom so that his crooked boots find footholds on either side of her stomach, and his tiny fisted hands, like the hands of a bell ringer, tug and tug on strands of her hair. Clarisse, Yvonne, and Sylvie hold each other and press protectively around Minouche and her child, as if their crowding bodies might shield small Déodat from the heat of the fire above and shield themselves from the certainty that all, all is lost. The men are helpless. The women cling together in their circle of grief. Our five women, dressed for sleep, huddle together beneath the windows and the night sky that rains with fire, and their feet are bare, their hair is loose, they are becoming transparent within these sheets of light.

"Come down, Bocage," they call. "Virginie, come down!"

In the street below us, in the brighter and brighter light that each moment heralds more sharply the disappearance of Bocage and me, how can they know that within our smoking corridors and burning chambers there is in fact the would-be rescuer, who prowls forward with his bucket and feels his way hopelessly toward the naked person of Bocage and the small naked person of Virginie where they lie burning? But yes, Monsieur Malmort, old and awkward, faithful and loyal, who came to us nightly in the rain, the snow, now Monsieur Malmort has braved our fire to become our rescuer, down hot corridors and in rooms ablaze. Now I hear the sloshing bucket and dragging step of Monsieur Malmort.

But it is not to be. Should his bucket prove an eternal spring, still there are not waters enough to quench our flames. Or should he not burn alive and should he in fact burst stumbling through the livid curtain and stand ready to empty his bucket and save his Virginie, still I would make a sign to Monsieur Malmort, who then would nod, set aside his bucket, and lie down beside my burning nightdress to die in peace.

"Flee, Bocage! Flee, Virginie!"

But it shall not be.

Thus I am only the child before the woman, the insubstantial voice of the page that burns. Thus I begin and thus I end.

But see Maman! She who set the fire stands in our doorway blocking entrance to Monsieur Malmort. Holding her empty fuel tin, and indifferent to her skirts on fire, she towers in our flaming doorway in a voiceless rage, no longer conscious of the fire she ignited in her determination to destroy at last what for all this time she could not prevent or even condemn aloud in human speech. Oh, what a wonderful rage possesses our mute Maman!

Reflection and memory are usually denied to the life of the child. These are the attributes, they say, not of the child but of the adult. There is not yet time in the life of the child for dark corners or distant hills; the child lives in a world of personal invention and has not the means to engage in figurative analysis of the life she leads. But I reflect and I remember, though I am only in my eleventh year.

So I remember the bee that was buried in the hibiscus, and the way Maman used to sit beside her flower cart on her folding stool, a beautiful big waxen figure in the sunlight, while I selected this flower or that from the bright masses overflowing the cart. I curtsied to this person, who was not quite a stranger, or to that one, and proffered the flowers and accepted the payment, an egg in paper or a thin coin. I tended all the flowers in the bed of the cart; I admired them; I sprinkled on their scented surfaces water from the copper watering can with its thin neck and its handle that was a ribbon of red gold. Together we worked on our street corner beneath the old plane tree, Maman and I, and still I remember the wheels, so much taller than I, wedged motionless with the same small stones day after day, and the effort it took me to reach the selected flowers or to give them water, and the majesty of my Maman, who sat in her many skirts and shawls like an aged noblewoman on a milking stool. The plane tree cast down its shade and among the smells of the passersby and the lines of bicycles I was always able to detect the breath of the forest and the brisk self-centered call of the morning cock. To me even the city that never ended contained its brief evidence of pasture, farmyard, shady glen that I longed to know. The breath of some distant rural landscape was always there to be discovered in the dust of the city and its rusted rails, its boarded windows, its old stones.

The task of Maman was to push the cart, which I was not able to do, and then to take her place on the stool, to nod occasionally, to say a few words, to accept the greetings of those who regularly bought their flowers from Maman. Only her presence was required for the success of our enterprise, because if it was I who busied myself about the cart, exerting myself and with my beauty enticing the world to flowers, still it was Maman who had selected the jealous families of violets, the bright bunches of freesias, Maman who selected her flowers and upon whose knowledge depended the lives of all those flowers for the given day. Only the genius of Maman determined whether our day's investment should thrive or die, stay fresh or droop.

"Virginie," she would say, "you are my flower."

She was imposing. She wore only the heaviest of clothes. Rarely did she speak except to call me her flower. Never, never did she smile.

"Yes, Maman, I know," I would answer, and skip to my scissors and stiff paper, avoiding the thorns, and smell the wood smoke from the country through the fumes of a passing truck, and tremble happily in the love of my Maman.

And when I was not there? For the immeasurable time before the life of Virginie? When Maman was her solitary self, except for Bocage, who was always at the wheel of his taxi painted bottle green and black? What then of our Maman and the flowers she handled as little as possible and never raised to her nose? What then? But even I knew the answer to this question: There was no difference. She loved me. But before I was born I made no difference to Maman. Had I not been born, still she would have pushed her cart, arrived at her corner, unfolded her stool, accepted compliments just as she accepted the happy ministrations of her only daughter. And if I had ceased to be, she would have sold her flowers alone. But

I was in fact her assistant, and unessential though I was, she loved me.

The plane tree, the familiar cart, the dry pond in the hidden park, the bank clerks in shiny shoes, the shopkeeper in his apron, and the aged flower seller and her little girl: could this be the stage and these the characters of a catastrophe? Here in the sunlight while Maman and I sold flowers? Yet it was exactly here and on an ordinary day that Maman was struck down.

"Quickly, Virginie," she said. "Run for Bocage. . . ."

I turned and watched as Maman rose to her feet, lifted one hand to the side of her head, and then, with no change in expression, slowly resumed her seat on the stool. She did no more than that, and again her enormous white hands were in her lap; no passerby gave her a glance; the fierce impervious expression on her broad face was unchanged. Yet now I saw dark shadows; the breath in her mammoth chest was deeper than ever; her great brow was suddenly wet in the sun; her expressionless eyes were turned to mine.

Hurry, hurry, Virginie, I told myself, and I dropped my copper watering can, flung up my hands before my face, and ran off through crowds, through cyclists and vans, through the bright congestion of late morning, and never was I so slight, so short, so sinuous, so fleet of foot, and never could there have been a faster little messenger of doom.

When we returned, Bocage and I, surging this way and that in his bulky taxi, we found Maman still seated beside the half-empty cart, though now in the midst of a small crowd that had collected. We rumbled up, Bocage and I; we alighted; the crowd parted and Maman caught sight of Bocage and me and made again her gesture as if to stand.

"Help me, Bocage," she said. "Soon I shall be unable to move. Then, and almost as soon, I shall lose the power of speech. Now for once I shall be a passenger in your taxi. And you must be quick!"

But she was wrong (she who was the august spirit of our family and was never wrong) because, as it turned out, she first lost her power to speak and only later, at the end of the day, after we had put poor Maman in her bed, only then did she finally lose her power to move. In fact, it was while she was still seated in the back of the taxi with me at her side that Maman became, suddenly and in midsentence, unable to speak, and from that moment never spoke again.

"Bocage," she said, "I charge you to care for this child as you would a daughter, as if this little Virginie . . ."

There she stopped. We heard a honking of horns. I raised my face and stared into Maman's great face, that was glowering down at mine. Her mouth was open, her jaw was set, her eyes were violent. With my own eyes I saw a phantom hand on an invisible arm reach forth its fingers into her open mouth, and while I watched in horror, pluck from her mouth and throat the power to speak. She made a deep murmurous sound. Involuntarily I clutched her arm. Then she closed her pale lips to speech forever.

"Bocage," I cried, "Maman is mute!"

By the time we had parked in our large courtyard (long ago a château's sandy courtyard where tall horses stomped and sucked up water) and helped Maman to climb the spiraling steps of stone and walk to her bed in its bare chamber, still Maman had not lost her power to move. Even Bocage might have cowered before her great strength, though he did not.

As soon as we stretched out poor Maman, as soon as I removed the first shawl and Bocage the second, suddenly she raised her right arm and crooked it, began to swing it backward and forward before her chest and face, staring at Bocage and swinging her arm as if to drive her own son from the room at the moment he was struggling, as was I, to save her life. Oh, what modesty had our Maman!

Together Bocage and I took down from its hook Maman's sleeping gown of the heaviest lace. Together we fixed the bedclothes around her great size. With silver brush and amber comb, we prepared her thick hair to accept the nightcap without which she could not sleep. In all this ritual and flurry, and even as Maman struck out at him one final time, throughout it all Bocage remained impassive, quite impassive, as his grease-stained figure loomed within the sanctity of Maman's bare room.

"Come, Virginie," he said at last, tugging his cap on his brow and wiping his mouth on his forearm and giving hardly a glance to our stricken mother, "we have much to do."

"Shall we bring the physician?" I asked.

"No, Virginie. We have no use for a physician. She will survive. But now the household of our Maman is ours!"

Happily I placed the pitcher of water on the black wooden night table, concealed the chamber pot in its flowered cloth tent beside the bed, and drew the white curtains about her for the night.

"Come, Virginie, that is enough!"

But when the curtain was nearly drawn on the right side of Maman's bed, while my hand clutched at the cloth which was only a face's breadth from the black bedpost, then my eyes met the eyes of Maman, who was propped on pillows I myself had positioned beneath her head and shoulders, and I saw in her eyes an expression of such anger, accusation, and disdain that I caught my breath and, in the next moment, became aware of a single tear in the corner of my right eye, that bore in its glistening symmetry all I felt for what I saw. Oh, the bloodless face that would make three faces of mine! Oh, the dark dilation of the nostrils in the great flattened nose! Oh, the loathing in the eyes of my Maman!

The pure day had given way to still purer rain, and in loud torrents it filled the courtyard, washed the cobbles, shook the green clumps growing out from the walls. I did not even bother to stand beneath the roof of the shed, so relieved was I to be quit of the stone rooms in which, until this moment, I had loved Maman and appreciated my own small life. Now all was changed and my long gray frock, appropriate to the most austere of asylums, as Bocage once said, clung to my body so that I knew that were I to confront myself at that moment in a full-length glass I would see my thin body revealed through the gray cloth.

Beneath the raised hood of his green taxi, Bocage struggled with an iron instrument and poured the contents of a dented tin down a thirsting pipe; with a broad smile he allowed the hood to clang shut and wiped his hands; after a moment he turned the engine over with a crank which, as soon as the engine banged and found again its sluggish rhythm, he cast aside clattering on the wet stones. Then together we entered the old taxi, in which Bocage wiped his eyes and proudly gripped the wooden steering wheel while I knelt on the seat beside him, as usual, and saw that his body was as wet as mine.

Dusk had fallen, night beckoned, the rain pelted the roof of our warm car with such a comforting thunder that I wished to seize Bocage's arm and hold it, though I merely gripped the door handle and the handle on the dashboard and peered through the wet glass at the intersections and grilled windows and stone house fronts that passed in the dark. I opened my window slightly and raised my already wet face to the randomly intruding gusts of rain; recognized Maman's corner and her empty cart as Bocage impassively drove on without faltering or looking back. Over the portal of the third subprefecture of police flew the guardian angel, and in a grilled window a little light burned. Two men leaned on their elbows at the counter of an open café behind a curtain of rain. And there in the middle of the street a bright rat in his silver coat was rushing home.

Another zinc counter, more lights gleaming on half-filled bottles, more music. But why had we stopped? Why here? The rain made me think of watery hands rending the night. Our engine idled. Men were laughing. Then I had the answer to my question, because in front of this second café, before which we had so abruptly parked, was a young woman wearing spectacles but no protection from the rain, and it was for her that we had stopped. She stood astride a stationary bicycle which bore on its rear fender a small and rickety metal seat where sat a laughing child. The mother carried on her shoulders a khaki sack, and like her little boy was laughing, though not at the night of rain, as was her child, but at several men who were calling and beckoning her to join them in the warmth and brightness of the café. I quickened to the sight of this vulnerable and happy pair braving together the night and enjoying the rain. "Pink" and "plump" are my favorite words, and in the light from the café the little boy was plump while his mother, it seemed to me, was pink. Her skin was white, her teeth large, her smile broad, the curls against her skull a familiar shade of orange. Laughing and shaking her head in the rain, she was, I thought, an image of candor such as I had never seen.

Bocage stepped down from the taxi. The engine continued its faithful pulse. He put his hand on the child's head and spoke to the mother. Naturally I could not have known what he was saying or why he had accosted this hatless pair in the rain, or why he spoke so earnestly into the woman's ear and held the hand of the child. Yet suddenly, and without knowing what Bocage wished of the young woman, while the men made laughing comments from within the café, suddenly I knew what I wanted: I wanted the little boy and the woman to enter our taxi. Why, I could not have said, and knew only that what I wanted was in fact inspired, as I well understood when Bocage opened my door as well as the rear door of the taxi on my side, and plucked the little boy from his seat on the bicycle and thrust him into my waiting arms, and helped the woman dismount, which she did by showing us her plain naked leg, then carried the bicycle to the rack on the roof of the taxi and helped the young woman inside where she sat luxuriating on the rear seat well out of the rain. The door slammed. We began to move.

"This," said Bocage to me, pointing with his heavy chin toward the grown woman now seated in the rear of our car, and speaking as if he had known her for many times the span of my own short life, "this is Minouche. . . ."

"And in your arms," the woman answered, laughing and speaking to me as had Bocage, "is my little boy Déodat!"

So they were. I hugged Déodat and smelled his wet breath mingling with mine. Minouche began speaking at once, telling Bocage, who nodded, what she wished to eat. Thus we drove on, discovering Clarisse in a darkened doorway; Sylvie, tiny and alone, on a vast street corner and wearing tight pants and a white beret pulled low on her head; Yvonne beneath the arch of a footbridge adorned with the sculpted skulls of infants; and Madame Pidou grimacing beside her hapless husband at an iron table upon which the rain was drumming before a café long closed in the now late night. By what stroke of fate Bocage was able to discover those five women in that short a time I could not know. But Bocage approached them, strangers all, and crowded them into our taxi filling with the wet bodies of homeless women. So we returned before the light of dawn and climbed the stone steps to the various empty rooms of sublime feeling which Bocage assigned them grandly, each to each.

"Now," he said, "now we shall have our charades of love!" Laughing, joyous, perhaps momentarily aware of the sound of his voice and of her whom that great voice must awaken, swiftly, cap still on his head, swiftly he strode into the kitchen and prepared to cook.

Day to night. Night to fire. Now all the time between the onset of Maman's paralysis and tonight, this night, when she regained her power of locomotion if not of speech, and fully enshrouded us in the power of her jealous flame, time that was my longest and most consuming, now that very time is over yet never ends. Now the scattered leaves of my journal lift, settle, and crinkle at the edges and disappear like the pages of a letter of amorous desire too fierce to preserve.

But what are these slowly approaching sinister sequences? These other sensual pages which I cannot remember having written nor bear to read? My nocturnal pages which burn as brightly as my pages of the day? Oh, what other life of the little child might they reveal? Read on, for I cannot.

Thus consummation prompts prior passion. Thus I both know and do not know that in the most secret recess of my spirit my prior life exists. There too the imprinted memory of my first journal, though I cannot and shall not remember it. So I am the authoress not of one journal but of two, and am the child not of one life but of two. In darkness instead of daylight, and with my left hand instead of my right, thus unknowingly have I made a fair copy of what I once wrote, though never shall I read it as I once did. Past life, past pages still exist. Oh, spare me both!

[1740] Morning of the Noblesse

"Awake, awake, Virginie," came the strong voice of Seigneur. "Noblesse is leaving!"

I awoke as bidden, I heard his voice, I uncurled in my usual place of sleep among the ashes still faintly warm on my cold hearth, and I sat up and blinked, gray child dressed in gray, and did not need to be reminded by the deep voice calling to me in irrepressible pride down the stone corridors that this was in fact the morning when Noblesse would depart, in her moment of ultimate achievement after how many arduous hours, days, months in this rigorous household, never again to return to Seigneur and me. Never again would our Noblesse, who was once as ordinary as I remain but who was now Noblesse and the fulfillment of her name in body and spirit: never again would this rare woman, more rare than any whose bejeweled casket is her château, stand without her clothes in the center of our courtyard on an icy dawn, or know the sequence of the dogs and pig, or learn the lesson of the bees, or submit to her necessary collaboration with Père La Tour, or view at last the otherwise concealed Tapestry of Love which even I, the privileged child-accomplice of Seigneur, have yet to see. No more ice. No more straw. No more rose petals on the oval pond. No more lying nude in tears. It is over, all over, and now she is Noblesse and leaving. What a momentous morning! What a day of gold!

"Hurry," said Adèle from where she was standing at the other end of our great kitchen and so far from me that I was hardly able to hear her lofty voice. "Hurry, or you shall be late."

But I was never late, and I could not have been more obedient, more eager to share the pleasure of Seigneur and his sadness too, and bestirred myself and shook off the ashes, used the cold water, and pulled the wooden comb through my soft brown hair that framed the white heart of my face. High on our vaulted walls the windows were open and, early as it was, I smelled the frost and the pungency of distant vegetables in their beds of manure, smells that mingled with the lingering aroma of the roast like a red log prepared the night before by Adèle with the help of Père La Tour, whom Seigneur had named our Chief of Stables. I smelled the far countryside and the long gardens close at hand, and I heard the crickets in the bushy trees, the rodents snuggling in the wild grass, the horses bumping in their stalls which, according to Père La Tour, were once inhabited by monks instead of horses. I listened. I filled my lungs. I noted that as usual on mornings such as this one, designated by Seigneur as the Morning of the Noblesse, the birds were still, as if they of all creatures understood the identity between their clear song and the womanhood of her who had achieved it, and hence withheld their music so that this woman should have all the more her day.

Then I thought of the gay scene that was approaching and ran to my pair of shears as long as my arm and heavy too, and quickly made my way to the west garden where the heads of the red roses were so dark that they resembled eggs stripped into broad soft petals of purpling blood. Wearing Adèle's gloves, which were much too large for me, and wielding my enormous shears, quickly I prepared the traditional armful of formal roses. They were almost too many to carry, but I wrapped them in the traditional length of white linen sprinkled with dew and intended to prevent any accidental discomfort to Noblesse on her last morning, though Seigneur would not have been pleased had those thorns made any painful marks on his Virginie. I carried that armful of flowers and, hidden behind the long white cone and massed glistening heads of red, away I went to meet Seigneur.

"Quickly, Virginie," he said with a smile. "I have heard the horses. . . ." I noted that he was dressed as usual, in his black shoes, white stockings, ivory-colored breeches tight to thigh and tied at the knee. His curious plain gray shirt was like some sort of punitive undergarment and, un-adorned except by the black band he wore at his throat, it offered a severe contrast to the luxurious breeches with their black bows at the knees. I noted also that this morning, as on all such mornings, Seigneur was not entirely composed here in our private cloister where a large cock scratched and a white dove nestled at the base of every column. There was a small table set as usual for two, since it was here that on this special morning Seigneur and I would take our morning meal together. But Seigneur had eyes for none of it: the cock's black sickle feathers, the dark wood of the table that shone like the flesh of a dark brown horse, or the heavy silver, or the three small yellow flowers in a thin vase, or the slender columns, or the green vine that was climbing one of them.

"Come, Virginie," he said in his soft voice that was serious though he was smiling. "Now it is time."

I followed him, flower-laden child of ashes, walking behind and ador-ing the immensity of his flesh so simply and richly clothed in gray, black, and ivory, and at such a moment wondering if Noblesse would forgive past cruelties in the splendor of this day.

In the courtyard, a vast floor of sand and stone walls the color of Seigneur's shirt and breeches, all was ready. The air was brisk, the light bright, the black iron cock on the gable as lively as the living cock awaiting us in the cloister. And there was Le Baron, whom I had not seen before, astride a horse so tall and black and perfectly proportioned that only such a high degree of equestrian beauty could so contain the obvious malignancy of the beast. Its hooves were oiled, its tail was a long silken plume, its eyes were honey-colored orbs rolling in a tight black mask of anguish. Standing behind Seigneur, attempting to minimize even my shadow, both arms filled with the bulk of the flowers almost as long as I was tall, I trembled to find my eyes on a level not much higher than the knees of the horse, and to find myself helplessly staring up at the rider himself. He was fat, clothed in pale blue, his silver spurs were barbed, his leer was as suited to his fat smooth face as was fury and anguish to the face of his horse. I did not understand such a leer, but it made me wish to free my hands and raise them toward the possessor of such an exact and energetic expression. Our two handsomely groomed white whippets were standing beside Père La Tour who, with sleep in his eyes, was holding by the bridle next to a newly scrubbed stone mounting block a small black horse that was a replica of Le Baron's horse, except that the small one was in nature the obverse of the large, and silkenly tame. These were the elements of our tableau, which lacked only Noblesse herself to be complete.

Then she came to us. The dark brown studded door swung open, we did not speak, and Noblesse in black boots and skin-tight costume of velvet the color of rusty nails (strange and vivid costume created by Seigneur and executed by the nuns of Sainte Angèle) entered our midst, strode to her waiting horse and, without glancing either at Seigneur or at Père La Tour, whose eyes were lowered, swung herself briskly into the little saddle made from the smooth tender skin of a fawn.

Père La Tour moved self-consciously away and waited. I stepped forward and offered the flowers, holding them as high as I could. Noblesse leaned down. She accepted them. She did not smile. Then at last Seigneur touched me on the shoulder and took my place, smiling at Noblesse, who in every way reflected the intelligence and taste of Seigneur and, I should say, was now someone I hardly recognized in her new beauty.

"Noblesse," said Seigneur in his gentlest voice, "we wish you well. Do not forget your lessons. And surely at certain times you shall think of me personally, instruction aside."

There was silence. The cock on his gable did not move. Even the horses did not move. We waited. Noblesse glanced down at Seigneur impassively. The air was bright. Side by side the two whippets grew softly paralyzed, from their pointed muzzles to the tips of their tails.

"Never!" cried Le Baron, wheeling about his great black horse so that the smaller followed suit and became its shadow, Noblesse not at all perturbed, as rider, by this metamorphosis from motionless tableau to frieze of action, holding her flowers and maintaining her seat with surest grace, surest strength. "Never!" cried Le Baron again, turning to shout over his shoulder and down at us: "This pupil, sir, has a new master!"

Together, without a moment's loss of time, the two horses clattered dreadfully out of the courtyard. It was only when the dust subsided, and the noise, that I saw that Noblesse had flung down my flowers which the horses had trampled under their vicious hooves. Even as I stooped and wept in the silence the birds began to sing.

"So," said Seigneur in a voice that was soft and unmistakably mournful, "so, she is gone. . . ."

"Yes," I answered after a moment in a voice that I tried to infuse with cheer. "Yes, she is gone. . . ."

Seated on our severe wooden chairs, facing each other across the narrow wooden table in the cool cloister where the birds were singing, together but in a silence most unusual we ate the meal prepared by Adèle for the Morning of the Noblesse: in the center of a pure white plate a bird cooked the color of oiled brass and no larger than the palm of my hand; next to the little savory bird a white unshelled boiled egg that was as large as the bird was small, so that egg and bird were the same size; and on the other side of the egg the thigh of a young chicken which might have laid the egg, this golden thigh prepared and trimmed so as to be precisely the size of egg and little bird. On the roasted morsels were single sprigs of parsley; in the tall goblets stood water that was clear and cold from a nearby spring; in a thin vase between us were the three small yellow roses bearing yet several drops of morning dew. When we cracked our eggs in their white cups, the yolks of the eggs were a soft syrup of flowing shades of yellow and orange that were exactly matching the melting brass color of little bird, thigh of chicken, and the three roses. Ordinarily we ate this simple meal, Seigneur and I, in never-diminished appreciation and with light hearts. Today we ate in silence; in silence we noted the harmony of colors; silently we drank from our goblets of cold water. The sun was full on Seigneur's dark hair, which, as always, was tied at the nape of the neck in a black ribbon corresponding to the one around his neck and the bows at the knees of his breeches. We were hardly aware of the doves that were wooing us or the small agile birds that were singing from every place of shade or shadow in our small cool cloister where a fountain played for our benefit and the cock scratched in the gravel.

"She is gone," he said at last, and then again, "quite gone. And she was not grateful. In the end she was unable to summon from her heart that I myself made proud the slightest sign of gratitude or affection. She forgave nothing. She chose not to recall the pleasure that grew with her development and that was an obvious recompense for pain. There is no living statue more beautiful than Noblesse. And what can we say of the statue that disdains the very sculptor who brought it to life? How sad it is, Virginie. How sad."

I tilted my head to one side, and I ate a silver spoonful of boiled egg and a taste of the little bird from the tip of my three-tined silver fork. I sipped my water and kept my eyes on my plate except when I stole glances at Seigneur, whose eyes were dark and whose breath was filling his great form.

"I must tell you, Virginie," he said at last, the strength of his deep voice belying his sadness, "that the man who creates women is an artist clearly comparable to artists who create images or coerce solid matter into new and startling forms. Is it actually not more difficult to work with a woman's living flesh than to squeeze paint from tubes or chop away at blocks of stone or chunks of wood? Oh, yes, the creator of women is burdened, challenged, inspired as no ordinary artist is: how can a lifeless work of art compare with a woman? Then too, if the ordinary artist fails, he merely throws out the stone or wood, obliterates the offending image from the unresisting canvas, melts down his horse cast in iron, and begins anew. But if he who creates a woman fails? When then, Virginie, what then? He cannot toss out the body which, at last, displeases his eye; he cannot destroy the mind that proves shallow despite all his care; he cannot kiss life into artless lips; he cannot blind the eyes that finally do not shine with the light that is his. No, Virginie, there is no turning back or starting over for the one who creates women. There is no higher form of art than this, no greater responsibility. And so failure, when it comes, is more discouraging. It appears that I have failed. . . ."

What could I say? I, a mere child in gray with sticky fingertips and on my white plate a tiny bare bone so perfect and glistening that it might have been one of my own? I touched my fingertips to the stiffness of my white napkin, noted that Seigneur had eaten almost none of his meal, and kept my eyes downcast and grieved for Seigneur who himself was grieving. After all, it would have been obvious to anyone that he had failed. And what resources had poor Virginie to restore his cheer? For the moment it seemed that Seigneur had lost his interest in my fidelity. What more could I offer beyond fidelity?

"But, Virginie," he said suddenly, beginning to smile, "perhaps it is not a charge of horsemen with swords!"

"Oh, no," I cried, on the verge of happiness, "oh, no, it is not a charge of horsemen with swords!"

"After all, Virginie, how many women have I created?"

And putting down my silver fork, raising my face, cocking my head, maintaining a serious expression but feeling inwardly small waves of joy: "I believe," I said, "that the total now stands at twenty-five."

"But, Virginie, twenty-five is a goodly number of women, wouldn't you say?"

"Oh, Seigneur," I cried, "it is a life's work!"

"And one out of twenty-five is not the greatest of all possible defeats. . . ."

"Oh, it is not, Seigneur. It is not!"

"Very well. Let us finish our meal and set off to discover five more women to take the place of those recent women of whom Noblesse was the last. I suspect that Père La Tour has already prepared the horses."

"But, Seigneur," I murmured happily, "let us not mention Noblesse again."

Whereupon he nodded, smiled, crossed his great thighs and, in obvious pleasure, ate the remains of the cold meal that adorned his plate. Upon leaving the cloister where we had recovered our repose, Seigneur and I, I glanced back over my shoulder and noted that the cock had leapt upon our table and, a stately silhouette of ferocious head and clump of black sickle feathers proudly asway, was sipping with his bright beak at the mouths of the yellow roses.

"Oh, Seigneur," I cried softly, "look at the cock! I have never seen a cock with such intelligence."

"Yes, Virginie," came the gentle and now cheerful voice, "he is surely a strange bold fellow, behaving in so human a fashion. But, Virginie," said Seigneur after a pause, "when I am dying, I would like you to remind me again of our final count of created women. When the day comes, I think it will help me to have the number in mind."

I nodded gravely and then skipped ahead to the courtyard, where, exactly as Seigneur had said, our horses were waiting.

The sun was high, the sky was clear, the air was replete with that brisk appeal called by Seigneur "the breath of Virginie," a phrase that embarrassed me whenever Seigneur gave it voice, and the great chestnut horse and my own plump pony Cupidon were never more eager to cross the fields or venture together, strange winsome pair, down our country roads. Yet on that day we did not have good fortune, as if the absence of Noblesse accomplished in such an unexpected and hurtful spirit had become a dark presence on a beautiful day in late summer. She might have been saying in her voice we could not hear: Now that I am gone you shall have no more. Of course we cantered together and walked and trotted, confident that by the day's end we should have discovered one or several or even all of the women we required for Seigneur's proud enterprise. The great chestnut cast my plump and pearly Cupidon in a vast protective shadow that determined in its motion the pace of our gait, while Cupidon himself, broader than ever to my outstretched bare legs (for I, like Noblesse, was allowed to ride astride), shook his short head and snorted and lifted his stubby graceless hooves and trotted or ambled beside the chestnut down shaded aisles of tall trees or paused to sip at roadside springs. Sly, wise, sleepy, comfortable, alert, with lowered head and bouncing flanks, he carried me through that unproductive day, I with my own head level with Seigneur's knee, so that I was forever tempted to glance up at the immense black saddle, the ivory breeches covering the muscles that clove to that black saddle, and higher still to the man's pure head and shapely face from which the lofty eyes scanned all the terrain across which we journeyed and which, that day, revealed not one single woman who conformed in any way to our requirements.

We perspired, we stopped and waited at the first crossroads, we stopped at the village inn, we approached the farm well-known for its orphaned girls: nothing. We called to each other across the fields green or golden, we remounted and cantered all the way to the second crossroads, where ordinarily the coach passed but today did not. On foot we approached a clear voice behind a tall fern only to discover a thin boy as young as I. On the other side of the haystack: nothing. In the cool of the shepherd's stone hut: nothing. Inside the small and rarely frequented church beside the bank of wild roses: nothing.

By the end of the day Seigneur was once more silent; our mounts were wet; I knew that a slight discouragement was evident even on the face of Virginie, and so I tried to hide my face from Seigneur. But we were unsuccessful not only on this day but on the next, so that it was only on the third day that we found Magie, as we knew in advance she would be called, whom Seigneur took by the hand and Cupidon nuzzled. Only on the third day did we find Magie.

Down the hill we raced to what were surely cries for help. On this early dawn of our third day in search of five women each one of whom would become, eventually, a new Noblesse, Seigneur had stopped at a curve in the sloping road, listened attentively, then knowing I would follow, and with a flick of the rein and a mere touch of his heel to the chestnut's flank, proceeded down the hill at a gallop toward the scene that awaited us, as he well knew, just out of sight around the curve in the road and slope of the hill in a dell of wet trees and tender grass. Such unfortunate incidents had rewarded us before, and now in all haste we proceeded toward the vines that bind in martyrdom the feet of the night-ingale that sings so hopelessly for love, or toward the clear young face that rises to the call of the ax, or toward what would beyond doubt prove to be the site of the victim. And, yes, those were certainly cries for help, voiced in tones that came to us from the fluted throat of someone who could only be a young woman in pain. And there they were, a single towering fat horse for plowing fields, two unkempt men who looked like porcupines, and (we were not disappointed), loosely roped to a thick tree, indeed a woman and precisely the woman for whom we knew at first glance we had been searching. Her empty wagon and bay horse stood at a distance.

"Allez-vous-en!" cried Seigneur. "Allez-vous-en!"

One man, with bowed and hairy legs, left his trousers at his victim's feet and turned to flee at the sound of Seigneur's voice, while the other, more modest, managed to gather up his trousers, which were filled in the front with torn clods of earth, before he too fled, joining his companion on the rump of the brown, filth-bespattered beast which then carried the two of them to safety at a solemn trot. Together we dismounted, Seigneur and I, and together we flung aside the ropes and released the young woman who smiled through her bright tears and attempted to

27

cover her bared breasts, which Seigneur and I had both surveyed and judged to be near perfect specimens of those plump creatures that dance their happiest dance in the boudoir. Seigneur and I exchanged glances in which we conveyed to each other our mutual approval of the young woman's curling hair that was light brown tinged with pink, her ordinary oval face in which the eyes were honest and the expression suggestive of goodwill and flowing streams, and our approval of the fair breasts that had about them no lean look of arrogance, no opposite fattening with lust or despair. We judged her suitable, though she could have known nothing, of course, of the doubly good fortune that was befalling her, and while Seigneur chafed the red wrists and leaned to the young woman's smile framed in curls, and with his own dark hands assisted in restoring her body to its modest state, I proceeded to calm the small bay horse that was harnessed to the standing wagon, though the bay horse was already eating the grass with lowered head and thus sweetening the air. I noticed a blue blanket heaped on the floor of the wagon and detected movement, or so I thought, beneath the blanket. But I held my peace.

Seigneur laughed and hung the attacker's soiled and abandoned trousers from a low broken limb of the victim's tree, and in all his impressive contrast of black and ivory, and moving gently in his best of humors, for some time he whispered into the young woman's ear, lifting away her airy curls, then gently he took her hand in his and drew the young woman to a clear spot among the ferns where he, still standing, seated her within arm's length of the head of her horse and the unobtrusive figure of Virginie, whose fingers were now shyly caressing the velvet of the horse's ears.

"Now that we have effected your rescue," said Seigneur in a serious voice (but did I then see the briefest look of disappointment on the young woman's honest face?), "and now that I have explained to you this child's sense of potential womanhood, and revealed that judgment of you which I share with her, now I must explain at length the stipulations and purposes of that rare offer I now make you and which I hope that you, of your own accord and in full knowledge of the arduous life I am proposing, will accept.

"Very well," said Seigneur, glancing toward the far trees while the young woman reached out her hand and with it touched my own where it lay fondling her horse's ear. "Very well. . . . If you accept what I propose, you will be but one of five women in all, and hence will have no undue privileges, and will receive from me no favors; in the course of our days" (and here I marveled at the simple curls and the brightness of the young woman's eyes, which were more honest, more open, more inviting than any I had ever seen) "you will find me cruel, exacting, dogmatic, brutal, even from your point of view perverse, as well as inspiring. The regimen of true eroticism is strenuous. You shall be made to rise early, to practice special and occasionally painful devotions appropriate to the astounding purpose of our retreat, which is nothing less than to create of you, and the others as well, a person of true womanhood: a person, that is, indomitable in taste, speech, intelligence, and the art of love, which is to say the very art of life as only a woman brought to the fulfillment I propose can know it. There shall be punishments, both mild and to you unthinkable. You shall be trained in music as well as in the multitudinous forms of the erotic embrace; you shall know the beasts of farmyard and field" (and here my new companion gave my hand a squeeze) "and you shall be expected to write in a journal, in prose but never in verse; you shall have human intimate experience not with myself, ever, but with a partner or partners whom I shall designate; until through such long and difficult exertions devised by me, supervised by me, you shall attain at last that shape of womanhood which is art itself, and then, as Noblesse, become at last the prize of someone even higher in rank than Seigneur. Now," said Seigneur softly, but with perhaps a moment's less certainty, "do you wish, under these conditions, to join my household and attain the glories I propose?"

She smiled and reached for her horse's other ear. She raised her oval wholesome face to Seigneur, who was staring down at her in shadowed seriousness, and for the first time and in a voice as lively and limpid as her attractive self, she spoke: "I could wish for nothing more," she said. "But I must tell you that I have a child, a little boy, Dédou, who was fathered by the wind, as they say, and who is hiding there in the wagon to keep himself out of the way of my molesters. . . ." Here the child obtruded his tiny face from under the blue blanket and looked at us with eyes that were replicas of his mother's. "Don't worry, Dédou," said that young woman. "Your mother shall never forsake her little Dédou."

"But, Madame," said Seigneur, smiling and, I thought, relaxing somewhat, "the child is not at all a difficulty. We shall assign him to the tutelage of Père La Tour so that he shall grow into a stable boy of manly proportions."

"Very well," said the young woman quickly. "We are yours."

"But I must propose a final stipulation, Madame. There are five qualities I expect the person of true womanhood to possess: anger, wit, voluptuousness, delicacy, and magic. In my household these qualities become the very names of those I undertake to create as women, thusly: Colère, Bel Esprit, Volupté, Finesse, Magie. Upon entering my household, Madame, you abandon your own name and accept the name bestowed on you by me—until you become Noblesse. Should you now accept my proposal, you would immediately and henceforth become Magie."

She smiled, waited, patted Cupidon's nose. She glanced at me and at the head of Dédou, who had climbed down from the wagon into her lap. With all her goodness she looked up at Seigneur and extended her hand, which he seized. "Very well," she said again, in the flush of her good fortune. "Very well. I am Magie."

Later that day and on the next our own good fortune continued at this high pitch, so that at the farm for orphans we discovered Bel Esprit, and at the village inn, Finesse, and behind a rotting haystack poor Colère, who was much older, and in the distant asylum for women of all ages, which we visited only as a last resort, there we discovered Volupté in all her flesh. "Now," cried Seigneur, when he had found these additional women and spoken to each as he had to Magie, and at last had gathered his five new women into the waiting courtyard, "now we shall have our charades of love!"

"Back to Dédale!" he cried. "Again to Dédale!" And as our small throng rode clattering through the wide gates and into this château as into the sun itself, suddenly I was pressed all around by tall horses ridden by eager women, and in their midst was suddenly so lost and forgotten among them that now, this moment, I too was a woman, with all the prospects of a woman though I in fact had none. So for a moment I too spurred on my mount, clapped my heels to my pony's flanks as if I were a woman and he a horse, and trotted on laughing and talking to her on my left, to her on my right, knowing at last the joy of being a gay rider in a small high-spirited throng of women who were following, every one of them, the sound of the voice of the man on the chestnut horse.

Oh, but I spy myself, and distantly! and small! in flames! But where? And when? And whose voice cries "Virginie" and why do I yearn? For what? For whom? Now time's curvature and earth's as well are as taut as my own tenderness, as I stretch and yearn toward some fiery end of silence and clear space. I am transported, though I cannot be!

〖1945〗 The first charade

I have become the burning bird in a burning cage, bird and cage indistinguishable in that intensity which is the nature of fire and in which the light of the burning object becomes more real than the object disappearing in its own display. Cage to room, bird to flaming child: thus I have never been closer to extinction nor yet more real.

Now I am only a memory in my burning mind, content, for reasons I cannot hope to explain, not to languish but instead to writhe, to writhe still more, in the light, the heat, the climbing and descending ladders of fire that must lead, as now I somehow know, to darkness, the dead hearth, ashes. Why? I ask myself. Why am I able, even eager, to brave the fire in order to achieve my true destiny, which lies in ashes? Why is mine a destiny of warm ashes on a cold hearth? I cannot know. I do not know. But I am content. Now the person whose body burns on mine is moaning. "Virginie, Virginie, Virginie," moans Bocage, and happily and without answering I cling to him.

"So," said Bocage, rising at the head of the table in our hot and vaulted kitchen. "So I have something to say, as you can imagine. . . ."

The others smiled, knocked forks to glasses, knives to plates, and raised shiny eyebrows, tossed back their hair, continued to eat. But at once I placed my metal fork on the edge of my plate and folded my hands and, where I sat to the right of Monsieur Pidou, raised the small white heart of my face to survey in admiration and anticipation the figure of Bocage. He was wearing his leather taxi driver's cap and soiled apron, which he no longer bothered to remove, and puffing one of his yellow cigarettes and holding high a glass half-filled with red wine. His lips were thick, his cheeks were wet, his hands betrayed their usual signs of engine oil and flour for baking.

"Yes," he said again, taking a drink of his wine, "yes, Bocage has something to say. Are you listening? Are you paying attention?"

"Of course we are paying attention," said Madame Pidou, a mouthful of her dinner concealed inside one gleaming and protruding cheek. "What do you want?"

"Be quick about it, Bocage," said Sylvie, "because when I am finished at this table, which shall be soon enough, I am going back to my book."

"We love you, Bocage," said dear Minouche, shaking her curls and smiling at each of us in turn, "so take your time. . . ."

He nodded, stroked his jaw, drank from his glass of wine and began again.

"Well," he said, and tilted his leather cap away from his eyes, "it is simply this: for weeks now, and more than that, we have grown accustomed to each other's ways and found our niches, so to speak, in this household. For instance, we know that Madame Pidou is not averse to working in the kitchen when I insist on it; that Déodat has discovered how to paste his little drawings to our stone walls; that Sylvie enjoys her book which she is slowly reading; and so on. But where, I ask you, are the charades of love? The tins on our shelves are fewer and fewer, our supply of wine is low, Yvonne has still not shown us her sumptuous leg or Madame Pidou her bosom—forgive me, Monsieur. So the time has come. Tomorrow is Sunday, and we shall attend together the Chapelle Sainte Angèle, and then Sylvie and Yvonne and Clarisse as well shall wash our stone floors and make the beds, and all of you shall wash your hair, and Madame Pidou and I shall prepare the feast while Virginie shall fetch a large basket of flowers from the flower market. And so tomorrow night we shall be ready. Tomorrow night we shall have the first of our charades, which I myself shall orchestrate."

Bocage nodded around the table, allowed a soft smile to sit on his heavy lips, and drank the last of his wine.

"But what about Minouche?" asked Sylvie, making a clatter of knife and fork. "Why have you assigned all this work to the rest of us and given no work at all to Minouche?"

After a long pause taken, I thought, on the stage of triumph, Bocage gave his answer. "Tomorrow night," he said, "Minouche will be the principal actor. That's enough. . . ."

Did I sleep or wake in that long night? I was not sure. Perhaps I merely dreamed that Déodat was laughing in his sleep and that I crept from my bed and tiptoed to the open door through which, by the light of the street lamp beyond the window, a single lighted bulb in a casket of glass, I could see and hear Déodat laughing deeply, for so small a child, in the crook of Minouche's arm, though both were sleeping. Perhaps I dreamed as well that I crept to Sylvie's room and listened patiently, heard nothing, then crept to the room of Monsieur and Madame Pidou, whose age had only enhanced her beauty, and heard the poor man weeping in his nightshirt, the laughing of the child oddly reversed in the weeping of the man, and then crept away to the room of my Maman, where I found her staring at me through the darkness. Did I dream the darkness that wears soft the stone, like sheep in the narrow passages of a labyrinth? (The darkness that changes in density and moves, magnifies the smallest sound, and lies so curiously alive yet unsatisfying between the sleeper and all the activity he awaits with the sun.) In my sleep I was inert, certainly, yet impatient too, tossing or lying still, stealing from room to room as if to find in the dreams of Yvonne or in the sounds of Bocage's breathing a sign or token of what I did not know was to come. I was not afraid of Maman; I rolled over carefully, so as not to disarrange my bed; I heard a far bell in the night, and felt a tingling throughout my body, and somehow knew that even in my sleep I was envying Déodat for having Minouche to hold him in the crook of her arm when he laughed or sighed. Oh, it was night, when everything and nothing happens, and I longed for the dawn though for me it was only the tone rather than the content of what Bocage had promised us that drew me on.

Then the first light, orange in color and lying full in my face, brought me suddenly awake, though of course I could not remember why I had yearned for morning throughout the night, could recall no reason for my happiness. Sylvie began complaining in a high voice that Clarisse had awakened her too soon, and Bocage began yawning, and it was Sunday morning, I knew, and none too early to rush to the flower market, holding Déodat with one hand and in my other carrying the basket that was like a curved shield upon which would lie the bunch of long-stemmed flowers. So Déodat and I procured the flowers, bells rang, our entire household, except for Maman, joined a small congregation in the Chapelle Sainte Angèle. Later, much later, we feasted, as Bocage had promised. The stones became perfumed with their own cleanliness. Our heads of hair, when we dried them in the open windows (except for Sylvie, who sat alone in the courtyard), grew soft and airy in the sun, while Bocage whistled in the kitchen, and the day waned.

"Costumes for the actors," called Bocage, standing in our vaulted salon before the hearth so large that he could enter it with the merest stoop. He too had bathed and was bareheaded and gave off a fresh strong smell of lime, and in his heavy face there were signs of eagerness. We gathered about him, among the shadows cooling on the stone floor, and to each of our five grown women Bocage presented a paper sack bearing her name carefully penciled in a blunt hand. Even Clarisse, young woman of few words, and thin, angular, with her short hair and narrow face as appealing and as deliberately undemonstrative as that of a handsome youth disguising his shyness, even Clarisse joined with the others, reached out her hand, received her own paper sack. And Yvonne, whose smile was as comforting as her great knees, she too pressed into the group and held out her hand, causing Madame Pidou to say: "Don't push, Yvonne. There is something for everyone, as you can see." Except, I thought to myself, that there is no paper sack for Virginie. Nothing at all for me to open and exclaim over in unexpected pleasure. But then, at the first sight of what Bocage had purchased for his five women, as he called them, I was so surprised and pleased that I forgot about myself, as usual, and again found all my happiness in that of others.

"How foolish!" cried Sylvie, having ripped open her sack with typical impatience. "Do you think I could ever wear such foolishness? Sylvie," she cried, "Sylvie does not wear the frilly underpants!"

The sacks were torn open, the pieces of bright cloth were raised on high and everyone, Sylvie excepted, held the furry or tasseled bits of underclothing, for such they were, against their bodies. I too might have tied about myself with joy such butterflies or sprightly flowers.

"Sylvie," said Clarisse, who hardly spoke and never smiled, "you have no sense of humor. You are not clever. As for me, I shall wear this costume or not, as I wish." Whereupon she stuffed her set of intimate apparel back into its sack and, approaching Bocage, and keeping her face expressionless, extended her free hand and gave his arm a squeeze.

"Exactly so," murmured Madame Pidou. "You are a person without much appreciation, Sylvie. Do you not realize that these garments are sewn of silk and satin? The cache-sexe speaks eloquently of what it hides."

"Imagine how we shall entertain each other," said dear Minouche, "when we are all standing together nude except for these little dazzling things. What games we shall invent and play!"

"But I will not fit!" cried Yvonne and they all laughed, while I saw that on the contrary, her body, large as it was, was not at all too large to be contained in the elasticity of the ribbons and fringes she was now stretching comically across her bold curves. And how like Bocage, I thought, to choose an ensemble in the color most appropriate to each wearer: red for Yvonne, orange for Minouche, white for Sylvie, violet for Clarisse, and then the shiniest and richest black for Madame Pidou! How strongly it all appealed to a fanciful mind! How strongly I found myself yearning, suddenly, to see them in their costumes, now, this moment, garbed like swimmers on a beach with no ocean or like sleepers in scented rooms without beds.

"Soon," said Bocage, rolling down his sleeves and touching my shoulder, "soon, and Monsieur Pidou and me excluded, it will be time to procure the indispensable element: men."

He laughed, there was mock clapping, while Bocage winked at Monsieur Pidou, from whose two hands his wife, rather gently I thought, removed her black gifts, which he too, apparently, had wished to inspect. The day waned, and our vast and vaulted salon was filled with the smells of soap and departed sun, and Madame Pidou breathed deeply at an open window and Bocage brought forth his small radio with its bent aerial and dull black finish. He lit the fire he had set on the mammoth hearth, though it was summer, and surveyed the long stone room and its recessed windows, the rude beams overhead, the fat and shabby couch that faced the hearth, the chairs he had arranged near a squat table bearing dusty bottles of red wine and chunky glasses.

Then Sylvie spoke, proudly and to herself. "Sylvie is not going to like this party," she said. "I am sure of it."

Over all the city lay the hood of night, and in this darkness, deeper than ever, the stars shone fiercely and the street lamps, so widely spaced, were now dim, now incandescent, but clearer and more lonely than on our former nights of driving these same avenues. I knelt on the seat beside Bocage, we traveled at a pace so slow that I could hear the turning of the tires and, through the window which I had lowered, the rattling of one dark rear fender like a broken wing that shuddered when finally we drifted to a stop at the foot of a small high-crested bridge that spanned one of the narrow tributaries of the dank canal. Here the air was offensive, the water deep, one of the balustrades of the clearly unused bridge had long crumbled away and fallen beneath the dark waters. But on the other low balustrade and at the top of the bridge, the squat misshapen figure of a man was leaning.

"One moment, Virginie," whispered Bocage, "only a moment. . . ."

With careful steps Bocage ascended the short way up the bridge; I saw his tall silhouette join the short round silhouette of the leaning man. A match flared, and even from where I waited I smelled the thin smoke. They smoked their cigarettes, Bocage and the man, who appeared to consist entirely of shoulders and belly and to have no head, and they smoked another pair of cigarettes before strolling off the bridge and joining me. Both were laughing when they reached the taxi, arm in arm, cigarettes aglow, and Bocage opened the rear door and held it open while Monsieur Moreau, as he was named, leaned down and blundered with all his weight into the comfort and security of our old machine.

"It is quite true," he said, apparently for the second or third time, laughing and dropping the remains of his cigarette out the window in a display of sparks. "I had no thought of suicide. Not at all," he said, slapping a thigh that sounded wet beneath the blow. "It's merely that that little bridge is my private place, and unlighted, as you. saw. A perfect spot for musing when one is bored. And I am bored all the time. So it was boredom, you see, and not suicide. But your invitation is interesting, nonetheless. . . . And this," he said, leaning forward suddenly, and touching me on my shoulder and then my neck, "and this is Virginie? Your sister? What a peculiar child!"

So it was that initially I found myself uncomfortable with Monsieur Moreau, and only later that night, and on nights to come, discovered in him those soft and lively qualities that aroused my compassion and gave me happiness. For now, he did nothing to allay the fears with which I had begun this drive.

"Well," said Bocage, laughing and clutching the wooden wheel, "I had my suspicions about you, Moreau. You can understand. But if I can't be your rescuer, at least I'll relieve your boredom. But look there," he said, pointing off into the darkness. "There is just the fellow to complete our picture."

With these words and the halting of the taxi, and the hurrying way Bocage and Monsieur Moreau rushed off leaving me alone, my spirits fell still further, as if in a context of strangers Bocage himself had become a stranger, preoccupied with thoughts appropriate to men but not to me. I frowned. I could see nothing. From far in the darkness I heard the sounds of laughter, thick laughter, and the clink of glasses and a deep voice telling, I supposed, an amusing story. I wished I were lying in bed or helping dear Minouche to bathe. That I had surely been forgotten I could not deny, and now I wondered how long I should have to sit alone in the darkness before Bocage remembered that I awaited his return and that tonight of all nights he was obligated (in ways known only to himself) to dear Minouche and Sylvie and Clarisse and Yvonne and Madame Pidou.

But voices? Three voices? And drawing closer? Yes, distinctly I heard the voice of Bocage, and suddenly out of the darkness they came, Bocage and Monsieur Moreau helping between them a man who was taller than Bocage and broader, and was wielding in one massive hand a pair of wooden crutches which he carried rather than used because of the support Bocage and Monsieur Moreau were giving him with their own arms. There had been no change in the light. Darkness prevailed. Yet I was able to see the dirty cast on the foot and ankle, the vivid crutches, the coarse handsome mouth, and Bocage and Monsieur Moreau both voluble and eager to bear the tall man's weight.

"Virginie," cried Bocage from what I took to be their circle of light, "is not our Lulu splendid?"

Dropping his crutches, lunging forward out of the helpful arms of his companions, and wrenching open my door and sweeping me into his own strong arms. "And this is she?" the man known as Lulu cried. "This is Virginie? Your sister? Well, Bocage, she is my sister too!"

I smelled the oil in his hair, felt myself clasped in his arms, held high, hugged and hugged again, and so in an instant I was transported from gloom to pleasure, from uneasiness to happy trust. "Oh, she is beautiful, Bocage, beautiful indeed! Just the sister for a fighter like me!"

Fighter, I thought. All the more reason why I should gasp and hold him around the neck and over his shoulder murmur to Bocage: "Oh, yes, he is splendid, just as you say. . . ."

Tumbling (all four of us) into the taxi and hastening away on those cobbled streets so dimly lit by our weak and yellow headlamps, and leaning on corners, accelerating down deserted avenues, thus again we reached our courtyard and mounted the spiral staircase and all together entered the vaulted room where waited the fire, couch, bottles of wine and, all alone, Minouche.

It was then that Lulu, while I watched, gave way to that habit which, in days to come, I never ceased to find startling: he simply raised his arms slowly, grandly, and allowed the crutches to slip from his armpits and fall clattering in whatever crooked direction they chose to take. Down went the crutches, out went his arms, and Minouche (for whom this pantomime was enacted) was at his side, caught him, and helped him, as he knew she would, to reach the broad and broken couch where down he sprawled with our Minouche beside him.

"Bravo!" cried Bocage. "Bravo!" From a dusty cupboard he brought forth a cracked tray with amber-colored bottle and little glasses, while Monsieur Moreau sat himself uncomfortably on a straight-backed chair. Gone was the pretended enthusiasm with which Monsieur Moreau had entered Bocage's taxi. Now, wearing his suit of damp material, with hands clasped and feet together, he stared at Minouche and Lulu clutching each other on the couch as if he could not bear the sight of them yet could not bear to close his eyes or look away.

Bocage and the cognac, for so it was, and Monsieur Moreau's discomfort and Bocage's secret pleasure, which now I recognized, and most of all Lulu's grand gesture: suddenly I understood it all, because all of it was for Minouche, who had indeed inspired in her visitors fear and adulation both. Minouche had bathed, so much was evident in her soft white skin and oval face; the flames of the fire were in her hair as well; and her steel-rimmed spectacles but disarmed the more the brown eyes that could only belong to a face as ingenuous as hers. Her feet were bare, her smile wide. Stuck into her orange curls was a red rose. But in our absence, and most important of all, Minouche had dressed herself deliberately for this occasion: from the hips down she was clothed in her everyday pair of tight and faded khaki pants, but her lovely torso was entirely naked and somewhat glistening except for that portion of the orange costume which she had decided to wear and which, a mere slight orange wired halter on her chest, now plumped up her breasts and bared the rounded tops and buds as well. Tight pants, tight and fluffy halter making naked the very flesh it might have concealed, and laughing young woman unselfconsciously asprawl beside Lulu on the sinking couch: no wonder those men could not look elsewhere except at dear Minouche. Her every movement, even as she sat, conveyed the weight and shape of the legs and hips contained in the tight pants; every movement intensified the fulsomeness of the upper body, bare but for its trace of color. From where I sat I smelled daylight in the tight pants and nighttime powder muting the white skin.

"Lulu speaks!" cried the injured man, clutching Minouche's far shoulder with a rough hand. "Tonight," he cried, "this creature is mine! To defend my declaration," he cried, "I would fight a roomful of men as big as Bocage, there. Broken foot and ankle notwithstanding, still I would beat them all to defend my right! You know it now," he said more softly, "I am a fighter! And I am attracted," he murmured finally, "to this girl, who is mine!"

What a fine speech, I thought to myself, where I sat on my hassock and pressed my knees together and pulled the bottom of my gray skirt to the floor, and how clever of Minouche to prepare herself as she had, since

Lulu was in every way her match, thanks to his sleeveless black-and-white-striped shirt that clung to his chest and left exposed his muscled arms, and thanks to the green tattoos that covered entirely those massive arms, and thanks to the long tight sailor pants so darkly blue in color as to be nearly black. Even the filthy cast on foot and ankle, by enlarging or clubbing that enormous foot, only exaggerated the vast vigor of the rest of him. Perversely, I thought, and smiled to myself, Lulu's crude cast had an effect on his body that was not unlike the effect of Minouche's orange halter on hers. Yes, I thought, Lulu was worthy of Minouche.

"Oh," Minouche said then in her normal speaking voice, that was .the sound of a cheerful disposition and good health, "oh, so you are a fighter, Lulu? I like that word."

She sipped from her golden glass; Lulu emptied his; Monsieur Moreau, whom Minouche was watching unobserved except by me, was holding his untouched glass in his small and tapering white hands. Now Bocage was playing lively music on his radio and taking an interest, or so it appeared, in the flowers I had placed about the room in all the old jars and crocks I could find. I wondered only in passing about Sylvie, Clarisse, Yvonne, and Madame Pidou, who were noticeably absent and silent as well, and only in passing about Monsieur Pidou, who had not dared to leave his hiding place in the kitchen, and about Déodat. And Maman's door? Wide open, I knew, yet I did not care.

"Fighter?" Lulu laughed. "Yes, it's a good word. And if I had the use of both feet, I would stand up right now and give you a demonstration of shadow boxing that would make you catch your breath in your throat. In fact," he said then, drinking down another glass and beginning to struggle free from his seat beside Minouche, "perhaps I shall just give you my demonstration anyway."

"But that's not necessary," said Minouche, restraining him and running her fingers over the glorious green scenes on his arm. "I can see by your tattoos that you are a splendid fighter. I can well imagine you dancing and punching in the boxing ring, your muscles gleaming and your gloved fist striking the face of your poor opponent." Then turning her lips and eyes away from Lulu's forearm, and glancing at the perspiring man seated on the hard chair created as if for a child: "And what about you, Monsieur Moreau?" she asked. "Why are you seated so uncomfortably and so far away? Come here to Minouche. . . ."

The radio was loud, the long vaulted room smelled of the fire and living flowers, and Lulu was drinking yet another glass of cognac while Minouche continued to look at Monsieur Moreau and pat the thick dusty cushion at her side.

"Oh, no," said Monsieur Moreau. "I won't stay. A mere moment for my boredom. I am a widower, you see, and all I have in the world is my daughter. Yet I find my daughter so boring that I can't even keep her name in my mind."

"Well," said Minouche, "I shall hear about your child, Monsieur Moreau. Now come and sit by me. I want to have Lulu on one side of me and you on the other. I want to be the pink slice of meat in the sandwich!"

"Do what she says, Moreau," murmured Lulu, who had drunk a considerable quantity of cognac and was now attempting unsuccessfully to roll himself onto his hip. "Don't talk to me about boredom. We're not interested in your boredom. Not a bit."

"Yes," said Minouche softly, and sat up, shook her curls, held out a hand to Monsieur Moreau so that he began to rise. "Come sit close to me, Monsieur Moreau."

Oh, but of course, I thought to myself quite suddenly, and concentrated with all my energy on the timid footsteps Monsieur Moreau was taking, of course this poor man with his fat body and small and pointed hands and feet deserved as much as Lulu or even more, I thought, to have the pleasure of pressing himself against Minouche, who was now rubbing Lulu's chest but beckoning toward Monsieur Moreau with her warm eyes and round and flashing spectacles. But perhaps Minouche had really cared all along not for Lulu but for Monsieur Moreau. Could she now be kissing the mouth tattooed in green ink on Lulu's forearm, I asked myself, only in secret appeal to Monsieur Moreau, who had at last taken his place beside Minouche in the light of the fire? What then of my earlier allegiance to the handsome Lulu? At that moment, and stretching my gray gown still tighter to my body where I was rocking to and fro on my stolid hassock, and with my chin on my knees and my lips compressed, I realized that Minouche was far more important to me than either man, and quite admired the way she demonstrated her affections for the one while engaging the other in mere play. I hugged myself stock-still and ceased my rocking when Minouche drew her face away from the green lips on Lulu's arm and touched her own soft lips to the plump cheek of Monsieur Moreau. Then I sighed and rocked once more as Minouche laid back her head and laughed and held hands with both Lulu and Monsieur Moreau.

"Yes," said Lulu, speaking to all of us and somewhat thickly in the pause between two songs on Bocage's radio. "Yes, tonight this young woman belongs to me, no matter who she sits with or whose cheek she kisses. But I must tell you," he continued, now speaking directly to Minouche, "that I am hard to please. After all, there's not much I haven't experienced in the way of women."

"So," murmured Minouche, "our Lulu is a man who wants new tricks?"

"I'm only giving you a warning hint. Just think of the women who have clamored for me after my victories. There's not a type I haven't known or a way of taking a woman I haven't tried. Being a fighter is my first advantage; being a good one is my second; being tall, strong, and glamorous in all my battered features is the final blow that's made me irresistible since my earliest manhood."

"Lulu," said Minouche, interrupting him and at the same time unbuttoning one button on Monsieur Moreau's soiled shirt, looking at Monsieur Moreau while speaking to Lulu, "what a challenge you are. How can an ordinary girl compete with the hordes who have followed you from match to match? Yes, I see you are a serious challenge. I'm sure that Monsieur Moreau will agree that there's something of the devil in you, Lulu. How can I possibly appease your devil?"

"It will not be easy, I assure you. . . . ."

"Well, Monsieur Moreau," said Minouche in her most natural voice, "what do you think: shall I try? Shall I risk the wrath of Lulu's devil? risk humiliating myself amongst the shadows of all his past admirers? Really, Monsieur Moreau, I need your advice."

"What can he know," said Lulu, drinking again. "He's only a dull man bored by his own child."

"Monsieur Moreau knows more than you think."

"I can only say you've got a job on your hands," said Lulu. "A tough job."

"Lulu," said dear Minouche, rubbing her cheek against the green lips on his shoulder, and thrusting her hand into the tightness of Monsieur Moreau's shirt, "I have just the thing for you. The steaming exercise. Surely that's what he needs, Monsieur Moreau. Don't you agree?"

Bocage stopped rearranging my flowers and stood still. Again I stopped my rocking and held my chin rigidly against my knees. For some reason I found myself enumerating Lulu's tattoos: the mouth, the anchor, the dancing girl, the serpent coiling around his entire arm, the rose on a short stem containing one giant thorn, the two women rising in a soft balloon and holding aloft a banner that bore the words Bon Voyage. We waited, Bocage and I, and all the artistic array on Lulu's bare arms was not enough to deflect my attention from Lulu himself in his handsome black arrogance or from Monsieur Moreau with his heavy shoulders and disproportionately small head and face on which I saw the faintest expression of hope in the midst of bafflement and fear, or most of all from Minouche herself who seemed to be swelling imperceptibly inside her skin. The rose in her hair was like a pocket of flame; her spectacles were flashing; with her left hand she returned Lulu's enormous hand to his lap. What would she do, I asked myself, this Minouche whose body strained inside her pants and whose breasts, supported only on their undersides, were so pumped up with life?

"Virginie," she called in a breath of pure amusement, "fetch the kettle. We are going to introduce Lulu to the raptures of steam!"

With those few words she increased my anxiety yet broke the spell, and gathering up my skirts and stepping forward, I promptly seized the handle (how hot it was to the touch!) of the iron pot on the hearth and carried it as quickly as possible to the kitchen, where I held it interminably under the trickling stream of the small and crooked spigot and waited, conscious of Monsieur Pidou who, in a corner behind my back, was holding Déodat on his knee and humming. Then away I went, stumbling with my wet and heavy pot which I finally hung on the great hook that was like an iron jaw above the flames. The scene that greeted my return was rife with paradox: Lulu all but lifeless on the couch; Monsieur Moreau breathing heavily, watching my every move, and making an attempt to close the shirt front which Minouche had opened; and between the two men the empty space still bearing, I knew, the hot impression that was like a handprint in a dish of wax. As for Minouche, no longer was she the repository of her own unselfconscious languor. Instead she was on her feet and laughing and, with a great pair of shears, was cutting into long strips various scraps of flannel that filled the basket resting beside her feet. She held high the cloth, took aim with the shears, and squinting in girlish pleasure cut the cloth into broad strips which she dropped, while stooping and reaching for still more flannel to subject to her shears. At her feet, and along with the increasing mound of soft cloth, lay a heap of flower heads which she had apparently pulled from their stems the moment I had left the room.

The pot began to boil. Minouche sat back on her heels and, with a loud clatter, dropped the shears.

"Beware, Minouche," said Bocage in a soft and serious voice. "Be careful. We don't want to lose his patronage. . . ."

"But, Bocage," she answered, "Lulu is going to enjoy his punishment!"

The radio was loud. The fire was at its brightest pitch. The hour was late and yet I had no need for sleep. Having deposited the boiling pot within Minouche's reach, I returned to my hassock, and leaning this way and that in my attempts to watch Minouche's every move, suddenly I understood that my dear sweet Minouche was a priestess readying herself for a performance which I longed to see.

How deft she was! How quick in her preparation! Monsieur Moreau was leaning forward, as was I, as was Bocage, to see.

"Now," said Minouche, "in go the roses." As she spoke she scooped up handfuls of the effulgent flowers and flung them into the cauldron. "And now," she said, "the bandages." These too she thrust into the boiling pot. "And now I stir my broth," she said, working into the steaming mass the head of the wooden spoon I had also fetched from the kitchen. "And now," she said, "we are ready."

Bocage took a step closer. I ceased my rocking. Monsieur Moreau was beginning to assume an expression of the most painful eagerness, and I was well aware of the artificial tooth in the front of his mouth and the black hair visible in his open shirt.

"Oh, the endless buttons of sailor pants!" murmured Minouche, who was now kneeling, now squatting between Lulu's legs and unbuttoning each black button on the front of his trousers as though picking bright berries from their prickly clumps.

I watched the ministrations of Minouche's quick and kindly hands. I knew that I had been forgotten for the second time this night. I felt all the anxiety of the child who has not the privileges of the adult. Yet I stayed where I was and remained silent, breathing only in the smallest breaths and marveling at Minouche's bright and lively naked back and her mysterious movements.

But what exactly was she doing? Even as I asked the question there came to me an answer that was not entirely wrong. In the same instant, that is, I had seen Minouche tugging open the front of Lulu's pants and had noted, all too briefly, my first sight of what looked like a short white piece of rubber hosing beneath the hood of Bocage's taxi, and which I associated immediately with Bocage and "going to the back of the garden," as he called it, though I had never seen him thus engaged. This was precisely the moment that Lulu began to moan, as might a man in deep fever, while, simultaneously, the hose between his legs changed color, became enlarged and, so tenderly encouraged by the touch of Minouche's fingers, swayed upright from the sunken loins.

"And now, Lulu," whispered Minouche, "the steam!"

Lulu moaned. Monsieur Moreau remained indifferent to the dryness of his open mouth. Bocage kept silent and tugged on his cap.

Strip after steaming strip Minouche pulled from the cauldron and, with circular movements, she swathed Lulu's hose in the flannel which was hot and wet and smelling of the oil of the roses that had already decomposed. She laughed, our dear Minouche, as she pinched between thumb and first finger each strip of cloth and held it high before wrapping it round and round what now resembled, I thought, a miniature mummy which, except for the bare head, was swaddled wetly in white. The poor creature was, I saw, so thickly bandaged that it could no longer sway. As for me, the forgotten observer, I was well aware that I was confused but filled with a new clarity of mind; that a welcome terror was roaring inside my head; that I too was a fated yet willing participant in a charade that had summoned forth all of Lulu's being and focused it for us all to see. There it was: large and helpless in its bed of steam. My own being leapt forward from the cage of myself. The two female balloonists were waving, and the moist green tattooed mouth was gaping, while Lulu's own real mouth was opening in a cry we could not hear.

But oh, the naked night broke into fragments of activity like a small bird shot apart in the sky. Minouche stood up, and with little pulls and tugs removed her tight pants, and seizing Monsieur Moreau by the hand, drew him firmly from the room. Lulu rolled over like a ship capsizing. From the kitchen came Monsieur Pidou, bearing Déodat on his shoulders. Suddenly, at the far end of the room and in the open doorway we rarely used, appeared a small and shabby man who carried in a strong sack three battered unlabeled tin cans. Then, oh, then, Clarisse and Sylvie and Yvonne and Madame Pidou came into the firelight laughing and wearing only the halters like Minouche's and the tight and tasseled underpants to match. Together they surrounded the stooping man. Together they swarmed upon him and concealed him among their bodies that were all but bare.

"Monsieur Malmort," I heard the intruder say in self-introduction. "Only Malmort, a worn and aged man with an unfortunate name. . . ."

The night ends in smoke and darkness in which I keep watch over the sleeping figure of poor Lulu, who might have been chiseled from the portico of a blackened church. In this way I spend the night of our first charade of love.

〖1740〗 An amorous bestiary

As the bird cares for its nest so I cared for my hearth. I banked the coals, I swept its vast warm floor with a broom of twigs as long as I was tall, and I shoveled out the ashes with an iron shovel I considered to be my own, stooping and pushing and scraping my shovel like someone tending the hot lair of an unappeasable beast. As for the iron pots great and small that hung from hooks and chains like ranks of bells in a tower, these I removed one by one, systematically, with considerable effort, and scoured inside and out at the stone trough in Adèle's kitchen, and then one by one replaced where each belonged, so that my hearth was always filled with scrubbed iron vessels that I knew by touch as well as sight. My hearth was so large that I could move about within it freely, at will, avoiding the hanging pots and applying to both chains and pots the slightest caress of my fingertips. But mine was not a life confined to the hearth; no one exiled me to sleep in the place where the fire roared and the flames died. I was not a captive relegated to the blackened pit, the lowliest and ugliest and most frightening chamber of the château, since I myself chose to inhabit that enormous hearth. Precisely for the sake of paradox I became the keeper of the vault of fire. The very paradox of child and hearth, small girl and revolving spit, thin creature and arch of stone, was exactly what provided my sense of self and gave me pleasure. Chosen freely, the hot dungeon became for me the cell of my contented solitude, and I wished for no other. Around the hearth I worked for my own amusement; inside the hearth I slept in the warmth and comfort of the forest turned to ashes, the tree to smoke, the ringing ax, the sledge loaded with wet logs, the music of the invisible bird or hidden spring, the charred beef brought to table. Well I knew that all my associations of the hearth signaled, for me, the presence of Seigneur. It was he I tended in sleep or in my waking hours. It was he who was my secret reason for loving the hearth.

Though womanhood was not for me, sometimes I thought that everything Seigneur imparted to Magie and to Finesse, Volupté and Colère and Bel Esprit, he was imparting, actually, to me. Sometimes I thought that I, the child without past or future, was actually the object of his most severe and ardent interest. No wonder I was the constant shadow on his black or roaring hearth. Not a single person could know what I was thinking, not even he. But inevitably my thoughts gave rise to but one word: fidelity. No woman who passed through our château could claim that word. Fidelity.

I awoke quickly, vividly, silently, of my own accord. I shivered as I usually did upon arising, for the dead hearth in the morning never failed to provide me with the brief thrill of all that was gone, and then I crept forth and shook myself, performed my ablutions, and seated on a high stool ate my buttered bread and drank my spring water from the stone crock. The air was cool, the day barely begun, the entire château lay around me like a labyrinth that only I might explore. Straight-backed on my stool, drinking and eating, I experienced a moment of that curious pride when she who is assumed to have no consciousness knows, for one instant, that she herself is the vessel brimming with all the world for whom, this instant, she does not exist. Hence I saw them all in the mirror that was myself: Adèle in her nightcap, Finesse and Colère and Volupté and little Bel Esprit and dear Magie all sleeping unclothed but under heavy sheets in their separate cells that were more austere and more sensuous than I can say, and Père La Tour who would soon be polishing his saddles, and Dédou alone and whimpering in the hay, and of course Seigneur, the first to rise, the last to sleep, now wearing only his ivory-colored breeches so that had the vision been actual and reflected in a real glass, I would not have looked.

I drank, I took a bite of my bread, with my other hand I touched the thick and bloodstained wooden surface, chopped and scarred, of the table that stretched away to my left and right so far that it might have provided fifty horsemen places at which to eat. But I sat alone and in the center of the single ray of light that came down thick and broad, like the blade of a weapon, through the high and vaulted window. Rivers were running within me, I tasted milk and grass. I allowed myself another thought of Seigneur tying the black bows at his knees, and donning his strange collarless and tight-fitting shirt. I saw the dovecote inhabited by cooing birds all of which were white except for a single male, dark purple and preening. I saw the soft nose of Cupidon poking and sniffing above the edge of the door to his stall. There I saw the sundial in the shape of the sun's face on a high sand-colored wall, and there the iron cock of the weathervane pointing in the soft breeze and the real cock strutting in regal loneliness in the cloister. Poplars and cool fields stretched away from us in all directions and it was dawn, I was awake, Seigneur was fully clothed at last. The doves made their sounds of burbling water and wood twisting in wood. I sat in the light and around me lay a labyrinth of light. What was it all if not the very domain of my purity?

But then the still morning erupted into all the fragments of its actuality, and I said good morning to Adèle, noting as usual the sleep in her eyes and the persistence of the little nutlike mole at the edge of her mouth, and carried to Seigneur his black coffee in its large white china cup that was molded inside a second skin of silver, and to each of our five new women I carried dates and bread and coffee and a single flower lying wet and freshly cut on each tray. As I went down the cool corridors of our labyrinth, and tapped on the narrow wooden doors that bore in bas-relief a sheep or sweeping hawk or head of a goat, and bid good morning to Finesse, Colère, Magie, Volupté, or little Bel Esprit, admiring anew each woman now unadorned and barefooted and wearing only the single ankle-length gown of her own color (violet, black, orange, red, and finally white, respectively), as I the morning's envoy went thus from room to room and brought to all of them this beginning of the new day, even then I had in the back of my mind two questions, as I always did: Who shall she be? What shall she be made to do?

I use the word "labyrinth" deliberately. It was Seigneur who taught me long ago the meaning of that word.

So inside the labyrinth I greeted Finesse and Colère and dear Magie and the rest, and carried my trays and collected them, and experienced once again the clarity of my morning perceptions, so that the very veins in the leaves of all the greenery in the enormous stone pots lining the corridors reached my eye as if in magnification, all those tiny veins as hard and sparse as the shining legs of little birds. I saw the sad expression on the face of a porcelain woman in a stone niche; I was aware of the occasional high-backed and empty chair that I came upon around a corner; I smelled the sunlight within our confines of warm stone. Yet even inside the labyrinth, seeing only what was before my hand or hanging on slender chains from the high ceiling above me, still I also saw our château as if from without and afar: the gates bearing their incomplete designs of ivy, the walls the color of dark sand, in one corner the single low tower that was plump to my eye and roofed in its gently sloping cone of black slate which, from near or far, looked always wet as in some cool clear shower of rain just past. Who but I could know what occurred both within and without? And all the while I carried in the back of my mind those small morsels of the morning that were mine alone: Who shall she be? What shall she be made to do?

Then through the noise of morning, a clacking of dishes and sighing of looms and neighing of horses and the laughter of a woman who might have been Magie, through all this I heard distinctly the cold tinkle of the bell in our chapel that was situated beyond the stables and which at this moment would be entirely empty, I knew, except for Seigneur. And so it was, when I arrived, although my anticipation had been too pure, too strong, investing in that scene an excessive emptiness, since when I arrived at the call of his bell, I found Seigneur not entirely alone but accompanied by the two whippets quivering on his either side in all their whiteness and uncertainty. But for the man and the two tall dogs there was nothing else in this white chapel which, before my time if not Seigneur's, might well have been furnished with prie-dieux for kneeling penitents, and golden icons, and an altar decorated with a single vast bouquet of dripping gladioli gathered by some humble retainer from our seas of those stately flowers. Now there was nothing except man, dogs, and on the air a trace of resin as if from some distant ceremonial of grief or joy.

"Good morning, Virginie," said Seigneur without moving, without smiling. "I would like to see Magie in Le petit jardin."

How strange, I thought as I always did, looking up at Seigneur's impassive face and showing none of my own feelings except in my eyes, how strange it was that most of our days began in a chapel stripped of every relic, every appropriate sign, and containing only Seigneur who always stood where once the altar had stood. How strange that from such a place, all the more devotional for having been rendered meaningless, should come the conception that so determined the pain or pleasure of our days. How strange to see the man flanked by his dogs in an otherwise empty chapel. But I had my answer, at least for the moment, and was relieved or at least partially relieved since I loved Magie already and, of all the possible places for our rendezvous, I much preferred Le petit jardin, in which no form of violence could occur.

Mere moments later the man and his two white dogs and the young woman in her orange gown and I the messenger and confidante, despite my mere ten years, were all locked together in that little enclosure of Le petit jardin, where we might have existed together for all time and all time to come. When the gate closed I could not help but feel that sensation of mystery induced as nowhere else by the man, the beasts, the seated woman, and most of all by the nature of Le petit jardin itself.

On four sides rose gray walls higher than Seigneur was tall; the gate was narrow and composed of straight and close-spaced iron bars; over two of the four opposing walls came the massive watery foliage of two weeping willow trees planted outside the garden instead of within, so that those of us inside Le petit jardin were sequestered among the heavy tendrils of trees we could not see. Along these same walls were cultivated rosebushes carefully pruned and blooming, no matter the season; in the center of Le petit jardin was a small carpet of the greenest lawn, upon which sat Magie in her high-backed chair that had a red cushioned seat and was carved with representations of climbing vines and the heads of animals never found in any field or forest. And then, as if flowers, green plot, intruding willows and anomalous chair and seated woman were not enough, the back wall, opposite the narrow gate, consisted of a family sepulcher of twelve ancient crypts. As always I marveled at the soft pure atmosphere of this little place. How wise of Seigneur, I thought, to bring us here. What better place in which to forge the first bonds between man, child, and seated woman?

"Magie," Seigneur said at last, "I want you to study the eyes of this child. . . ."

Smiling woman with her hands in her lap, and standing man flanked by his dogs, and the sun almost directly overhead and not a single bird or insect to remind us of all that lay beyond Le petit jardin: this was the context in which I once again stepped forward and raised my chin at Seigneur's bidding, and I thought that my narrow face was falsely modest, since I too had studied my eyes in pool and glass and knew them to be quite worthy of what Seigneur was about to say of them. But Seigneur positioned himself beside Magie; I faced them both; the two dogs stood so closely together that their bodies touched. Seigneur held out his hand as if to cup my raised chin—yet it was only an airy gesture since Seigneur had never touched me in any way, no matter how slightly. There I stood as always and looked not at Seigneur but at Magie whose pinkish curls were loose and who returned my gaze. I thought that Magie already saw in me what Seigneur saw.

"Magie," he said, "note the largeness of this child's eyes. Note the roundness. Note the deep shades of brown with which they shine, a color of the darkest brown that nonetheless in the proper light, this light, appears also to reflect the yellow of invisible daffodils growing not in a garden but in the mind. You can see these eyes as well as I can, Magie. You are already capable of noting how they dominate the face and hold the attention of the viewer like no other two eyes you or I have ever seen."

He paused, as always. He nodded, as he always did. He allowed himself the briefest smile while I waited, arms hanging and head raised, trying to keep my body still while Seigneur talked about my eyes as if they belonged not to me but to some other child who now stood in my place.

"Magie," he said, while I waited before the standing man and seated woman in all my outward shyness and inner pride, "the question is not merely one of beauty. Not at all. For now you must lean forward, without blinking, and see in this child's eyes what I myself have come to call the seven precious expressions in the eyes of innocence. Look closely, Magie, and concentrate. Know now that you are looking directly at the seven precious expressions which are, in the eyes of innocence, as follows: Joy. Attention. Calm. Surprise. Grief. Incomprehension. And finally the veiled painful accusation of her whom one must wound—inevitably. Do you see them? Do you understand the power of this child's eyes? But I want you to achieve in your own eyes these same expressions and to learn what you could not until this moment know: namely, that these same precious expressions which seem so rare to us in the eyes of the child are to be found, no matter your incredulity, in the eyes of a dog. . . ."

The crypts of the nameless dead were a somber gray, the willows were like thick falls of water, and the grass was serene, the clear light diffused, the pure air sweet with the "breath of Virginie." In all the suspension of this gentle place we waited, holding Seigneur's last softly spoken words still in our ears. Magie was smiling. Seigneur was not. As for me, I was by no means dismayed at his comparison since I too had knelt and hugged the two white dogs about their necks and used my eyes and hence already knew that Seigneur's comparison was exact and true.

"Yes, Magie," Seigneur continued, "I want you to court these rare creatures until you have seen for yourself that the innocence of Virginie shines forth, in fact, from the eyes of dogs. And now," he said after another pause, "now you must lift your skirt into your lap and woo my dogs. The degree of your success shall be determined by the dogs themselves. You see, they are private creatures and not easily aroused."

Had I been seated as Magie was seated on her high-backed wooden chair in what I thought of as this sacred place, I would have complied immediately with Seigneur's request so that my child's skirt would have been already lifted and my legs already exposed, if that was what he wanted. But Magie's eyes were still on mine; her receptive smiling face was unclouded by the slightest doubt; she sat without movement as if she were as much a fixture of Le petit jardin as crypt or weeping willow.

"Incredulity, Seigneur?" she said at last. "But you know I am not easily taken by incredulity. You know as well as I that this is one lesson I need not be taught, one trial I need not be subjected to. But no matter. I am happy to demonstrate what you have in mind."

Then with the simplest and easiest gesture Magie gathered the forward folds of her orange skirt into her lap. She no longer smiled. She sat with her legs exposed from lap to toe against the backdrop of that underportion of the orange skirt that came down behind her legs from the hidden edge of the chair to touch, in a simple silken curl, the grass where chair and naked feet were placed. Her legs and lap were bare; her hands were posed in the simple gesture in which she still held the bottom edge of the skirt; her milky thighs were swept, I saw, with a faint dusting of golden hair like pollen wafted from one white flower to the next. I knew that in this unhurried gesture of compliance she had quite forgotten Seigneur, where he stood to one side boldly, expectantly, with his hands clasped behind his back, and also had quite forgotten me, though mine was the very innocence, after all, that was both the object and the substance of this morning hour.

"Look at the dogs, Magie," he said in his lowest and most quiet voice. "Concentrate. Concentrate. The larger with the black collar is the male, the smaller with the yellow collar is the female. You must appeal to them both. You must win them over."

She did nothing, said nothing, and the dogs did not move. Yet the two dogs now pressed themselves against each other all the harder, and by their eyes revealed that they well understood that the atmosphere in Le petit jardin had changed and that now they had fallen suddenly under a scrutiny they could not ignore. How could I help but marvel at the whiteness and thinness of these dogs with their fragile bones and underbodies tightly shrunken to the purposes of speed? How not marvel at their uneasy eyes and gathering self-consciousness? Oh, but from where I stood at the edge of the green I marveled as much at the dogs' self-consciousness as at Magie in all her naturalness.

She leaned forward. Without knowing it, she had twisted her gathered skirt into a long roll which she now drew tightly backwards against her lower stomach and rounded hips. Without knowing it, she was looking steadily and even quizzically into the moist brown eyes of the dog in the black collar. How I waited! How I watched the shifting paw, the flickering of nerves beneath the white coat, the hardly perceptible movements of the long thin head to the left, to the right, and watched the dog's poor efforts to escape the steady scrutiny of dear Magie!

"Come, Le noir!" she might have said with her eyes alone, since giving a little lurch the poor beast pulled himself away from his mate and with tall broken steps complied exactly with Magie's wishes and crossed the patch of green between them. He stood beside her, looking desperately to the left, the right, then finally laid his thin head across her upper thigh in the peaceful, obedient, trusting gesture of the suppliant dog.

And: "Come, La jaune!" she might have said, again with her eyes, since after a moment's hesitation the dog in the yellow collar slowly followed the example of her mate until her own long head was resting across Magie's other thigh. Nose toward nose the two dogs pointed their still heads across the downy thighs of Magie, whose face appeared to me to be both pleased and pained.

"Well done," said Seigneur under his breath, "well done." But it was clear, at least to me, that Magie had not the slightest need of his encouragement.

So far these morning circumstances had affected my own consciousness, or lack of it, in exactly the way Magie's had been affected, since without knowing it I had clasped my hands and assumed a kneeling position on the edge of the grass, though I came to myself and realized the extent of my happy submersion in this morning hour as soon as Magie let go of her skirt, as she now did, and lightly rested her open hands on the heads of the dogs. Well could I understand the warmth she was feeling from each of the dogs' heads against her thighs; well could I imagine the sensation in her palms and fingers of the frail elongated bony skulls lying just beneath the living skin and coverings of white hair. For the moment she did not stroke the dogs watching each other across her lap, but merely rested her loving hands on their warm heads. It was a sight so stationary and paradoxical that suddenly it caused this question to come to my mind: mightn't the Tapestry of Love consist of some such scene, so that now I was viewing in life precisely what I had never been allowed to see in art? Perhaps, I thought, perhaps, since never yet had I seen whippets and woman so warmly and symmetrically arranged. There had been past times, in fact, when the dogs had cowered in the corners of Le petit jardin, or kept apart, or huddled against the legs of Seigneur, or approached the partially naked initiate only one at a time. Now animals and woman too were making order of this vulnerability. Now I myself had become their supplicant.

"Speak to them, Magie," urged Seigneur in a whisper. "Use your voice as well as your eyes."

But she did not, and yet she caused the dogs to lift their heads, turn their heads in search of her eyes, and then, simultaneously, to rise up and balance themselves on hind legs as brittle as dried bones, and simultaneously to position their front legs across the thighs where their heads had rested, so that now the two white bodies were stretching upwards, and the two white muzzles were very nearly in the same plane with Magie's face. Merely by lifting her gentle hands and holding them above the heads of the dogs in a gesture of benediction exactly the same, I noted, as that which Seigneur himself offered at times to the lowly animals, she had indeed caused the whippets to rest their front legs on her thighs and to elevate themselves so as to approximate in standing the way she sat. Their tails were tucked in nervously between their hind legs; they formed a white heraldic triangle over the naked lap; beneath her hands, now covering the shoulders of each beast, they stood as if paralyzed in comfort and made not a move except now and again, timidly, and in unison, to point their dry noses toward the fair face.

Unmoving dogs, seated woman, standing man, kneeling child: thus we remained immobile in Le petit jardin until Magie, who alone was mistress of all that happened, of all we saw, and who alone was the first to move, quite simply and slowly raised both her hands and in them clasped Le noir's warm and pensive head and with her own brown eyes stared seemingly forever into the eyes of the dog. I watched her face, the frowning of the forehead and the dimpling around the mouth. I watched as Le noir submitted his head to her hands and his eyes to her loving eyes. I watched as the smaller dog awaited without moving the attention that she too would receive, and did receive, from Magie, who was now lifting Le noir's ears, and breathing into them, and stroking the thin muzzle, and touching the tip of it with the tip of her nose, and above all else was peering again and again into the brown eyes of the whimpering animal. I saw what Magie saw: my own brown eyes and the seven coppery circles in the depths of them, and currents of air the color of an orange sun invisibly setting, and vast expanses of space the color of cut wheat. The longer she looked the more the dog whimpered. The more she smiled the greater was the agitation she caused in his breast. The greater her pleasure the wider the poor creature's unresisting eyes until, at last, she freed Le noir and with the briefest laugh, which was the only sound she made, turned to La jaune and with eyes and fingers lavished on La jaune the affection she had all but spent on Le noir.

The elk in snow, the swan on the pond, the blood-colored flower on a country road: all these and more she must have read in the eyes of the smaller dog, which, seemingly forever, she held in exactly that same thralldom in which she had held the larger. Then, quite suddenly, she ceased her stroking, her nuzzling, her kissing, and, allowing her hands to fall to her sides, shut tight her eyes and relaxed her naked legs and laughed her brief laugh, as if she could have known in advance that these were precisely the gestures with which to liberate the whippets from their constraint and to signal to the larger dog and smaller her receptivity to that eagerness which, until this moment, they had held in check. As if by a voiced command they fell to licking the fair smiling face of dear Magie and to nudging her willing head in her aroused affection, and all the while moving their hind legs, suddenly, in the tight and lively circles of an impossible dance. With wet and frantic noses they probed now the dancing curls, now the loose and unconcealed lap, La jaune kissing a partially hidden ear just as Le noir gave himself free rein to explore the open and inviting lap, the two creatures then reversing themselves from leg to cheek and cheek to lap despite the significance of the yellow collar and the black.

She allowed it all. She encouraged it. She smiled and kept tight shut those very eyes which the two dogs simultaneously or in sequence licked again and again with their purpling and excited tongues. How generously she received their ravishment, I thought. How blindly she accepted that close scrutiny which, only moments before, had been her own. At last, and when she knew by all her senses, excepting sight, that the dogs had finally forsaken her for each other, still she waited, blindly enjoying what Seigneur and I were the first to see: that bestial pantomime which might have been embossed on a silver coin or represented in a field of white mosaic.

"Open your eyes, Magie," said Seigneur in his most gentle and admiring voice. "Open your eyes and see what you have accomplished. In fact," he said, as if musing only to himself, "the sight of what you have accomplished tempts me to spare you the sight of what the end of this long day will bring. And yet," he said, in his suddenly quite distant voice, "I shall not spare you that sight or any other. In fact, I shall spare you nothing. Ever."

It was then that Magie opened wide her eyes while for me the sight of the white dogs gave way to the horror I foresaw at the end of the day.

Was I not the busy child? I who climbed the tower stairs to scan the terrain of sensuality that surrounded us? I who swept and swept again my hearth? I who wove another rose into the unfinished tapestry on the loom that was mine? And with my own hoe worked another furrow into my small portion of the east garden that I loved? And carried grain to the doves and wood to my hearth and paused periodically to watch the declining sun pass time on the sun's own face? Yes, I was the busy child shining pots of iron and pans of copper and goblets of glass that gleamed, and hurrying down one empty corridor only to return by another, my hands and body occupied by space and keys, flagons and baskets, while my thoughts went from task to task as though my hurried efforts might somehow surprise me with time safely past and the fated end of that day avoided. It was all impossible, I knew, and yet I kept to myself, and only occasionally stopped abruptly when the approaching fate of the day fell across my path like the shadow of a great wing brushing the earth, and then, and only then, I asked myself why it was that Seigneur did not relent, or told myself that perhaps this very moment he was in fact relenting, though I knew he was not. In all my experience of Seigneur's creativity, nothing, I thought to myself with the black wing stopping my way, nothing was quite so difficult to bear as what I had hoped he might dispense with or at least postpone this day. But even as the thought occurred to me, while gathering eggs that were still warm or turning the pages of my book of hours, still I knew that Seigneur was a man of principle and that I had only to prepare myself as best I could for what I could hardly admit to consciousness or allow to memory, though it was there, in my memory, like a barbed hook piercing a heart that throbbed.

The doves grew quiet. The looms fell silent. Inside their hive the very bees were stilled. High on its wall the sculpted face of the sun was now partially concealed by a shadow that no longer moved. As for me, I could not help but notice that we had reached that ending of the day when the light is clearest and the executioner is brave enough, at last, to don his hood and seize his ax and climb his scaffold where the waiting victim is already all but headless in the final and purest light of day. Then, reluctantly, I took myself to the courtyard, where the gates were closed, and all, I saw in a glance, was ready.

The high-backed chair so recently positioned on the green grass in Le petit jardin now stood alone, and how oddly, ominously, in the center of the courtyard, from which, I knew, there was no escape. Tranquillity had given way to barrenness, and there sat Magie with hands folded as before and the curls as resilient as before, in the morning, and on her face the same expression of smiling and ordinary confidence which conveyed all too clearly, I thought, that she had heeded no warning, had seen no ravens clouding her clear skies, had passed the intervening hours as if for her there could be nothing more arduous to face than a pair of white whippets in a secluded bower. For once the woman was more innocent than the pure child. Joining her and standing beside her as was my simple role in this grim scheme, I recognized in a breath her innocence, and my heart fell. Could she not feel the emptiness that filled the court-yard? Or note Seigneur's unsmiling countenance and his silence and the way he stood at a distance with his feet wide apart and that strange mechanical staff gripped in a firm hand, its butt in the sand and its small iron beak towering above his head on the end of the staff? Wouldn't this sight be quite enough to instill in most grown women the faintest shade of fear or the first unpleasant taste of apprehension? But it was not so, and there was nothing I could do but remain as best I could at Magie's side in the clear light, even as I understood that the moment had come, and that the day was at its fullest, and that the day was dead. Only in the prolongation of its death did this day exist. At times the clearest light, I knew, was indistinguishable from the darkest night.

"Magie," Seigneur called across the space between us, "at this day's beginning you enjoyed the pleasure of what I shall call the generosity of vision. Now, at its end, you must know what it means to see with the eyes of pride. No lesson is more essential, no sight more necessary to the womanhood you shall at last achieve. The generous eye is desirable, but without the eyes of pride the person who aspires to womanhood is blind. It is one thing to impart your natural generosity to a pair of dogs and thus, by the expenditure of natural innocence, to recognize in turn that the timidity of the united dogs is noble. But it is quite another to be the passive recipient and, further, recipient of the gift unwanted, and thus to discover that it is harder by far to accept the gift than to give it. She who is able to receive the gift, no matter the nature of that gift, is proud; the more unwanted the gift the greater the woman's pride in accepting it. And a woman's pride is the glory of the womanhood that is hers alone. It is pride that makes a woman loved, or makes her desired, and the greater a woman's pride the more she is loved. The heart of womanhood, Magie, is pride. . . .

"So now I am going to forge your pride: you shall not be touched, you have nothing to fear, nothing to do. Yet you must know that this day's final event is for you and you alone. You are the cause of this event, and its inspiration, and its center; what is to happen would not happen were it not for you, though you do nothing and say nothing and merely sit in your chair until this charade is over and the light fails. The amount of pain implicit in the gift is the only measure of a woman's pride. The greater the pain the more valuable the gift and the fiercer her pride. And the extent of her pride is the only measure of a woman's worth. So the gesture I am about to perform is an indication, at least, of the vastness of the value you represent to me. Accept what I am about to give, Magie! Be proud! It is all for you!"

This speech, so like a period of drums and horns, I thought, increased the distance between Seigneur and ourselves, and revealed the potential of the man's own pride, and with the last of its exclamation, died in our surrounding silence like the thump of the ax, the fall of the severed head. What, I asked myself, could be more ominous than the death of this rhetoric? My brief and somber sidelong look at Magie revealed that she too, at last, was beginning to appreciate the seriousness of this occasion. Gone was her smile, gone her faint flush, and visibly fading were all the happier aspects of the innocence that informed her life, no matter the adult she was or the fact of her motherhood. The silence that roared in our ears at the conclusion of Seigneur's speech was just as dark, I thought, or just as fraught with menacing cadences as the sound of the long-dead wave in the broken shell or the very shape and color which lone man, lone woman, lone child exacted from the space around us. In such clear light and heavy silence I was tempted to reach for Magie's hand and hold it, though I did not.

What terrible noise was this? For even as I heard the random blows of the hooves and heard the loud snorting of the beast that smells danger on the air, and as I saw the four attendants with their peculiar tools and saw Père La Tour leading into our midst the desperate horse that was taller and blacker than Le Baron's horse or any other such horse I had seen before, even as all the elements of Seigneur's cruelest drama filled the emptiness of our sad stage, even then as I remembered fleeting sights and cries from past performances and knew without question what was yet to come, still I cringed inside myself and in my mind attempted to deny, impossibly, what I saw and heard and what I would see and hear despite myself.

Seigneur made not a move, still facing us, as if he cared nothing for the horse and men behind his back, or as though they were not there, loud and struggling and tumultuous in the bright uncanny light of our dead day. Men and horse could not have more disturbed the emptiness of the courtyard, nor more destroyed the silence into which Seigneur's distant speech had fallen like a loud voice shouted down the deepest well.

"Don't move, Magie!" he called across the space between us. "But don't be afraid. You shall come to no harm."

Once again, as I had done before, I attempted to calm myself and brace myself by cataloguing on the very pages of my inward agitation all the particulars of this gathering scene. Père La Tour, for instance, was controlling the frantic horse by means of a short thick stick containing at . one end a small loop of rope into which the horse's nose was caught and held by the simple expediency of twisting the stick and hence the loop, which tightened around the tender nose, quite naturally, with every turn of the stick worn smooth with use. Whenever the horse attempted to rear, or attempted to lunge away from Père La Tour, or attempted to toss its head and thus dislodge the painful sensation in its poor twisted nose, Père La Tour had only to give his stick another turn to heighten the madness in the horse's eyes but also to subdue quite easily the urgencies that inhabited all the great weight of the struggling beast. It was a clever device, I thought, yet sickening.

As for the attendants, those four disheveled men whom I somehow recognized but could not remember, men who wore tight and faded shirts and knee breeches and old lumpy shoes long used to plodding in manure and raising dust, of these four frightened and bare-armed fellows there were two who were equipped with long and blunted poles of iron which, each to a side, they thrust against the heavy haunches in order to prevent as much as possible the lateral movements of the black horse, while their two comrades carried between them a great cagelike iron mechanism which in itself might well account for the bloodied flecks of terror in the animal's poor rolling eyes.

Still Seigneur made not a move. Still he faced us, as if the breathless and fearsome activity behind his back were no concern of his. The light held, like mercury in a column or rain in a cloud, while all around us lay the listening château and its silent occupants, each one arrested in what-ever her act of butchering, weaving, reading, singing, daydreaming at open casement, or producing sweet tones from an ivory flute—all quiet and waiting for the screams which, except for Adèle, they could not possibly know would issue suddenly from this near-empty courtyard from which, for the time being, they were excluded.

"Magie," called he who was master of this scene, "don't worry about our handsome but uncooperative animal. Once he complies with what I have in mind, and gives up his gift, which is actually mine as well as his, he shall spend the rest of his days among heavy and compliant mares in rolling fields filled with shadows and sunlight, green grass and yellow, and long meandering streams of clear water. Fear not for yourself, Magie, and fear not for the horse."

But what effect could such words have if not to increase our apprehen-sion? Yet I knew that this was not Seigneur's intention, and also knew that never did he say what he did not mean. So I nodded to myself and wished the horse away to his fields and Magie to her peaceful bed and me to my hearth, at the same time finding my attention more firmly fixed than ever on the commotion barely contained behind Seigneur's back.

The two men with the iron prods were moving them, I saw, and were muttering under their breaths in their now greater efforts to prevent the horse from thundering in a terrified half circle to the left, to the right, to the left, and from striking down his sweating tormentors with his glistening hooves. At the head of the poor beast the other two attendants were lifting high the great cagelike mechanism, which was actually a halter of sorts, but made of iron strips instead of leather, and, while Père La Tour turned ever tighter his rude but effective stick, were shoving and pushing and manipulating the iron halter so as to encase within it, finally, the horse's head. The black ears lay back, the eyes were white and bloodied in their sockets, the pink nose was so constrained and distorted in the loop of rope that the enormous creature was able to breathe only through the open mouth which, in turn, was partially obstructed by the wet tongue engorged with pain and also by the as yet muffled sounds the poor beast could not help but generate between his open jaws. Then they were done, the two thickset men, who were among the lowest underlings in our handsome stables, and Père La Tour (who loosed his rope) leapt back and flung aside his stick.

Now the true purpose of the iron halter could no longer remain a puzzle or be denied, even by me or, more importantly, by dear Magie, whose very self, I thought, deserved to be swept away this instant by some saving wind that would obliterate horse, men, seated woman, everything in fact except Seigneur and me. But there was not the slightest breath of wind to destroy or in any way obscure the now only-too-evident purpose of the iron halter imprisoning beyond a doubt the great handsome head of the poor horse. What was now inescapable, since I saw it and remembered it as well, was that the iron halter differed from an ordinary halter not merely because it was made of thick iron instead of supple leather, but mainly because it housed a ratcheted device which, something in the manner of the bit in a bridle, and something like a skeletal duplication of the beast's own jaws, sat inside the frothing mouth and compressed the tongue and held apart the mammoth jaws to any degree of openness desired. That was in fact the diabolical difference between this riveted and hinged device and the soft and comfortable halter which my own Cupidon and all our horses loosely wore throughout their peaceful days in our richly appareled stables. Now I could not help but see that the black horse's jaws were forced open to their fullest extent and perhaps beyond. The locked and gaping mouth, the chastened tongue, the large and yellowed teeth still wet to the watching eye: could there be any iron device more unnatural? any intrusion into the animal world more cruel? any spectacle more shameful to those compelled to see it? For a moment I thought to close my eyes, but I could not.

I watched, Magie was watching. In the silence in which time itself was suspended, and the clear light too, we heard the helpless unrhythmical pounding of the hooves, the unvoiced oaths of the attendants, the loud and labored breathing of men and horse alike. Père La Tour stood well out of the way and wiped his brow. Those to the rear of the horse poked and prodded the gleaming flanks. At the head of the poor beast the other two attendants, with straw in their hair and dung on their shoes, stood to either side of him fiercely gripping at arms' length the two long iron rods that were affixed in a swiveling manner to either side of the iron mask. All was in motion, yet nothing moved. With backs bent and feet shuffling, the four men fought the plunging and swaying horse to a standstill. The horse expended his energy as if at a gallop; the four men clung to their iron poles and kept him captive, great mouth high and open in the still air.

"Magie!" called Seigneur across the space between us. "Be brave! Be proud! In all your days to come, and without thinking and as a matter of fact, you must expect to receive from each and every lover, master, lord of your life, precisely that kind of gift to compare favorably, in quality, with the gift you shall now receive from me. Nothing is too good for you, Magie! Nothing too abominable! Nothing too rare!"

With these words he quite suddenly turned his back to us and, like a warrior brandishing his pike, grasped in both firm hands the iron staff, that had about it an aspect curious indeed, and frightening, and spread his feet, one slightly before the other, and bent his knees, gathered his strength, hoisted high the mysterious staff and faced the horse. But how could I have failed to understand, as memory and actuality joined again, and I saw that Seigneur was using both hands to operate, rather than merely hold, that which was no mere staff but was instead a long and slender pair of pincers all the more malevolent for its simplicity, its thinness, its great length, its sinister originality of design? Pincers, and I swayed in dizziness beyond my years while noting, nonetheless, that Magie's understanding lagged but a hair behind my own, since now she was standing up in a movement of surprise and defiance which could only have been prompted by that same recognition that had come to me and now had found its second mark and was rending the unsuspecting nature that was herself.

"No!" she cried, as Père La Tour stepped forward, at Seigneur's curt nod, and reached up his hands and, in one deft gesture, clamped the little ugly beaklike head of Seigneur's pincers to one of the two square teeth lodged by nature so tightly in the front of the black horse's long upper jaw. "No!" she cried again, as Père La Tour jumped away to safety and Seigneur squeezed shut his slender instrument and held it ready. "Injure me if you must," she then cried in a final breath. "But spare the horse!"

I saw the flexing of bold muscles, the shifting of feet, the motions of Seigneur's grand head, so violent as to shake loose the black ribbon binding his thick hair at the base of the neck. The horse squealed once, squealed again, as if a suffering pig were lodged inside its belly, and these sounds were so inappropriate to the great size and noble stature of the horse that they made me gasp. Then Seigneur leaned back on the end of the pincers. He applied all the tension he could impart to the upper end of the pincers. Thus, in sudden silence, the mighty horse stared down at Seigneur with a liquid steadiness that imparted to both enormous eyes a wild concentration which, in itself, must have spurred on Seigneur to the extraction that was the final purpose of this day.

I felt the sudden protective sweep of Magie's left arm and found myself smothered face-to-stomach against her warm body. I heard the splintering of bone. I heard the breathy expulsion of the man's relief. I heard the high protracted screech that issued once from the mouth of the horse in tones that were human. Sightless, I still knew that the light had failed.

"Your prize, Madame," Seigneur cried above the pain of the beast, and wheeled upon us, and extended the pincers. "Come take your prize!"

That night I forsook my hearth and spent the darkness seated beside the woman who wept in her sleep yet lay upon her bed as straight and unmoving as a stone effigy lying with folded hands upon its tomb. Though I could not see it, I knew that on a small and polished table next to the head of the bed there rested a silver bowl of spring water containing in the form of an eternal gleam that which, on the morrow, the waking woman would dispassionately remove, and dry, and enclose in the waiting locket that would hang from its silver chain around her neck.

In my single dream that night I heard the distant voice of Seigneur calling out to a group of new arrivals as he always did: "Welcome to Dédale! Welcome! The women you shall become await you here. . . ."

[1945] Sylvie's cache-sexe; the corset of Monsieur Malmort

I was mistress of our house. I fed Maman, I washed Bocage's back, I washed the slippery little body of Déodat and, on the wet floor beside the iron tub, knelt like the faithful busy attendant that I was and applied my hands to shoulder, thigh, forearm, shin, to all the warm shapeliness of Minouche, Sylvie, Clarisse, Yvonne, and Madame Pidou when this one, or that one, sat bathing. I filled our rooms with flowers in pots, jars, crocks, vases. I fluffed up Sylvie's pillows, spread smooth the coverings where Yvonne would sleep. I fired the stove, boiled water, wore my apron, handled the wooden spoon as long as my arm, on hands and knees regarded the reflection of my face in the stones I polished. I presided over all our meals, though it was Bocage who cooked them, and I preferred beans to peas, water to wine, salt to sugar, though both were rare, and if I enjoyed the little old woman I was in the day, which I did, then at night I reverted again to the quiet child alert in her corner, and watched and listened in utter wakefulness, while love in bright colors flew and fluttered around this one or that one who well knew, as I well knew, that partial nudity or nudity itself was the fact, the concept, the very world toward which all aspired: even I who thought of removing all my clothes but never would.

"Ladies!" cried Bocage, as he leaned over his greasy plate and rested his heavy elbows on the table and lit one of his yellow cigarettes and puffed the smoke. "Ladies! I have this to say!"

Around the disordered table we sat, Madame Pidou clothed only in her shabby robe like an actress, and Sylvie and dear Minouche and the others dressed in similar scanty fashion, sporting naked shoulder or bare neck or the wired halter heaving up bare breasts. All this, to my quick eye, but emphasized the more the distinction between our women and the rest of us, who were fully clothed and somewhat envious, perhaps, of our women who cared not a straw, I thought, for how they were garbed or not garbed or whether the light beyond our rooms was coming from the sun or moon. I sat straight-backed and rather prim between Déodat, who was not hungry, and Monsieur Pidou, who was silent and had eyes for nothing, I saw, except the potatoes and boiled cabbage still heaped on his plate.

"Ladies," said Bocage, puffing the smoke from his cigarette and wetting his thick lips with the wine in his glass. "What I have to say is this: you are not eating enough. That's the whole matter: not enough by half. I provide a full table, whether or not food is generally scarce and lacks variety. Obviously you are all aware of my hours at the hot stove, ladle in hand, and the ingenuity with which I stuff one rabbit so that it serves for two, and so arrange the white vegetables and the yellow on our hot platters so as to engage all the more your appetites. Still you do not eat enough. Not by half. I manipulate the tubs of dough, I bake and baste, I am more than generous with the tins of lard and pinches of salt. Will you deny it? Will you deny my sauces, so brown as to be nearly black or even purple and thicker by far than anyone's? Of course not. There is simply no question about the extent and savor of my cooking, so who can object to the pat I give myself now and then on my own shoulder? But why? you ask. Why this concern for food? Why doesn't he just cook and bring home the most interesting of men and be done with it? Why all the talk? Why does he care how much we eat or how little? Ladies, let me say it: you are all too thin. Even Sylvie, who is too small, you will say, to gain more weight, and even Minouche, whose shape is the closest, you will say, to the size of her spirit so that surely I have no right to complain of Minouche. But I do! I will! I must complain about you, Sylvie, and you, Minouche, and you, Madame, and you, Clarisse, and you too, Yvonne, though we are well aware that you stand the tallest and are in fact the largest of anyone around this table. But even you, Yvonne, have yet to achieve the fullness of the beautiful Yvonne I have in mind.

Now wait, don't interrupt," he said. "I know what I'm talking about and I will say it again: too thin! No matter what you think you see in the glass or feel when with your own fingers you test the extent of your flesh . . ."

Sylvie shut tight her mouth and flung down her knife and fork; Madame Pidou intruded a stealthy hand inside her robe; Minouche began to laugh and tossed a pellet of hard bread across the table at Déodat, who averted his eyes from such a playful mother; and Clarisse held back her slender shoulders and thrust out her chest, while Yvonne, the largest of all, rose to her feet, smacked her immense white thigh, looked from woman to woman for approval and, receiving it, resumed her seat. As for me, I too stopped eating, and with swift hands concealed beneath the table, swiftly I made my inventory of my hard knees, my legs that weighed nothing, my arms that were slighter than the twig that bends, my hips that were pointed, my stomach that resembled nothing so much, I told myself, as the smallest and driest of little empty sacks. I nodded inwardly, I clutched my poor elbows to my sides, I resolved to listen to Bocage's every word as never before.

"Too thin by far," he continued, raising again his glass and drinking and then taking two deep inhalations of the smoke which was blue, "too thin by far. And why all this concern for food? For weight? For size? Another easy answer in the form of a question: Have you ever seen an ordinary woman consciously aware of her own desire who does not, in one way or another, convey the fact of this desire in all she does and all she is? We find her everywhere, this woman, yet it is always a shock, a surprise, a delight to see her in a passing car, to brush against her in a crowd, to catch her eye as she strolls along with her husband. This is the woman who knows herself, who has seen the readiness of her craving in the oval glass, who is aware of little else, indeed, than that she lives for desire, and wakes, moves about, sleeps in the consciousness of her desire which is a boldness of mind and body that never dies, not for an instant.

"What is this woman's very person if not desire? What does this ordinary woman understand if not precisely this state of affairs? that she herself is desire, that she exists in the form of desire, that she desires generally and specifically throughout all the minutes of the day and in her dreams, which is to say that she herself is absorbed in the desire that is her self and knows, as only she can know, that her desire comes first and then the man. There you have it, ladies: the desire of the ordinary woman is not prompted by a man, does not have its origins in the glance of some passing man who melts her heart, invigorates the mind, calls forth desire. No, it is quite the opposite: in the true woman desire comes first, the man second. The woman, I say, is not dependent on the man. No, the woman in all her consciousness lives out her days until at last she is able to fit some man to her desire. And then another, and another, and another, vows and reason notwithstanding.

"But how, in fact, do we detect all this amorous receptivity in our ordinary woman? Does she have a pretty face? Or regular features? Some sort of attractiveness achieved at birth or artificially acquired? Never, never, ladies. That's my point. Precisely. How then does our ordinary woman convey to us her amorous receptivity? By being conventional! She dresses so properly as to reveal, to the discerning eye, her impropriety. She is so decent, I say, as to appear indecent. She holds herself on so tight a rein as to cause her secret self to sprawl invitingly at her side wherever she is, and whether or not she is seated or standing or strolling in our imaginary park. Tightness, ladies, tightness! There you have it. Our ordinary but amorously receptive woman takes such conventional but clever care of herself that she is 'bridled,' as I might say, 'bridled.' Her shoes are tight. Her stockings are a size too small. Her cache-sexe is only a little pinch in the proper place. Her dress is tight, her hair is so severely brushed and then pinned so tightly to her head that in our first glimpse of her, before she even knows we are watching, and is doing nothing more than standing still with her plain head turned away, we can't help but see her tightly modest head of hair as down, loose, freely falling about the shoulders that are always bare precisely because they're so tightly clothed. This woman of ours is bridled! It's exactly the right word. And to the discerning eye our bridled woman is nothing other than *unbridled!* The streets are filled with gloriously unbridled women for anyone who cares to look.

"But let me tell you, ladies, that all this tightness of the unbridled woman says that she eats! She eats! She eats deliberately and in such a way that the food no sooner sits on her tongue but what it fires up her skin, deepens her breathing, imparts to her very flesh the shape of her body. She chews, and we see at once that there is more in her mouth than food; she takes a little sip of wine and immediately the red wine becomes the light in her eyes. She shines. She beckons. She is soft and solid at the same time. She eats, you say to yourself. She takes her tiny mouthfuls as if gorging her face, you say to yourself. She eats for desire. She eats, and wine and butter and flour and fatty tissues of her midday meal lie in glistening languourous layers in her every curve. And the observer? The watchful admirer behind his newspaper? Let me tell you that he who watches such a woman tastes in his own mouth the very food she has only now devoured. In his own mouth he tastes the food that floods that woman's being. And what does he say, our watchful man? She eats for me, he says to himself. For me! No wonder we speak of appetite when we mean desire.''

He stopped. At last he stopped. In my admiring but stealthy glance, I saw the perspiration on his face and the trembling of the hand that still held the cigarette, though it no longer burned. I listened, I surveyed the table, hearing not one sound of fork on china or fingernail tapping glass, and seeing only the frowning or impassive faces of women who, according to Bocage, were not giving themselves enough to eat. Their chins were lifted; they did not speak, they did not move; what clothes they wore were hanging loose. All of them, and no matter the expressions on their faces, were staring at Bocage where he sat at the head of the table perspiring and rubbing his jaw. Then Bocage's audience erupted.

"Look at me, Bocage!" cried Madame Pidou, and from the white bowl she snatched up a white and faintly wet, faintly steaming potato and thrust it, as best she could, inside her mouth: she laughed, that ripe woman, though her mouth was full.

"Look, Bocage!" cried Minouche and even Sylvie and even Clarisse, who never smiled and hardly talked, as, following the example of Madame Pidou, they seized fistfuls of green beans or chunks of bread or the last of our fried fish, with which they crammed their mouths, crying, "Look, look, Bocage!" and all but smothering their laughter in the food they ate.

"Look at me, Bocage!" cried the impressive Yvonne, her naked shoulders shaking, as, for all to see, she wiped her bare hand around and around in her greasy plate that was not entirely empty, and then threw back her head and into her open mouth crowded her fingers which noisily she licked and sucked, while laughing louder than all the rest, who were reaching their hands now here, now there, and catching up bits of food and eating, laughing, knocking over thick tumblers half filled with wine.

"Look at us! Look at us, Bocage!" they cried, and leaned across the table and crushed the soft food and laughed and smeared their faces and soiled what fragments of clothing they still wore and vied with each other for handfuls of pasty cabbage and the flasks of oil, the flasks of vinegar, which they drank and spilled, and all of this in the best of moods, so that even Bocage himself began to laugh and to drink not from his tumbler, which lay in its own pool of wine, but from the black bottle which again and again he tipped on high.

"To the bridled woman!" he shouted, holding the bottle at arm's length above his head.

But in the midst of all their laughter I remembered my poor Maman. I slipped from my chair and left the table, as the hands reached and the food flew. Happily, and according to habit, I set about fulfilling my nightly duty and preparing the bowl of dinner for Maman. I seized the ladle, hearing the noisy storm behind my back. Vigorously I plunged the ladle into the pot, but then turned away from the bowl I held and listened, exactly as if I were still seated and not standing, as indeed I was, before the iron stove in which the flame was dying. Once more Bocage's voice came resounding through the steamy room, and I was so concentrating that my awkward ladle quite missed the bowl, though I did not care and did not bother to clean up what I had spilled. After all, I thought, touching the back of my free hand to my moist brow, I had only myself to thank for my own good mood, which was, I thought, as fragile as reason yet indestructible.

In my two hands I held Maman's hot bowl straight out before me. Calmly I walked from the raucous and glowing kitchen. Swiftly I went down the long stone corridor to the open door of the camphor-smelling room where Maman lay propped up and listening.

I entered the dark room. I left the door open as I had found it. Cheerfully I approached Maman, as if I were not still attentive to the high-pitched cries, the laughter, the shouts in which I distinguished now the insistent voice of Madame Pidou, now the suddenly eager screams of Sylvie. Ignoring those voices both loud and soft, near and far, sounds and noises I loved to hear, I crossed the room and stood beside the enormous bedridden effigy of poor Maman. Her glaring spirit inhabited that bare white room. The single window was curtained against the night. The combs and brushes of tortoise shell and silver, the photographs of faded faces, the white chamber pot in its brocaded tent, and the great bed itself were all exactly as I had left them, arranged in the absolute order that betokens a child's obedience and an old woman's mind. I held the steaming bowl in both my hands. As always I smelled the heavy linen, the little dish of dried flowers which were all that remained of poor Maman's once handsome blooms. Yet I could not help listening, despite myself, to the shouts of Bocage and the cries of the chorusing women who were still embarrassing Déodat and Monsieur Pidou in the hot kitchen where, I confessed to myself, I would have preferred to be.

"Maman," I said softly, as I always did, "open your mouth."

But what was wrong? What was different? How had she changed? No woman was ever larger than my Maman, and tonight she was as large as ever on her massive bed. She lay propped on the same aged pillows that were severely white; as always the great bare arms lay flat to her sides and heavy on the white covers which I myself had pulled up as far as possible and smoothed; as always her bulky body was shrouded in its lace nightdress so old and brittle that it resembled a garment woven of fine bones; and there on her head was the familiar white cap concealing or nearly concealing the lengths of black hair as wondrously thick as a horse's tail, which I had brushed and hidden as well as I could under the white cap. Her eyes were fierce, her large round face was proud. But how had she changed? What was wrong?

"Open your mouth, Maman," I said, patiently waiting for the head to turn and the jaws to part for my extended spoon. But nothing happened. She did not stir. There was not a tremor in all her majesty, undaunted as it was by days and weeks of paralysis in the high bed that was regal, I thought, and frightening too.

"Eat, Maman," I said, disguising my alarm. "You must eat what I have brought you. Please."

Then I took a step closer to the high bed. I put down the bowl on the

74

table that was in reach of the poor hand that could not move. I paid closer attention to Maman's expression, to her dark eyes, to the direction in which they were staring, as if the very look in her eyes could destroy what she saw. How had I failed to see what Maman was looking at with all the vehemence of her silent self? Yet there was my answer: for on the white coverlet at the foot of the bed lay a crumpled heap of satin which was, I knew in a glance, Sylvie's white cache-sexe. Of course I had not been able to distinguish this one white flake from the immensity of its snowy field. But now I saw what my Maman was seeing. Now I saw what I had overlooked. I understood that the appearance of Sylvie's cache-sexe at the foot of the bed was one thing for Maman, and for me another. How that little ruffled garment came to be where it was, or who had so lightly tossed it onto the bed, or why it lay where it did like a crumpled pigeon shot down from the sky, all this was a mystery I did not wish to fathom. And yet, and despite myself, at that moment I could not help but smile, as, with a pleasure I had not known before, I recognized this white scrap of an undergarment which, according to Bocage, had no function except to amuse the woman who wore it and to please whoever saw her wearing it. Sylvie had danced about our immense salon, garbed in little more than this same cache-sexe, and everyone in the room had enjoyed the sight and so, I admitted to myself, had I. But how peculiar it looked on Maman's bed, and yet how pretty.

So what could I do except step to the foot of the bed and between thumb and first finger of my right hand catch up the offending garment and, like the youngest of serving maids laughing and displaying aloft a little white rodent by its rubbery tail, hold high the flimsy cache-sexe for Maman to see?

"There, Maman," I said. "That's all it is."

Then I stuffed it into the waist of my apron and seized again the bowl and spoon and took my place beside Maman. She did not move. Her eyes were dark.

"It's gone, Maman," I said in my softest voice. "Now you must eat. I beg of you. . . ."

Slowly, as if peering deliberately into the dark entrance to her own sepulcher, she turned her head and stared at me and then without the slightest change in her scowling face, slowly she opened her mouth and closed her eyes. I was relieved at last. Spoonful by spoonful I fed Maman, who opened and closed her mouth in perfect harmony with the rhythm of my efforts, though she did not open her eyes to watch me, until at last we were finished.

I returned the spoon to its empty bowl. I leaned down and kissed the immensity of her solid and still frowning brow. Then, light as a whirling feather and leaving open the door to her room, I returned to the now-empty kitchen that was piled high with pots and pans and dishes and kettles that made me think of dripping cliffs and shining castles. Behind me, I knew, Maman was listening and her eyes were open. But then as I set to work I forgot Maman in all the pleasure of suds and brushes and rising water and the hot flames that were reflecting themselves on the wet walls of my bower.

Gradually the black cliffs, as I thought of them, decreased in height. Gradually my tall castles became mere ruins and then disappeared. Fiercely I swept the field, swiftly I darted from table to stone trough to the moldy bucket into which, without a moment's thought, I flung the scraps and tatters only faintly glued to white china and iron casseroles which I hefted in both hands and held to my stomach as I sped like a trapped bird, like a bird that appreciates nothing so much as its captivity, back to the enormous sink filled with water so hot that it reddened my arms and made me grimace. The steam rose, the reflections of the hot flames multiplied. I wiped my brow, I rested my wet hands on hips that hardly gave them purchase, I glanced about me, frowning, then set once more to work. I listened, paused for breath, rushed once more to the gleaming crockery now rising in the most orderly of stacks.

But I was done at last, and I flung down my wet towel and followed Bocage and the others into our salon that was both light and dark, warm and cool, where I saw my hassock waiting for me in the shadows. I came into the midst of that noisy company, where hilarity, quite invisible, whirled and bowed and skipped and set tingling the senses of everyone in our sensuous salon, myself included.

"Virginie!" cried Lulu. "There you are! Now come and kiss me," he cried, as if he had not seen me the night before and the night before that as well. He stood before me with his arms across the bare shoulders of Sylvie on his right and of Clarisse on his left, so that he was using

76

Clarisse and Sylvie in place of the painted crutches. He towered above everyone, this Lulu who did not hesitate to put his full weight on Sylvie and Clarisse while resting only the toe of his cast on the stone floor where he stood, and who did not hesitate to give me his full attention when, only moments before, he had been kissing Sylvie and rumpling with his handsome mouth Clarisse's hair. The fresh fire in the hearth was large and bright; Bocage's radio was loud; our salon, despite its size, smelled strongly of spilled wine that might have come pouring from immense casks smashed open in some fury of pure joy. Bocage was holding aloft a fresh bottle, and laughing at Yvonne and Madame Pidou who were dancing in each other's arms and singing as loudly as they could. Minouche and Monsieur Moreau, half undressed, were squeezing and embracing each other on the couch that made me imagine a wide boat low in a serene sea. I tried to think of all that had taken place in my absence, but could not because Lulu was towering above us all and, in his familiar bellow, was urging me to run at once into his waiting arms.

"Come to your Lulu, Virginie!" he cried, and I obeyed. But he did not exact from me the kiss he requested, nor did he offer me a kiss, nor did I incite him in any way to kiss me, since Lulu knew as well as I that he could speak of kissing me but nothing more. For me, he knew, it was enough to be hoisted high above his head in his strong hands. Tonight this pleasure was all the greater; tonight, and for the first time, I saw, Lulu was dressed in nothing but his clumsy cast, and the worn-down black shoe that had no mate, and the tight trousers. Tonight he was naked from the waist up, this Lulu of infinite surprises, had tossed away with his crutches his sleeveless shirt so that now his naked torso was indeed a match for the nakedness of Sylvie, on his right, and also for the nakedness of cold Clarisse who, on his left, had grown quite accustomed to her scant costume of the violet cache-sexe which she wore with ease. I waited one instant more, noting that Lulu's torso was triangular from the broad shoulders to the narrow waist, and that it was darkly burnished and oddly flexing in this careless light. But it was not Lulu's partial nakedness that made me think of a lone and slender tree bearing three yellow pears artfully arranged at different heights on the tips of bare branches, but rather the fact that Lulu's torso was so tattooed, so completely tattooed, that I could only think of my tree and pears as a measure of relief from the marvel of a human chest that bore on its every ripple and round of skin an entire colony of tiny women themselves as naked as the skin they covered.

I stared. No one, I told myself, could have thought for an instant that the two balloonists and other creatures and messages tattooed on Lulu's arms were only the merest hint of the extravagance of the tattooist's art concealed until this night beneath the clinging stripes of the discarded shirt. But women! Tiny women no larger than my first finger! Women leaping, sitting, lolling, peering from behind each other, lying recumbent in a warm sun! Women with tiny laurel crowns on their heads! Women clustered together on their hands and knees! Hour on hour he must have sat in pain! How he must have insisted that his muscled chest and back be adorned only with women! How he must have urged the tattooist to crowd them on all the surface of his dark chest!

He raised his arms. He held them out to me. Sylvie and the expressionless Clarisse clasped him and steadied him, like sylvan attendants to a great tree motionless in a raging storm.

"Up you go!" he cried, and seized me about the waist and tossed me high in that firm and unequivocal grip. On high I laughed and peered down into Lulu's face, while thinking to myself that no one but he would have made of his chest a rippling vision to so please a child.

"Welcome, little sister," he said in a voice that only I could hear above the din, and I hovered in my stationary flight above him and laughed and waited for him to put me down. But he did not, and for a moment longer kept me up there like his weightless weathervane. Then suddenly our smoky salon fell silent, except for Bocage's radio, and I raised my face and saw the figure who Lulu somehow knew was standing there behind his back in the darkness of the half-opened door.

"So it is you, Monsieur Malmort," he cried, and abruptly but also safely dropped me down.

"Come in, come in!" echoed Bocage, while Yvonne and Madame Pidou, half naked both, stood still in their interrupted dance, and Minouche looked up from kissing Monsieur Moreau, and I went to my hassock in the dark corner and sat down in my usual fashion to enjoy the spectacle of Monsieur Malmort.

In he came, as always wearing on his wasted body his worn and shapeless suit, and on his head and pulled down to his ears the sulky fedora which he had never once removed in our presence and which inevitably made me shiver in delight. In he came, indifferent to the warm light which fell in a glancing blow on Minouche's bare thigh, indifferent to the women dancing, and to the women captured in their efforts to support the proud Lulu, and indifferent to all the tiny women spilled across Lulu's torso like dancers on the stage of a little music hall built for a precocious child.

Now, and as never before, Monsieur Malmort was himself a comic actor, a poor twisted creature who dragged himself across a stage devoted to displaying naked women bathed in the rich colors of slowly revolving lights: like an actor playing the part of ghost or derelict, he pulled shut the door behind him, said nothing, raised one hand in silent greeting, took a few steps, nodded briefly at Madame Pidou, then looked away as if unaware that her robe was hanging open, and still more bizarrely, unaware of the incongruous sack which he held by its neck. It was this disreputable sack, quite empty it seemed, except for something moving in its dark depths, that caused the abrupt and momentary silence of Sylvie, Clarisse, Yvonne, Minouche, and Madame Pidou, who ordinarily met the nightly appearance of Monsieur Malmort by swarming upon him with laughter and bright voices and vying, each against each, for the opportunity of squeezing him with their loving hands. Lulu and Bocage were stilled by the sight of the small old man, and at the sight of his sack which appeared to be stiff and thickened with coal dust and dried blood. Even Bocage's radio fell silent in deference to the shuffling footsteps of Monsieur Malmort.

I leaned forward with my arms on my knees and with my white apron drawn tight to my ankles. I peered from my place of darkness, and not one thing escaped my rapt and eager eye: Madame Pidou, unwittingly raising a hand to her open robe; her husband, where he sat in shadows as protective as my own, lifting a hand defensively, I thought, to cradle against his breast the head of Déodat who slept on the timorous man's warm lap; Lulu scowling; Bocage gripping fast the neck of his black bottle as if about to drink. Still the radio was silent, and still silent were Bocage's women and the rest of us.

Monsieur Malmort stepped in front of the fire, turned to his audience, and raised up his sack and showed it; then with eyes downcast and face averted, dramatically he pulled loose the frayed cord and let it fall. Persisting in this behavior, mocking with deliberately saddened face the obvious theatricality of the sack, its contents, and the hushed and formal fashion in which he stood before us, carefully he inserted his free hand into the mouth of the sack, and then his arm, frowning, raising his eyebrows in skeptical anticipation, groping until at last he seized what lay in the bottom. He grimaced and then, with considerable effort and a final flourish, at last he pulled from the sack a large black cock and gripped it by the golden legs and held it high, inviting gasps of surprise that remained unvoiced and applause which was in fact withheld. The cock's wings were clipped, the legs were tied as was the beak, but rebellious vigor shone in all the feathers, so black that they might have been polished with a soft cloth. Even upside down that glorious black cock gave vent to his anger through eyes that gleamed but never moved. His breathing, I could see, was even, despite his struggle; his comb and wattles were sharp configurations of bright blood.

"For your table," said Monsieur Malmort and dropped the poor creature to the stone floor where it lay in a heap. I heard its thud; I watched as even then the living heap of that discarded bird struggled to move.

"Wait," he said, raising his free hand to stifle laughter or cries of horror, or to call for silence in the midst of what was already an atmosphere of the thickest silence. "Wait," he said, glancing around him and feigning complicity with all those who watched. "Wait, please. I have something more."

Again he groped, again with skeptical expression he followed the progress of his cautious arm as it entered and then descended slowly into the depths of the sack. We hardly recognized the sour smell that Monsieur Malmort had once more released among us. Minouche leaned forward, bereft of her passion for Monsieur Moreau. Even Yvonne, as large and shapely and nearly naked as she was, stood beside her forgotten dancing companion and followed the movements of Monsieur Malmort. Only little sleeping Déodat was not exposed to the performance of Monsieur Malmort.

He tugged once, tugged twice, our Monsieur Malmort, and drew his arm half from the sack and paused, looked to his left, his right, and closed his eyes with effort, and tugged again, lost ground, scowled at the sight of elbow disappearing once more into mouth of sack, then shrugged, abandoned his amusing tricks, and simply, without more fanfare, pulled from the sack and into view something gray, something limp but stiff, something which for moment upon moment no one could name.

He dropped the now-empty sack. He glanced in all directions. Then he seized with his right hand what he had been holding with his left and shook it somewhat. With the tips of the fingers of both his hands he so displayed his unprepossessing thing of cloth, if mere cloth it was, that I too shared the consensus of our salon and saw in the shape of that ugly but engaging thing the unmistakable torso of a woman who had once been real but now did not exist. To not the slightest degree had that distant woman resembled Sylvie or Clarisse or Minouche or Yvonne or Madame Pidou, so old and stiff and worn was the corset (for it was indeed a corset) with which Monsieur Malmort was attempting to entice them all, I thought, to some mysterious end. How wide it was to cover imaginary hips! How small in the waist! How fat and angry in its upper portions! How rubbed and molded of ancient bones it was, and how dry and gray its dead material that was once the finest of golden silk! And how amusing, I thought, yet frightening too, those laces loosened in their rows of eyelets and still demanding to be tied by cruel hands and fingers of someone other than the wearer. How immense she must have been, that woman who had been much larger than Madame Pidou, and in her corset how proudly imprisoned she must have been, I thought, as I watched Monsieur Malmort appraise that tough and faded garment dangling from his fingers.

"So," he said into the silence he himself had created. "So, who's first?"

No one answered. No one moved, though Bocage looked to Lulu and Lulu to Bocage, while Minouche and Sylvie and Clarisse and Yvonne were all staring fixedly at Monsieur Malmort and licking their lips.

"So," he repeated, peering from face to face and shrugging. "Who's first?"

At that moment Madame Pidou disengaged herself from Yvonne and stepped forward, tossed her head, drew wide her robe, surveyed her audience with ill-concealed pride, and let fall her robe. Beneath it she was nude.

"I am!" she cried as she flung wide her arms and lunged in an urgent faltering step toward Monsieur Malmort. "I am first."

They faced each other. He nodded, his old hat bobbing up and down. She took another step. Her face was radiant. His own was shining in pretended impassivity, with all its wrinkles looser than ever, and there was no mistaking the satisfaction that caused him to cock his head as might a crow caught off guard in its cleverness. Victim or victor, Madame Pidou took one final step and abruptly turned her back to him, instead of embracing him as I thought she would. Slowly, after another glance around our hushed salon, she lowered her arms. All was ready. Silence was everywhere.

"Mathilde," came the quiet voice of her husband, a voice no one could have expected, since he was a man long broken to her will. "Mathilde," he said, "will you do it here? In this room? When I am present? When I am holding on my lap this sleeping boy?"

She glanced once in his direction. She was magnificent.

"You!" she cried. "Poof! I say. Just imagine you're someone else and enjoy yourself! Now, Monsieur Malmort," she said over her shoulder in the beguiling voice of a woman much younger than she, "now I am yours!"

Never had I thought to witness such a spectacle, and I could not help but think that no one was any the less surprised than I. The radio suddenly found its voice, softly and in the middle of a song that made me think of a night of rain, a lighted café I could not see, the pleasure of kneeling inside Bocage's taxi and peering out at the rain. But from my corner I was watching as eagerly as the rest of them.

Monsieur Malmort stood behind Madame Pidou and with a swift and single movement wrapped her, loosely, in the corset. Into her armpits he pulled the sharp and cutting top. With strange efficiency he tugged the corset into the narrowness that was her waist; and holding it closed with one hand and as best he could, with the other he slapped the corset tight to the hips. It was too large, corset once fitted fresh and supple by some happy maid to the shapely body of her large and waiting mistress. It was too stiff and ugly to please Madame Pidou, I thought, yet still it did.

Old and brittle and shabby man. Corset that was much too large. Woman whose nakedness was all the more pronounced inside the menacing garment in which it was partially and slackly draped. But now Monsieur Malmort seized in both hands the unruly laces, which he wrapped about his palms and began to pull. He pulled again. Again. He fought to stifle the loud breaths of Madame Pidou. He discovered straps where none had been, and buckled them. He returned to the laces. What power in his skinny wrists! What signs of determination in the wrinkled face! And Madame Pidou? Clearly she had lost all awareness of herself, the corset, the old man struggling behind her back. And her breath came in fervid gasps, her face was half raised in sightless bliss toward the dark ceiling she could no longer see. Her neck was flushed. Her chest was pink. The blue veins in her long legs were bluer still. She turned herself each time Monsieur Malmort tightened the laces behind her back. She turned, he followed; he tightened still more the corset, which made her turn. It was impossible to know who was leading, who following. But in rapturous symmetry they turned together as might a statue of two embracing figures on an ever-revolving pedestal in the garden of night.

Suddenly the corset that had been too large now clung in a winsome fit to the upper body of Madame Pidou. For all to see, the corset was now changing color from gray to ivory as it molded the flesh of Madame Pidou to the swellings of an hourglass blown to her very size and filled, in its top or bottom, bottom or top, with pink sand. Her eyes were closed, her nostrils dilated slowly and fully with each impassioned breath she took. Her gray hair fallen to one side, her bony feet, her poor calves thin and hard, and long and naked thighs, and the darkness where the meeting thighs met the corset's lower edge: never had she looked so uncomfortable, so distraught, so in danger of collapsing there on the stones, no matter her rosy cheeks and helpless smile. And all this because of an old corset that had grown happily petite, I saw, and as smooth as silk? Perhaps it was not Madame Pidou revolving crookedly and raising one wet hand to her neck and pinching an inner thigh with the other, and through her open mouth moaning for mercy: perhaps it was instead that woman of a different age who, once wearing on a summer night only this same shiny corset, wanted nothing more than to tear it off in the presence of the man she craved. Straining forward in the darkness of my own concealment, little figure as warm and rapt as those that were large, at this moment I too was more possessed than puzzled.

"There, ladies," said Monsieur Malmort. "There she is. The lady who's never too old for kisses. What else?"

But he allowed no answer. He refused to acknowledge the single word of objection uttered by Monsieur Pidou. He took one step away from his proud creation and pointed, as if that woman staggering and clinging to herself and then reaching out an empty hand and clutching the air, woman both young and old, slack and firm in her corset that had once again changed color, from ivory to pale gold: as if that woman needed pointing out to those other women, who were as short of breath and as flushed as she. Where else could they possibly look, I asked myself, if not at her?

"Take a good look, ladies," said Monsieur Malmort. "Don't give up hope. Your turns will come. . . ."

He took another half step backward. He tugged down the brim of his fedora. His hands were hanging limp at his sides, he was smiling at Clarisse and Sylvie, Yvonne and Minouche, and even Virginie, though his eyes passed over me quickly in my nest of shadows.

Then, oh, then, a chair, his favorite rickety chair, appeared from nowhere at his side. Had it been thrust forward by Bocage? by Lulu whose hands were holding the shoulders of Clarisse and Sylvie and leaving red marks on the pale skin? I did not know. I could only watch and wonder at what I saw, until what I wanted to see prolonged forever came to its end.

First the chair appeared. Then the baggy trousers fell and gathered about the knees. Then he sat down, still wearing the tortured hat, the rumpled coat, the shirt that had long lost its collar. But something was different. Different indeed, I thought, and so it was: Monsieur Malmort sat slouching backwards on his rickety chair; his thighs were bare; his knees, buried within the mass of the fallen trousers, were spread as wide apart as possible. And there, leaping like a warrior from the naked loins, there was the old man's zizi (as Bocage had told me it was called) and tonight it was not the pathetic thing I had seen so often in the past, but rather was so ripe and ruddy, hard and soft, pink and plump, that it might have belonged to a man much younger than Monsieur Malmort. In fact it might have been the twin to Lulu's own.

"Come to me, Madame Pidou," said the old and seated man, while sucking through his teeth the air we breathed.

She turned, though her eyes were shut. She moved abruptly and awkwardly on her long bare legs. With accuracy and abandon too, she straddled the old man's waiting thighs and floundered forward into his embrace, though she could not see.

"No, Mathilde," murmured Monsieur Pidou, "no, no. . . ." But even I had not much patience left for Monsieur Pidou, who was speaking under his breath and wiping his eyes and cradling Déodat's little head against his chest.

Swift on the heels of her husband's voice, Madame Pidou's own voice cried out in a volume much louder than that of the radio and yet in a broken rhythm that matched the tempo of its lively song: "So hard, Monsieur Malmort?" she cried. "So young? So hard? So filled with gusto? So serene? Oh," she cried, "I could continue like this forever, and so could you, Monsieur Malmort, you with your generosity, your virility, your wisdom, your sense of humor. . . ."

She gripped the stiff shoulders and retained her seat. She wobbled from side to side and to and fro. She tossed in unintended circles, lunging now up, now down, while on the stones at her feet the poor black handsome cock marked time to the radio and the united pair by flapping as best he could, I saw, his clipped wings. On, on rode Madame Pidou, crying aloud, snorting for breath, staining the silk corset with great streaks of sweat, riding the ferocious Monsieur Malmort like a woman unskilled at horseback riding yet in love with her ride.

"Bravo!" shouted Bocage, no longer able to contain himself. "Don't stop!" shouted Lulu, and clutched Clarisse and Sylvie and, in boisterous empathy, limped and stumbled about as in the boxing ring.

"Henri!" cried Madame Pidou at last. "I do it for you, Henri! But I am done!"

She subsided. Trusting herself to Monsieur Malmort, she kept her seat but leaned back gently in the circlet of the frail arms that grasped her waist. She sighed. She breathed more evenly. She opened her eyes.

"Now, Monsieur Malmort," she whispered loudly, "now you must liberate me from this villainous garment that has caused a grateful woman to experience publicly her joy."

She disengaged herself. Stiffly, awkwardly, she regained her feet. Shrugging his familiar shrug, Monsieur Malmort stood also, pulled up his pants, closed his coat, with nimble fingers unlaced the corset, which had now returned, I saw, to its original shapelessness and dull color. With roughness he pulled and peeled the ancient corset from Madame Pidou, and stuffed it, that extraordinary garment, back in its sack.

Monsieur Malmort resumed his seat. Madame Pidou walked swaying but with head held high from our hot salon.

Then the night proceeded on its downward course. Monsieur Malmort beckoned me from my place in the shadows to climb upon his lap as usual. While I listened and the old man dozed, and his distant heart beat on beneath my ear, I saw that Sylvie and Clarisse were with wet tongues licking all the tiny women who ran and sprawled in luscious congestion on Lulu's bare chest, while waves of heat and noise came and went, came and went, in our darkening salon.

Later, much later, when I was alone at last, and when I had regained my awakened state, in this the darkest hour of the night, I thought of myself, at last, and wondered what it was I seemed to want when I was my own child and quite alone. Not exactly knowing what I was about to do, I crept down the hall to the small light burning in Maman's room. Her eyes were closed. With impunity and decision too I seized her silver hand mirror and returned to the kitchen. I studied the darkened emptiness of that room I knew so well. I thought of myself and, turning to the still-warm stove, heated myself a little saucer of milk. Then, bright as a bird, I laid the hand mirror where I wanted it on the polished floor. I pulled up my long gray skirt and holding it with one hand, and the dish of milk in the other, carefully I knelt with my bare knees straddling the mirror. I lifted the dish of milk between my legs and pressed it gently up and up again, while there, as I told myself, I drank and drank again. I set aside the dish. I knelt still closer to the glass, upon which I began to drip my little drops of milk. Then I bent down my head and looked. There was not much to see, dear self, but I loved what I saw.

Later, still later, I slept with Sylvie's white cache-sexe beneath my pillow. Once, from the courtyard, came the squawk of the cock with the fatal thudding blow of Bocage's hatchet. I resolved to eat with more conviction, though I knew that I was doomed to eternal childhood and would never grow into the woman I longed to be, would never attain a noble womanhood like Madame Pidou's, no matter how much I ate or what I might have yet to see.

〔1740〕 Land of Love;
Colère and the pig

The future. A new life. Another life. But shall I become a second self?
Shall I awake to a consciousness I cannot recognize as mine? Shall I find
myself unable to tolerate my second life, and so with increasing frequency
slip backward to inhabit once again the precious self that was the first
cast from its earthen mold? But whether or not I shall recognize myself in
sequences of prose like these: what if I manage to embrace both selves,
and having done so find them both the same? Mightn't my second self
be quite as innocent as the first? To discover only in the distant future or
distant past that one is destined to remain forever imprisoned in the same
self: what then? One self and then another, yet still the same? Still innocent?

This much I know: I am the child within. I am this unchanging child.
I am her voice. Who listens?

"These little creatures," I said to Dédou, holding his hand and leaning
over the better to inspect the clusters of small fat chocolate-colored things
growing there at our feet, "these creatures, Dédou, are called the Farts of
Nuns!" The end of the bright morning was emblazoned boldly on the
world. Hand in hand we stood, Dédou and I, bending over to study this
collection of miniature mushrooms, for such they were, that had but the
day before not existed here, at this very spot, on a path that always
appeared to me to have no end, no beginning, no matter how often we

followed it, Dédou and I, over the gentlest of hills and through fields that were green or brown, yellow or lavender. Overhead the blue of a clear sky; on every side and as far as one could see, sloping fields of every hue; and behind us the small far cluster of gables, tiles, shining roofs, and chimneys that looked like fingers, which signified the labyrinth of the château known, to farmers and villagers alike, as Dédale. From the low and slate-roofed turret flew the familiar pennant: a white and two-tongued background bearing a blue heart. The pennant was outstretched and beating; higher yet a handful of white doves circled and reflected from their soft and soaring bodies the warmth of the late morning sun.

"See them, Dédou," I said, bending still closer with his hand in mine and with my other pointing out the treasure growing there at our feet. "Notice how small they are, how closely they pack themselves, how light of weight they are, and how in their conical heads they represent the entire range of their color, from the faintest caramel to the black of some sweet candy burnt in a fire. That is why Seigneur has given to these mushrooms the name they bear. The Farts of Nuns are the smallest of all mushrooms, Dédou, and the lightest, and shiniest, and tastiest. Do you understand?"

But answer? Ask a question? Comprehend a portion, at least, of what I had said? No, I thought, he would do none of these, and I would not be disappointed in his lack of liveliness. He was the smallest boy I had ever seen, and the youngest, the plumpest, and except for his round face and fair hair, which gave him a false appearance of angelic intelligence, he might have been some mute and stunted version of Père La Tour since like him Dédou wore always a gray and collarless shirt fit for the stables, and puttees that concealed the chubby flesh of his little legs, and chunky boots. So how could Dédou be the least concerned with what to him were mere mushrooms, mere path, mere field, but was to me the very landscape of paradox itself where contradiction grew and truths flourished?

"Now, Dédou," I said, giving his placid hand a tug, "you must not step on the mushrooms. . . ." Guiding him around the chocolate colony, holding and swinging his hand in mine, off I led him at a brisk pace up the path climbing the gentle slope of this rounded hill. Over its crest, in a patch of green, grew a family of bright daffodils, and now I wished to pick a few of the tender stalks and yellow cups. Today the wild daffodils would be brighter than those that stood in their straight rows in the garden designated by Seigneur as mine.

"Look, Dédou!" I cried out, shaking him into attention and pointing toward that clearest of all horizons we were striving to achieve. "There she is! Do you see her?" Side to side, shoulder to shoulder, free hands shading our eyes, again we saw the stately woman who was dressed in black, as always, and who cajoled her dappled horse into a slow and unvarying canter, as if the horizon was hers alone to follow on a journey that would never end.

"Quick, Dédou!" I cried. "Back to the stables!"

We had only to race straight down the hill in order to precede by several moments the arrival of the monumental woman and her snorting horse in the otherwise empty courtyard of Dédale. So down we ran, forsaking entirely the narrow path for the broadness of the slope itself, while far from us yet Dédale came closer, loomed larger, while behind us the dappled horse rocked across the horizon like a child's rocking horse which, once set in motion, would forever maintain its artificial gait. All around Dédou and me the colors slowly changed from green to yellow, brown to lavender, the tint of one field shading into the hue of the next, until we came to the last field that lay between ourselves and the mustard-colored walls of Seigneur's château. But this was not the way we had come before. This was a field I had never until this moment seen, and only as we leapt to its edge did I perceive that in this flat field the cows belonging to Seigneur must have browsed for several days on end before being herded to some other.

"Faster, Dédou!" I cried, seeing that we had no alternative but to run directly through the center of this vast field, and feeling already our children's feet trodding the unlikely surface that lay in our path like a golden carpet; and suddenly I embraced this opportunity to dash headlong across a field which, otherwise, I would have circled. With delight I pressed ahead to skim the crust through which Dédou abruptly sank with each labored footfall of his clumsy run. I tugged his hand, I dragged him on, I marveled at the immensity of this smooth sea.

Thus I skimmed while Dédou floundered, despite the grip of my hand. When we reached the courtyard, both breathless, Dédou was quite bespattered from top to bottom, head to toe, while I, still savoring our flight, was as fresh as ever.

"Watch her, Dédou!" I whispered. "Here she comes. . . ."

I stood as close as I could to Dédou and put my arm around his shoulders and hugged him tight to my side, and with the hem of my gray skirt wiped his cheeks and dabbed his eyes.

But had Père La Tour heard the hoofbeats of the horse? By what sign could he have known to open the gates and bow to the entrance of the dappled horse and its rider attired crisply in black, from flowing hat to flowing skirt, and then again to close and bar the gates when they were once inside? But there had been no hoofbeats, as there never were, and there had been no sound of breathing, no cry, no rattling of silver chains, no sounding of horns, nothing to herald the arrival of this phantom pair which, safely within the courtyard of Dédale, became fearfully and imposingly the living woman and her living horse. I held Dédou; together we huddled against the warmth of the wall; together we stared at the arrogant woman high above us on her arrogant horse.

"Oh, you servile creature," said La Comtesse, for I knew her name if nothing more. "Oh, you are still servile," she said to Père La Tour as she always did, while her dappled mare, as large as Seigneur's chestnut horse and more ferocious, shied and tossed her head and danced and frothed in a spectacle that caused Dédou and me to cling still tighter to each other against the stone.

"Servile. Servile, as always," continued La Comtesse, addressing Père La Tour as if in the distant past he had become forever worthy of her contempt. "Oh, I cannot bear servility in a man, even in one who has fallen from high to low, and I would not allow you to so much as touch my horse's bridle except that unless you seize her bridle and hold it, I shall not get down! So I allow you and even order you to catch hold of her, if you dare, and keep her at a standstill while I dismount."

The tall and handsome horse (showing off, I thought, her bloodied eyes, pink gums, gray tail, jaws champing or yawning wide) now reared and flung herself this way and that, sidestepping in ever-tightening circles around Père La Tour. Still La Comtesse sat unperturbed on her dashing beast. Her feathered hat was like five ravens perched serenely and with outstretched wings upon her head; her enormous face was white and glaring; her black skirts hung unruffled, concealing all the majestic shape and size of her lower person except for the toe of one black boot, which stood in the stirrup and peeped from under the voluminous blackness of the long skirts that betrayed not the slightest movement of the bad-tempered woman on her unruly mount. As for Père La Tour, he did not flinch from the horse's viciousness or its rider's disdain, but waited in all humility for that moment when he would catch the singing bridle and hold and calm the now openly rebellious mare.

Sparks flew. Showers of gravel came down everywhere. But who was La Comtesse? I asked myself as I always did on these occasions, and why was Père La Tour forlorn and submissive in her presence? as if our Chief of Stables (which was what he was, despite his work in the kitchen) concealed within a different man too gently noble for his station in the life of Seigneur's Dédale.

But had I heard correctly the imperious words of the imposing and wrathful woman who had suddenly turned her attention to Dédou and me? I stared up at her, disbelieving what I had heard, and feared that this towering woman might spend her vengeful energies on Dédou and me.

"Remove that child," cried La Comtesse, speaking to Père La Tour while focusing on me or on Dédou or on both of us her blazing eye. "Remove that boy-child, I say, and quickly. Can't you see what a filthy little man that boy-child is? Away with him, I say. Out of my sight. . . ."

The horse allowed Père La Tour to leave its circle. Dédou began openly to cry. I stared up at La Comtesse with an expression of justified remonstrance on my heart-shaped face. I looked up so at La Comtesse, and gripped my little Dédou, besmirched and weeping, still tighter in my protective embrace. However, Père La Tour did as he was told, approached us gently and lifted Dédou into his arms and carried him off into the sweet darkness of the stable. La Comtesse deigned to look down at me once, twice, again, and not unkindly, I thought, though she said not a word.

Père La Tour came back to us. In an instant the dappled horse put off its fury and became as tender and trustworthy as Seigneur's two whippets. Père La Tour took hold of the bridle, and in a fine show of blackness and in complete indifference to me and the somehow vanquished man now stroking the silky nose of the dappled horse, La Comtesse dismounted. They spoke no words, he who led away the docile horse or she who stood alone and taller still and beginning to smile, by which I knew immediately that Seigneur himself had arrived to welcome her.

Without so much as a glance toward me where I pressed myself against the wall in the full light of the sun, and with his longest stride, and showing us only his most serious face, and with the merest shade of haste to temper the formality of his approach, in this way Seigneur strode through the studded door and in the next moment stood close enough to La Comtesse to give her a kiss, which he did not do. Handsome? Oh, yes, this man was never-changing, always the same, and yet each day was more composed, more fully complete in his bearing, his frame, his muscles, the simplicity of his dress, and thus more handsome than he had been but one day before. Black hair tied back; black ribbon banding his neck; shirt loose yet tight enough to remind the viewer of the power implicit in those heavy shoulders and shapely chest and well-proportioned arms; and the satin pants the color of old ivory or clear amber and tight to the thigh and chopped off firmly at the knees where they were tied; and the calves like the calves of a statue in white stockings: surely his was the beauty of authority in all its vigor!

"Madame," he said, and no word ever conveyed more devoted deference. "Madame," he said again and gave La Comtesse his arm, in the crook of which at once and without hesitation she placed her hand. From this moment forward I knew what to expect, what they would do, how in the subtlest ways they would reveal the regard they were now feeling for each other. These tête-à-têtes occurred only at great intervals, but with regularity, and I had been the silent witness to them all.

First the two of them would stand arm in arm and heads together for as long as I could hold my breath, and longer, and would then remove themselves from this walled and empty area of sand in the strange compatibility of total silence. They did. I followed. Then they would go to that same cool cloister that was sacrosanct to Seigneur and me, visited only by the two of us and then only on the Mornings of the Noblesse, except when, as now, Seigneur introduced into our cool cloister this very companion, who was much older than he, though all the more beautiful for the age she bore, and with whom he walked around and around as often as he did with me. Hidden behind a slender column, I watched them stroll side by side, shoulder to shoulder, around and around the pebbled garden path meant for Seigneur and me.

I knew that once secluded they would talk and talk, in tones too soft for me to hear, yet with such concentration that mere speech would become the severest intimacy, mere words more personal than the literal touching of hand to arm or of lips to lips. So they walked, as I knew they would. So they voiced in words the stored-up contents of their hearts and minds, as I knew they must.

As always they commenced their rendezvous at noon, when the sun was overhead and the black cock crowed, on the very stroke when ordinarily Seigneur and I and the women in Seigneur's charge gathered together, as we did at no other time of day, to consume the only meal that we shared. It was a time I cherished, and now this Rite of Noontide would be delayed, for as long as an hour, as I well knew.

La Comtesse arrived at Dédale at noon, inevitably. She stayed an hour. She went as she came, head high and hand on Seigneur's arm. But who was she? Who that our noontide rite must be delayed for her? Former inhabitant of Seigneur's château? Unidentifiable Noblesse who had left us one day in a past too distant to remember? No, I told myself. Impossible. This was not a woman who had known the fire, taken up the bees in her bare hands, watched the agony of animals for her sense of pride, aroused even the sacred father in his confessional, learned to make of flowers cosmetic ointments, scorned everything that did not contribute to sensual knowledge, suffered with selflessness the purest teachings of our Seigneur. No, I told myself, she had never lived with us. She was not such a woman. Then who? Perhaps La Comtesse had managed to form her own tempestuous depths of womanhood before Seigneur acquired his art. Perhaps she was somehow prior to Seigneur's art or even his life. Perhaps she herself was the fount of all that Seigneur knew. But I did not know.

So for the time I gave up my vigilance. They would walk, they would converse, they would part with their secrets undivulged to me. Seigneur excluded me from this mystery in much the same manner in which he kept me from any knowledge of the Tapestry of Love.

There was no more to see. I knew it all, and nothing. Their tête-à-tête was not finished, was no more than halfway toward its conclusion, and I was growing weary while La Comtesse talked and Seigneur listened. So I crept away, and avoided Adèle's domain of hearth and cookery since, in the Rites of Noontide, I was a participant instead of the favored servant I was when other meals were prepared and served. I avoided the stables, and I had no desire to visit the garden that was my own, or to work my loom. I languished. I leaned against a column. What could I do? How pass the time? With nothing profitable, I told myself, since I was no longer tuned to surprises and secrets, and had lost my usually productive mood. I wanted only to know that La Comtesse had left, and nothing more. What could I do?

Suddenly I heard the bells. And a cacophony of women's happy voices. The triumphant sounding of the black cock, though he had already announced the midday an hour before. And needles stopping and looms shutting down. And the book closing. And the winging of the white doves. The crackling of the roasted boar we were soon to eat. And best of all, the burst of hoofbeats that in the next moment was gone.

Briskly I entered Dédale's dining hall and was not the last. Once more I was aware of the objects that from every corner, every angle, every wall, leapt out specially to incite the child's mind. Two long narrow tables were positioned parallel to each other and lengthwise on the polished floor, and were dressed in heavy cloths of the deepest blue; places were laid only on the sides of the tables nearest the walls, so that the diners sat together in two facing rows. One monkish table was set for two, the other for five, so that seated side by side at the table that was always ours, Seigneur and I were centered, so to speak, on the row of five women who, when seated at the table that was theirs, could smile at us across the space between the tables. Seigneur was already in his chair, as were little Bel Esprit and Volupté. And the rest were coming.

The symmetry of this hall as long as a wooden ship propelled by oars went far beyond the situation of Seigneur and his confidante and the women who had vowed apprenticeship to love. Oh, far beyond our situation went Seigneur's passion for symmetry and need for order. Two tapestries of blue sequences on fields of white complemented each other on our facing walls; and overhead there were two rows of chandeliers (with candles lighted despite the bright day) instead of one; and even Seigneur's whippets comported themselves in accordance with his designing mind, since La jaune sat stiffly on the polished floor at the southerly end of the women's table, while Le noir sat similarly at the end of the table belonging to Seigneur and me. But there was more than this: for adjacent to the northern wall, and in the space between our tables, and equidistant from each, there stood the serving table, and beside it Père La Tour with knife in hand, and on that burnished table, lengthwise and filling a silver platter so heavy a single person could not carry it, the roasted boar whose inner cavity and open mouth were stuffed with bunches of green grapes. And more, still more, and what I loved the most: for there, on blue plaques affixed around three walls and as high as possible, where white walls met the white and blue-beamed ceiling: there, and side by side around the walls, hung the stuffed heads of the largest of the boars Seigneur had killed. The bristling, ferocious heads had open mouths and curving tusks, long and blackened snouts, and big eyes the color of Seigneur's favorite shade of blue. The tusks were gilded, the blue eyes fixed. Disdainfully did those shaggy heads look down at the beast still steaming on its platter. I joined them in relishing such a sight.

No longer did it matter that our meal was late. Seigneur's visitor was gone from Dédale and all but gone from my mind, where she yet excited me faintly to a longing I could not explain and to an utterly unfamiliar fear. But no matter. She was all but gone. With each stroke of Père La Tour's long knife she faded. With each forkful I raised to my lips a fragment of her image disappeared. And then another, and another. I ate with more than my usual pleasure; I glanced at Seigneur and put my napkin to my mouth with care; I sipped from my small portion of dark wine. The wine was of the deepest taste of wood, of stone; the flavor of the meat made me think of hot blood in a cave. The women across from us were exempt, this hour, from the obligations imposed upon them by Seigneur, and were talking to each other in soft voices.

The immense but tranquil dining hall received the sun, made use of it, sustained on its temperate air the fragrance of perfume, the tang of the prostrate beast, as if these aromas were musical notes surviving in the ear long after the disappearance of the song. We ate. We drank. Back and forth went Adèle with blue plates now filled, now empty, now filled again. Père La Tour did not cease his carving. He smelled of the stables and had come directly from stables to dining hall; nonetheless he concentrated on his carving and did not allow his mind to take one direction and his knife another. He worked deliberately, as I well knew, if only because he gave Seigneur the boar's left cheek and me the right, and Seigneur had told me often that the cheeks were the prized portions of any roasted animal or fish.

I looked at my plate, glanced at Seigneur, raised my heavy fork when he raised his. I sat as straight as I could on the edge of my chair, and surveyed the company, smiled at Père La Tour but made no sign of recognition when Adèle took away my plate and brought it back, took it away again and then, each to its blue dish, served the pears. Great yellow pears they were, and without stems, without cores, without blemishes of any kind. No other fruit could have proven so perfectly translucent beneath the skin, and on the tongue so sweet.

"Mesdames," said Seigneur at last, remaining in his seat but lifting his goblet in a prolonged salute, and speaking with only enough volume to command attention, "I drink to you. To you, mesdames, as you are now, already in the midst of change, and as you shall be, one sooner, another at a slower pace, but inevitably as you all shall be: deliberate in your employment of caprice; submissive to all the posturings required of you in the Land of Love, as it has been called by an old and fanciful cartographer; and stronger willed than the very men who exist for nothing more than to guarantee you your freedom by imprisoning you in the Land of Love . . . So, mesdames, to you!"

With shrewdness he glanced from face to face of those to whom he was paying tribute. He toasted Finesse, Magie, Colère and Volupté and little Bel Esprit. He put his full goblet to his lips. He drank. They did the same. Serenity was what the Rites of Noontide were intended to achieve, and once more I recognized the serenity in which all present were enveloped and which issued, with the words he spoke, from the mouth of Seigneur.

"Now, mesdames," continued he who in this hour had become soft-spoken, "now, as you might guess, I wish to explore none other than this domain of the precious sentiment. But why Land of Love? why not Terrain of Sensuality? or even Lust? You know my inclinations. By now you understand that when I speak of love I have lust in mind, as when I

97

speak of lust I am thinking of love, with its winged infants and crowns of flowers. And why not? I am convinced that the map-maker shared my view, no matter his choice of words."

More wine. Pears superseded by cakes containing in their centers nuggets of honey. Cut flowers carried to our tables by Adèle and Père La Tour. But cakes, wine, flowers: now they were of no importance since for all concerned there was only a single sweetness, which was Seigneur himself. We ate and drank unconsciously, fixed only on the sound of Seigneur's voice.

"Mesdames," he said, "we begin on what our privileged maker of maps has designated as the Plain of Indifference, a sterile landscape rolling from horizon to horizon and occupied by nothing except a strangely forbidding country fair. At this fair we see only homeless creatures whose great hoods hide their faces and who do not talk. We too wear hoods. We do not talk. The fair is a marketplace for sacks of resin, boxes of ordinary stones culled from the fields, cages meant for birds but filled with wasps. It is a barren plain, and we keep well to the edge of the listless crowd attending as if forever its useless fair. I must tell you that that hooded crowd, admiring the wasps and buying stones, is composed of those who exemplify three kinds of indifference. First there is the young and unawakened woman whose hesitation is mistaken for indifference; she is not long at the fair. Then we have the woman who feigns indifference, and feigned indifference, whether inhabiting a desperate or merely a clever breast, is ultimately transparent and best avoided; our feigning woman stays longer at the silent fair. Then we have that woman old or young who has feigned indifference for so long and so successfully that her mask has become the face it was once meant to hide, and thus hers is the face forever pocked and pitted with true indifference, which she now detests but cannot put off; she is a familiar figure inside the flapping tents, no matter how thoroughly she cloaks her face. But there is one more. This is the woman whose indifference comes and goes according to her will, and is a strong and serious attribute by which alone she is assured of selfhood; this woman, of whom I have spoken in the past, is frequently seen at the windy fair on the Plain of Indifference, but never for long.

"So much for indifference. Its domain is intolerable and soon enough we discover the hidden road that leads away from the desolate fair on its windy plain. In such a place it is not long before we of spirit are driven into our lovers' arms and hence escape.

"Thus you see, mesdames," he continued, sipping again his wine and raising his eyes to scan the row of bestial heads high on the wall behind the women for whom he spoke. "Thus you see that even the start of our journey is arduous. But we have begun. We are fortunate. We hurry on. Where next do we find ourselves? Why, in the Wood of Assembly, which is a pretty place where gentle and ageless instrumentalists sit beneath pale trees and play their lutes, and where silken goats feast on green leaves and where horses graze. It is pleasing enough, this Wood of Assembly, but worthy of only the shortest stay. So too the Hostel of the Gentle Look. Though it is situated well off the road and is a friendly house, it beckons most to lovers untried and young. One tires quickly of its numerous attendants and of sunny rooms in which there are no devices for making fast the doors. We are impatient, all of us, to be on our way. We proceed. We are still eager. Yet we have already learned enough to skirt, as if it were infested, as in a sense it is, the Valley of Declared Love, as our map-maker has so aptly named it. We know well enough what would await us in the Valley of Declared Love: an entire colony of righteous couples so burdened by the need for sanction that they suffer inflamed throats and runny eyes and fits of hoarseness such that no one can hear the endearments they whisper to each other throughout the day. They wipe their eyes, strike their stomachs and, in voices all but lost, swear the honesty of the love they must every hour of the day profess. They declaim their virtue yet have nothing to show but faces flushed in shame. We do not want the company of such as these. But it is hardly better in the Fields of the Wounded Heart, where the sentiments of abandoned women turn tattered windmills that pump no water, grind no grain. These women are not for us. We skirt their distant windmills and again step out on the road that is always ours to follow.

"Ah, but, mesdames," he said and paused, raised his goblet as if to drink, then set it down, "at last, and as weary as we are, at last we gain the place we have been so very long in seeking, the place where there are no dreams of love but love itself, and no laws of love but the art of it. Its name? The Citadel of the Desire to Please. It is a secret principality unto itself, as we shall see, and here we stop and here it is that we discard our hoods. It is a principality of pleasure, this citadel, and just as various as the landscape we have only now traversed, but more coherent. No sooner do we pass through its gates than we stand before a château which, in former times, was but moderately defended. It was known as the Château of Resistance. It lies in ruin. Not for long do we inspect this ruin. Instead we turn and proceed directly down the shaded avenue that takes us to the garden lying in the center of our sacred citadel. A labyrinth, this garden as darkly green as fir trees or as brightly green as the first leaf unfurling, it is nonetheless a labyrinth in which we cannot lose our way and to which we constantly return throughout our stay in the Citadel of the Desire to Please. I am speaking of the labyrinth of Surrender All. Obviously there can be no pleasing without surrender, no surrender that does not please. The labyrinth is to the citadel as the fountain is to the park. The garden of green confusion, which it initially appears to be, is in fact as orderly as the citadel itself; the greenness of the labyrinth determines all. Everything in the citadel is held in its proper place, attains its balance and hence its meaning. Across from the merchant of sweet lemons and acidic oranges, there is he who has brought jellies from far countries and is matched in turn by he who creates sweet essences. Here even the chickens hatch only in the light of the sun and sing only for the pure of heart. In this citadel's cathedral flying babes consort with birds of blue glass; in its place of learning are wise authorities on such subjects as clever words, enchanting stories, and the cultivation of flowers that arouse the senses. Now we are no longer weary. We bring to the lecture hall the receptive residue of passions undertaken in the labyrinth; in the golden hall we listen attentively to impassioned lectures that return us, newly inspired, to the labyrinth. No form of love is excluded here; all forms of love are spawned, cultivated, scrutinized, enjoyed. In the mauve light of the cathedral in which we rarely kneel, we see our lovers and ourselves prefigured in stained glass; silent choirs reassure us that no love is too immoderate to share, no desire so gentle as to deny its impending violence. Even the golden babes sailing in the darker light above our heads have themselves but come from flying down the green corridors.

"But no one is ever satiated, mesdames. In the Citadel of the Desire to Please there is no such thing as satiety. She who stuffs herself on the food of love has room for more. Surely it must be obvious that the desire to please can never in itself be sated. Amorous desire is self-inventing. Tranquillity must not be confused with satiety. It is not satiety that drives us from our citadel. Yet we are so driven. Indeed we are.

"The answer, mesdames? It is all too easy. She who achieves the citadel begins to forget that she too was once tempted to indifference. . . ."

Here, in sadness and anticipation too, I thought, Seigneur ceased to talk. His pause grew longer while we waited, as if forgetfulness had descended upon Seigneur, as it had on the woman in his narrative, and had quite destroyed the very account which, initially, had given rise to this same forgetfulness from which he too seemed to suffer. We waited. The shadow of his silence grew. My eyes were turned to my plate, and yet I saw that the women across from me were doing exactly what I was doing: searching their plates. My discomfort was no less than theirs. Still Seigneur preserved his silence, resting an elbow on the table now empty but for wine and flowers. He glanced at the whippets, and smiled to himself as if indeed he had forgotten what he had meant to say. Then, without explanations and still bemused, or saddened, as I thought, quietly he resumed his recitation, though after the first few words his raised head and gentle smile signaled once again the authority that was his and on which we, his listeners, were so willing to depend.

"We are indeed driven from that citadel," he said, sitting straighter in his high-backed chair and inflecting his words with still deeper tones of certainty. "Indeed," he continued, "that is the case. And why? Not from satiety, as I have said, but merely because she who achieves the citadel begins to forget that she too was once tempted to indifference. There comes to all of us that day when in the midst of bliss the merest fragment of memory slips into view and beckons. Our lips are moist with the taste of our lover's desire to please and with our own; the birds of blue glass are poised on twigs that do not bend; sensuality reigns in the Land of Love. No matter. The day has come. The hour has come. We have only to allow the briefest memory to obtrude into our contented woman's bliss than she is ready to throw over bliss, contentment, rapture, sensuality. Suddenly she knows she had a former life and yearns to recover what she has lost, yearns to regain the entirety of all she has forgotten in the Land of Love: no matter that what she yearns to recollect will prove to be only misery itself. She has but to remember congested wasps or to see in memory a single stone and she is off. On a clear day she abandons all that she has lived to attain, and leaves the citadel and sets out to rejoin her past, no matter what that past contains, and so completes the circle and begins anew the journey. So you see, the prospect of more life, even the life of the past (for those who have no future), is so strong in itself as to pry the most faithful mistress from the naked embrace she still adores. More life! We must have it!

"So love, no matter how inspired and whether given generously or stolen, is no match for the dullest memory. So she finds herself, courageous woman, once more on the windy plain and more than ever receptive to the imminence of a forgotten kiss. She is off. We wish her well. She is a zestful traveler. So let us have more life, mesdames. More life!"

He stopped. He drank long and fully from his goblet and then set it down. He was finished, fatigued, satisfied. In our silence there was unheard applause, as Seigneur leaned back in his chair and looked from face to face of his admiring women, and allowed himself to accept unstintingly of the pleasure they intended their shiny faces to convey to him. The sunlight in our hall was still a pink ray shot through a prism and diffusing among us unchanging light; the boar was gutted on his platter that was still held motionless at the head and foot by Adèle and Père La Tour, whose progress had been arrested by Seigneur's clear voice.

"But, mesdames," he said suddenly and in a lively manner, "who in the golden hall delivered his disquisition on lust and love?"

"You, Seigneur!" cried little Bel Esprit at once.

"But who took his place among the sheep and doves depicted in the stained glass?"

"You, Seigneur!" cried Magie before anyone else was able to reply.

"But, mesdames," he said, and indicated that he would ask his final question. "Who made the map?"

The silence with which they met this question was answer enough, and was so unmistakable and sufficient that Adèle and Père La Tour carried off the boar and the light dimmed. In profile Seigneur's face was larger than it had ever been, and the harmony of his features still more pronounced.

"Very well," he said, and nodded. "Now, who is to read aloud to us today from her journal?"

"I," said Colère, and rose at once and opened to the place she had marked in the volume which she had been concealing beneath the table. Seigneur smiled at Colère, who among the women gathered in our hall was the only woman of middle age, and had not read to us before. But why was she standing when Seigneur had not? When no one else had ever stood to read? Was standing so necessary for Colère? Was it to show us her height and the extent of her black gown? Was she then so nervous? Or was it that she thought too highly of what she had written in privacy and was now ready to read to us aloud? Nervousness or pride, she caused me to glance uneasily at Seigneur, but he had not moved and his expression remained unchanged.

"Seigneur," she said, "and mesdames. You might think that what I have written came to me in a dream. But such was not the case though I wish it were. Nor do its women derive from any of you seated at this table and with whom I share our secluded life. As far as I am aware, my composition has no source, refers as little to memory as it does to dream. How did it come to me? I do not know. If it is so enigmatical, having no correspondence to my own life, such as it is, or to any life I am able to recognize, do I still dare to present it to this audience, intimate and receptive though it is? I hesitate, as you see. But without understanding of what I have written, I yet stand before you and I shall do my best. Could it be that what I have written concerns my age? Or the concern of any woman for age? I am not sure."

The open book trembled in her hands. Her voice was faltering. But she commenced to read.

"Three sisters," she began, "sit by the edge of a stream talking of love." Here she interrupted her reading, though she had hardly begun it, to say that she had no sisters. Somehow it was an admission appropriate to her quivering figure, her uncertain voice, the darkness beneath her eyes, the courage, as I now saw it, with which she stood before us. She took a breath. She plunged on in her trembling book as if to find in it that sadness that should prove the source of her awkward pride or else bring her to tears. "Three sisters at the edge of a stream," she said, "are singing softly. The youngest is dark-haired: 'I would be distrustful,' she says, 'of a lover with dark hair. But my hair is dark and I shall have a dark-haired lover.'"

She paused. She marked her place with her finger. She stared at Seigneur with not the slightest recognition. She too might have been hearing for the first time what she was reading aloud. Again I glanced at Seigneur: he was unmoved.

Colère looked to her page. "Three sisters," she said, "sit by the edge of a stream and sing softly. The second one calls to her friend Pierre: 'You have already taken me into the dark wood. Take me there again!' "

Once more she stopped. Her lips were parted. She searched our dining hall so avidly and with so little comprehension that I feared she might leave the table, walk from the hall, and leave us behind in her silence.

"Continue, Colère," Seigneur said at last.

"Three sisters," she repeated in a rising tone of voice, "three sisters sit by the edge of a stream and sing softly. The eldest" (and for a final time she stopped and again continued), "the eldest says: 'A woman must love when she is young. She must take care to keep her love when she has it.' "

She closed the book. She remained standing. Her eyes appeared to be quite sightless. At last Seigneur pushed back his chair, stood up, and faced Colère. The hall might have been empty but for the two of them.

"Colère," he said in a voice that was firm yet neutral. "Those who keep journals at Dédale are forbidden to express themselves in poetry. The poet's medium is the single word; the prose writer's is the sentence. The word is the gem, but the sentence is the entire crown. Yet what you have read to us is poetry, despite its sentences. But sentences like yours may move the best of us to tears. I had not thought you capable of such a view of love. I hope your poignant sentiments attend you this afternoon."

So saying, and followed by Le noir and La jaune, he strode from the hall.

"Père La Tour," cried Seigneur, gripping my hand and walking with strides thoughtlessly long, "prepare the salon. . . ."

Flown the hawk of dawn. Fading the day. The distance was short enough between the arbor, where Seigneur and I had been sitting in silence on our bench of stone, and the narrow door by which we would reach that cold corridor which in turn would take us to the locked salon that was our destination, and yet Seigneur proceeded at a pace unnecessarily swift. I noted that his mood had remained exactly the mood he had put on suddenly at Colère's first words. When he was brusque, when he was precise, when he was most peremptory, and when the reach of his authority soared far wide of our needs, then the only word for Seigneur's mood was sinister. Now his pace and bearing were bright with sinister intent; the very substance of his person was sinister. But I did not fear this dark mood of his.

The corridor was lit by tall tapers. When we reached the locked door, Seigneur produced the heavy iron key and applied the brutal key to the small and shining intricacies of the brass lock. We heard a terrible rumbling in the little lock; the door swung open silently to Seigneur's push; before us lay Dèdale's salon. No room in Seigneur's château was as grand as this one, as richly appointed, or, to me, as curious. There before us on the hearth still larger than the kitchen hearth was the immense fire feasting on logs the size of a child and burning in midflame, though the door had been locked. Six tall narrow windows of leaded glass, three to a side, admitted into this room a light that was ever the same and waxy; yet near the top of the middle window to the left was sharp evidence of a broken pane. Against the right-hand wall was a table heavier than a throne, on which lay a volume opened apparently but moments before. Between the windows and flanking the hearth, all the walls supported row on row of books in leather bindings; yet all this roomful of books concerned but a single subject, as Seigneur had said, were books which he himself had had prepared in a uniform edition and were devoted each and every one, in texts and etchings, to depicting woman in her various amorous lives from glory to despoliation. Most of these volumes were green with mold. A dusty ladder climbed to a high place where a single book was missing. Was the missing book that same one on the table? I did not know. I did not wish to know. I much preferred the question to its answer, no matter what that answer was.

But oh, how intriguing was our salon, readied as it always appeared to be for guests, yet empty! lavishly arranged in thick rugs of intricate patterns and a gilded cross atop the mantelpiece, yet exuding in all its surfaces the staleness that perfumes only decaying rooms in châteaux long abandoned! The furniture had been moved aside, leaving the vast center bare except for the largest and softest rug, which had been soiled and cleaned and soiled endlessly, so that its pinkish color suggested both the blooming and the fading rose.

Seigneur took his place at once, with his back to the fire, hands clasped behind his back, legs apart. His sturdy thighs and calves were silhouetted by the fire; he had all the appearance of a man who had in fact emerged unscathed just now from this very fire. As for me, I went straight to the small black upright piece of furniture that was unlike any I had ever seen, that existed as it did for me alone, and that served what I took to be the most curious of purposes: that of concealing me inside it. My black box was for me like an upended coffin in miniature, whereas Seigneur inevitably referred to it, and with evident pleasure, as Virginie's confessional, which perhaps it was, though no one ever spoke to me when I was seated behind the flimsy door which I myself hooked tightly shut from within. Seigneur assured me that my little confessional was intended to contribute to his own satisfaction and not to mine, and in ways which he preferred not to explain.

No sooner was I seated than I began to tingle in my self-confinement to the darkness that was mine alone. Legs together, back straight, hands in lap, skirt to ankles, face as close as possible to the black lacquered netting that filled the perfect square so cut into the flimsy door as to accommodate with ease my eager face: so I positioned myself and readied myself for what was to come. Invisibility was its own treasury, I somehow understood, yet I did not know why.

There I sat. There stood Seigneur. The heat of Seigneur's fire filled my box, while he before the fire was more than ever preoccupied with the sight of my white face which he could no longer see.

From the corridor came the rumbling sound of wooden wheels rolling on stone. Suddenly, and as always and just as startling, the emptiness of the immense salon gave way to activity, to all the matter-of-fact activity for which we waited, Seigneur and I, and which appeared to have a momentum of its own and to be quite unrelated to Seigneur and me, though all that happened did so in accordance with what Seigneur had willed.

The wheels rumbled in primitive prelude to the most dazzling of incongruities. Seigneur leaned forward to thrust himself into what he had himself devised. Père La Tour appeared at once in our salon, paying attention not to Seigneur or to my black box, but only to the whippets, which he led on a double leash, and to a young pig extravagantly large despite his youth, which Père La Tour held on an old rope that was tied in near-throttling fashion about the pig's fat throat. Even as the animals betrayed incomprehension, attempting to entangle themselves in leash and rope, the narrow cart came slowly into our midst with one of the assistants of Père La Tour walking backwards and pulling on the wooden tongue, while the other, a shorter and more sturdy man, leaned all his weight into the clumsy wagon from behind. Seigneur had no need to speak to Père La Tour, nor did Père La Tour address his attendants, who positioned the heavy wagon at the edge of the faded rug as they had done before. No word was spoken as Père La Tour kept the whippets on a gentle leash and tugged at the pig's rope; in silence the attendants, with their eyes downcast, set to work without a care for what they were doing or for the nature of the sumptuous salon in which they worked.

The pig was white, yet also pink. The drooping flap of his left ear had been snipped away and replaced with a perfect duplicate of gold. Did I prefer the left ear to the right? Or the aristocratic dogs to the splendid pig? I did not know. The wooden cart was filled to overflowing with straw so glazed and yellow that it could never have lain thickly strewn beneath a horse's hooves, and now the two attendants, one short and broad, the other lean, applied their wooden pitchforks to the straw in the cart. Under the watch of Seigneur and Père La Tour (and of me as well, had they but known), they drove their pitchforks deep into the glistening straw, lifted high their forkfuls, flung their yellow clumps upon the vast pink field of the carpet, and turned again to the wagon. The whippets huddled together while the young pig emitted muffled and urgent squeals, choked as he was, and attempted to escape his rope. Seigneur looked on as impassively as did Père La Tour, though I knew that Seigneur was but concealing his concentration whereas Père La Tour was more than ever stooped and distracted under some burden of the distant past. He did not see the wagon. He did not care what his attendants were doing. The fire burned, and a page of the open book rose of its own accord and fell.

The rug was gone from view. The straw that concealed it was shin-deep and golden. The attendants sent their wooden forks clattering into the empty wagon, and sweating in the extent of their efforts pulled the wagon from Seigneur's salon and down the corridor until there was nothing more to hear but silence. High overhead, near the white ceiling supported by squared beams ornamented in blue and gold, a cool breath blew down upon us steadily from the broken pane. Now even the pig was silent and had visibly accepted the tight rope and ceased to move.

The animals announced the arrival of Magie and Colère. The two dogs turned their heads in unison toward the narrow doorway; at once the pig abandoned his submissiveness and lunged forward on the end of his rope, and mustered again his fatness and threw himself toward the doorway in unmistakable recognition of Colère, whom he had never until this moment seen. They were arm in arm, Magie and Colère, and waited just inside our warm salon where they were welcomed not by Père La Tour or by Seigneur, but by the pig and dogs. Magie freed her arm from Colère's and prepared to leave; Colère stood listening to Magie's soft voice, while staring in alarm at the frantic pig.

"Good-bye, Colère," said Magie. "Remember that we have all done what you are about to do. Most of us have done it more than once. May you succeed immediately and thus spare yourself unpleasant repetitions of the trial you shall undergo today. Now, good-bye."

With these words Magie kissed Colère's white cheek, retreated silently, pulled to the narrow but heavy wooden door, and was gone. We heard the tumblers of the brass lock falling in place, though Seigneur still possessed the key. The door could not be forced.

Colère took a faltering step. Another. She avoided the lunging pig. With large uncertain eyes, and in silence, she questioned Père La Tour, questioned Seigneur, stared with still wider eyes at the bed of straw, glanced hastily at the walls of books, glanced more briefly at my black box.

No woman could have been more alone than Colère was now, standing but barely inside our locked salon, and confronted only by men who refused her greeting and animals whose friendly ways were trivial to her, or startling, and nothing more. Again she looked toward the books, toward the constant fire, toward the pig, more than ever distraught in his eagerness. Again she shied back, lifted a long hand to the bosom of her black gown, appealed equally and in silence to Seigneur and Père La Tour to release her from ignorance, muteness, humiliation.

"Colère," said Seigneur at last, and not unkindly, "come closer. I see that I must address myself to your hesitation. Let me insist that there is nothing in this salon that I have not already described to you with care and clarity. Long beforehand you have known what to expect. Is it then so unfamiliar? Animals, warm light, Père La Tour and me: is it not exactly as I promised? With nothing taken away and nothing added? Then why surprise? Why timidity? To participate in this charade is no more difficult than to read aloud a poem. Now, Colère, I must ask you to advance."

She looked left and right, over her shoulder, down at the fat pig. She stirred. She clasped her hands before her prayerfully, attempted unsuccessfully to keep to the front her strained face which, against her will, kept turning to this side or that. But she went forward, reached the edge of the straw, went further, shook her head, found herself up to her knees in the straw and stopped.

"Seigneur," she said, in a tone as worried as the wringing of her long hands, "tell me again. Tell me why again." No longer did she notice the wisps and thicknesses of straw into which the bottom of her black gown disappeared. Already she was summoning that strength of spirit which I knew was hers. Despite wrinkles, agitation, clasped hands, youth was returning.

"Very well, Colère," he said. "A word or two. No more." The pages of the open book were turning. Seigneur took a breath, exhaled, looked at Colère with kindness in his eyes, then spoke.

"No creature is too deformed to love," he said. "No act is too unfamiliar, too indelicate to perform. Repugnance has no place in the heart of a woman such as you. By embracing an animal, or several animals, you do no more than to embrace the very man, those very men, for whom you are now preparing yourself in the art of love. Adoration cannot live without debasement, which is its twin. I must ask you to disrobe."

"But, Seigneur," she pleaded in a still firmer voice. "If for my own sake you are to see me triumph over bestiality, will you not as well be pleased? Will I be pleasing you? Tell me. Will you be pleased?"

She waited longer for his reply than I had thought she would. From without, the breath of the ending day came down to us from the broken pane. The fire burned steadily behind Seigneur, without diminishing, fueled not by the heavy logs on which it flared and danced, it seemed, but fed instead by an inexhaustible jet of some light or vapor we could not see. Colère's body was twisted in the torture of anticipating the reply she hoped to receive. Finally Seigneur nodded. That was all. But nothing Seigneur had ever done or said bespoke such eloquence.

"Then I shall do it!" cried Colère at once. "I shall disrobe!" she cried, drawing her gown over her head and flinging it aside. "I shall do it," she cried, "and even more!"

In all her nakedness she turned and faced Père La Tour. She flung wide her long arms and kissed the air. Impassively Père La Tour bent down and freed the whippets, tore loose the rope from the pig's neck, draped rope and double leash over his own shoulders and folded his arms, leaned back against a row of moldy books to await, with no interest whatsoever, the outcome of the event we were now, all three of us, to see.

The light of the fire and of the late day crawled in serpentine fashion through the straw, burrowed into the straw, rose and lay in flat strands and pools atop the straw. Exact simulations of each other, except for size, the two white dogs waited side to side at the edge of Colère's rustic arena in its sumptuous setting. With the back of her bare body turned to me, again Colère flung high her arms and shook down the black hair pinned up on her head in wave on wave. All at once the pig lunged into the straw, surged forward in leaps and bounds, one moment completely visible, the next submerged entirely so that I could mark his progress only by the straw he sent flying upward as he tunneled and swam to our tall Colère who stood with a hip thrust out boldly and a hand pressed upon it. In a loud voice she both taunted and encouraged the fat and youthful pig now noisy and frantic in his pursuit of the woman who was so clearly his. He romped. He fell. He shouldered away great gouts of straw and grunted in a voice that was all but human and screamed forth his joy as he reached Colère and flung himself upon her, rising on hind legs too small to bear his entire weight, and heaving the underside of his fat body upon Colère's firm thigh, and grasping Colère's thigh with his front legs and little dangling hooves.

"What! You wretched creature," she cried. "Would you mount me thus? Climb upon me thus without a yes or no? Hop upon me upright, you foolish creature? Capture and subdue and use only my naked leg for your selfishness? Off, you brute! Get off!''

So saying, she kicked her long leg. She laughed. With nothing more than a kick of her leg and twist of her hip she rid herself of the now rabid and snuffling pig. Up he got. Again he caught her leg, clung to it, attempted to assuage his desperation against her gleaming leg, and again she kicked him away despite his weight, and again he returned to his attack.

"What! You exhausted thing, will you not learn? Have you a mind for nothing else? No other way? No subtlety? No humor? And wrong! Mistaken! But here," she cried and kicked him off. "Now let Colère set you to rights, poor beast. . . ."

She whirled away from him, laughed and stumbled, bent over, escaped him, with her strong bare arms swept together huge heaps of straw until she had made a lengthy mound, a bright plateau, a shelf, a bed. Down went Colère upon her back, laughing, kicking up her legs, raising her head, looking about for the pig, spreading wide her upraised legs in flashes of light, curtains of falling straw. Again the pig risked failure and drove himself head-on into her naked ribs.

"Ah, poor brute," she gasped, "you're wider of the mark than ever."

With a swift hand she seized one of the pig's hind legs. The pig squealed. He pulled away as though to tear off his puffy leg and leave it behind in Colère's firm hand. But he could not, and she did not let go. Instead she arched her back, thrusting high her burnished stomach, and rolled partially over, and in a dexterous darting of her free hand, caught the second of the pig's hind legs, at which he squealed unremittingly his helplessness and worked his front feet as if only to paddle as far and fast as he could from his victim turned in all her treachery to victor.

Colère held fast to the little legs. Slowly, and not without a struggle, she contorted herself so that her arms were stretched full length behind her hidden head, the hands still keeping their relentless hold on the pig's legs. So she maneuvered the angry animal until pig and captor were oddly coupled, a single beast with a pig's head and a woman's feet. Now Colère dragged the pig's captured legs across her shoulders, so that were she but to stand the pig would be hanging headfirst down her back, rear legs gripped over her shoulders as if she were the rewarded hunter and he the prize. But they were prone, and Colère's face was buried beneath the pig's hindquarters in the straw. Still she laughed her raucous laugh while the pig evidenced surprise, squirmed less and less, grew still. I missed nothing. My hands were spiders on my knees. I was veiled. Unseen child that I was, I saw it all.

"Le noir," came Colère's muffled voice, "come here." Both dogs, in stately fashion, obeyed her summons. "Not you, La jaune," she said in mock anger. "I am able to accept Le noir, my poor La jaune. But not you, as you can see.

"Come, sweet monsters," I heard Colère say, and then I discovered that male whippet and male pig were much alike, though the dog was held fast between Colère's thighs and the pig was swaying languorously above her hidden head. But I valued the pig's commitment over the whippet's elegance. The pig's barrel belly and outlandish snout and little stationary haunches were suddenly, for me, more worthy of attention than was the familiar beauty of the dog. Oh, the young pig was white, but had been so severely scrubbed with a cruel brush that his whiteness was shot through with pink! How clean he was, cleaner even than Le noir! And his golden ear, which fortunately was the ear that I could see, how it hung flashing! though the pig was now so still that his rearward half appeared to be mesmerized while the rest of him trembled as if giving vent to what the sinking hindquarters could not allow. Above those hindquarters stood his curly tail.

The pig turned to me his dizzy face. Le noir's eyes were closed. But the pig's eyes were blue and round, and fast becoming more blue, more round, above the fat pink nose with its black holes through which the white pig was no longer taking or expelling breath. Still he looked at me, our bedazzled pig indifferent at last to his own bemusement. Le noir, with eyes still closed, began to howl. His howl was as long and soft and slender as he himself. At this moment Colère's body, or what I could see of it, convulsed on her bed of straw and an arm thrashed free. Slowly, still peering in my direction, the pig's blue eyes began to close, the body shuddered, and the creature's awful snout and mouth became a smile. Then the pig fell forward and lay still.

Colère disengaged herself and, her nakedness enhanced by wet light and clinging straw, climbed to her feet and once more turned away from me.

"Now, Seigneur," she said, and raised the back of a hand to the victorious face I could not see. "Now, Seigneur, are you satisfied?"

In the blue of night I sought out the pig, and found him standing alone, as I knew I would, in a corner where two low stone walls met. I leaned on the rough cold top of one of the walls and in my drowsiness stared at him and was pleased to detect the glint of his ear, though there was no moon. His front legs were pressed tightly together, as were his legs behind. His head hung. His back swayed. He was smaller than I had taken him to be in our salon.

"So, Virginie," came Seigneur's voice from the darkness, "you too are here."

"Yes, Seigneur, I am here." He approached so close to me that I could have clasped his hand if he had offered it. "But, Seigneur," I asked, as suddenly I knew I would, "why must I be confined when in the salon? Why may I not be as visibly present there as are you and Père La Tour?"

The blue light deepened. The white pig had turned in color from blue to gray, and was motionless. In the distance, in the sleeping stables, one of the horses was slowly and monotonously knocking a great hoof against what was surely stone.

"Virginie," came the familiar voice at last. "Life's first principle is love. But the first principle of love is secrecy. In the salon," he said, and stood closer to me than he ever had before, "you are my secret."

〚1945〛 The Sex Arcade;
Monsieur Pidou seduced

"Come down, Bocage! . . . Virginie, come down, come down! . . ."

I hear but do not listen. My own voice speaks to me in stronger cadences: the fire that moves within her when she moves . . . the smile that lies behind the grimace on the fiery face . . . the heat that rises inside her body where it lies . . . the love that burns . . . But what is this, dear self? Can it be? The fire that burns without is but the fire within? Passion? Passion? Is that the word I say at last? At last admit that I feel it in captive arm? in spread thigh small and bare? but most of all in my place of longing that has all but consumed itself and so become the very sensation of which it is the source and with which I ache, and which Bocage has found, though now it does not exist yet floods me? But what is this? still more? another voice that speaks to me more insistently than my own? than theirs? *The colors of passion, Virginie*, it says, *are these. These are the names of passion's primary colors: first the color called Belly of the Devoted Nun; then that known as She Who Waits; then the supreme suffusion called Widow's Climax; then the grainy color familiar to everyone as Waste of the Goose. Recite them*, says my distant voice, *commit them to memory. You have only to say to yourself these names to see the colors. . . .* And I attend this voice as no other, even my own, and hear it within me where it gives me counsel. But long have I been drenched, child that I am, in Widow's Climax.

Maman is a widow, I tell myself, or as good as one, and I have only to turn my head to see her standing in the doorway that is aflame, Maman become the fiery sunset in its burning frame, wearing the heavy night-dress which she does not know is flaming as fiercely as the walls around us, and bracing herself with outstretched arms, with hands pressed flat and firm against the burning sides of the doorway in which she stands. But I refuse to turn my head. Again Bocage calls out my name, and vacantly I am pleased that Maman can hear his voice.

"Belle soeur! Belle soeur!" cries Bocage, whom I had not thought capable of creating such a name, but I refuse to listen to Bocage or look at Maman. But which prompts her to greater fury, the sight she stares at from the doorway or the words she hears?

Suddenly I know that I am prone, borne down, pained and contented. For I remember that I was alert when they thought me drowsing, clear-headed and quickened both when Bocage lifted me from the lap of Monsieur Malmort and took me heavily, clumsily, to his own; alert and pleased when Minouche caressed my cheek with the backs of her long cool fingers, and Madame Pidou cupped in her palm my head and pressed it still closer against Bocage's chest, where it already lay; alert and frightened when Sylvie knelt at Bocage's feet and with hands as small as mine raised my poor aproned skirt above my knees; alert when Bocage stood up and lifted me into his arms and turned and carried me off to this little room in which I shall never again find sleep. But I was awake! So too was our Maman!

So was our life then all for me? For Virginie that Bocage gathered them together and cooked, filled glasses, proposed his toasts, admonished the women and humored the men? For me that he invented Bocage's Sex Arcade, as he came to call it, in which he waited until he knew by instinct that I had seen what there was to see and would see no more? Why else? Who was better able to accept his gift? to be the sole object of his rare plan?

"Belle soeur!" he cries, knowing that in this minute or the next we shall be no more. "Belle soeur! Belle soeur!"

"Monsieur!" cried Sylvie, changed person that she was. "Bathe him in front of the fire tonight! Bathe him where his Maman and your Madame and the rest of us may form a circle around you and little Déodat and watch!"

"Oh, Monsieur," cried our large and generous Yvonne, "tonight you must bathe the little boy in our salon!"

"Henri," said Madame Pidou, amidst the assenting laughter of Minouche and even cool Clarisse, "you must do as they wish. . . ."

"Voilà," said Monsieur Malmort, the first of our habitués to arrive on this occasion. "Wash him in here."

As for Bocage, his grudging silence proclaimed quite clearly enough, I thought, his disapproval of Sylvie's proposal. But why not? I asked myself. Why not a moment of domesticity in our salon?

All day Bocage had been hammering closed our tall ill-fitting windows, and stuffing the emptiness of broken panes with rags and crumpled paper, and blowing on his hands and scowling at the ice outside. Now his fire on the hearth was fat and full, a great nest of flames that swayed and leapt and spoke in hollow voices. The hearth was aglow; the stones of the hearth were hot; large as it was, our salon would once more prove tolerable, I knew, to those who would bare themselves in the hours to come. All day I had followed Bocage and assisted him as best I could, and had stood on my toes and peered out at the world of ice. Now, as I prepared to fetch the tub, the lump of soap, the scrap of towel, and to bring the water to near boiling on the hearth, quickly I stole another look at the darkness that had turned to ice. Facing stone wall like a ship's prow; unraveling threads of electric wire; old street lamp with its broken glass: everything I saw was bright, brighter even than in the day, slick and glistening in its skin of ice, clear and stark, unnatural with the appearance of wetness on something dry, thanks to the faintest film of ice which, in itself, could not be seen. No wonder I pressed my face to the glass and had my look at all that invisibly frozen darkness from which we inside were safe.

I carried in the tub, a battered tin thing in the shape of a shoe, that caused me to hold my breath, muster my strength, walk in little steps with my thin back swayed. And the water. And the towel. And the soap. When all was ready, and Monsieur Pidou and Déodat approached the waiting bath hand in hand, Sylvie and Yvonne and Clarisse and Madame Pidou and Minouche all gathered around the man and boy and knelt, or sat, laughed, fell silent, leaned forward to see, enjoyed the sight, gave way to nostalgia which I plainly saw brought out on their faces by the fire. I smelled the hot water, the warmth on a bare knee, the light in Minouche's hair. The heat was rising from the water; the salon, lit only by the generous fire, was warmer still in the night that was growing deeper, darker, more silent. I thought of ice.

Monsieur Pidou removed his jacket in movements angular and shy and rolled up his threadbare sleeves deliberately, frowning the while as if there were not five women and Virginie pressing closer and closer around his little stage of light and stones where he, who was surely aware of manhood as he undertook what was conventionally a woman's work, lowered himself with dignity and a series of the briefest of bodily spasms which he tried to disguise, until he knelt awkwardly but without self-consciousness beside the patiently waiting Déodat. Could there be grace in a lonely man's long and bony fingers fumbling with the buttons of a child's shirt? turning the child by plump shoulders, sighing, smiling a crooked smile, then undoing the buttons with long fingers which were oddly foreign to this task yet not unpracticed? Yes, I thought, grace was what informed Monsieur Pidou as he parted the child's shirt, let fall the pants, offered his amusing smile to the small boy, who saw that smile and liked it, was used to liking it, despite his passivity and unresponsive eyes and mouth.

With modesty Monsieur Pidou now drew the naked Déodat against his own chest, face to face, so that we were able to see fat shoulders, small rosy back fatly cleft for the short and tender spine, fat buttocks like a baby's cheeks, fat legs, but nothing more. Déodat put his arms around the neck of Monsieur Pidou with the obedience of habit, it seemed to me, and allowed himself to be shielded and transferred from naked light to pool of sheltering water which Monsieur Pidou had tested first with his fingers. Submerged to well above his wrinkling waist sat Déodat, but I thought that he would not have cared had his zizi been exposed to his audience of admiring women.

Monsieur Pidou was smiling more for his own sake than for Déodat's, as he knelt beside the battered tub, took up the soap, leaned forward to wet the still dry upper belly and chest and shoulders, and apply the soap. Déodat was turning pink, his hair was an inverted saucer of bright gold, and seated patiently in the water he was unmistakably content, though there was yet nothing to be seen on his round face except its changing color. No small painted ducks to bob about in this child's bath, no boat in miniature, no shouts of delight or fat hands splashing the water, no familiar signs of joy that ordinarily accompany the child in his nightly bath: only Déodat sitting still and silent in the water I had drawn, and alone, content. I too smelled the steaming water and felt the heat that is like no other and shared the luxury of the child enjoying indifferently the spectacle he had in fact become.

"Look there," whispered Sylvie. "See how gently Monsieur Pidou uses the soap!"

"And little Déodat," whispered Yvonne, "how buttery he is, and red!"

"But, Henri," came suddenly the voice of Madame Pidou, "how womanly you are, my dear."

Monsieur Pidou did not reply, though now there was more sureness in his movements as he thrust wet arm, wet hand, wet soap into the water, and retrieved the slippery soap and, holding Déodat with one expert hand, used the other to make slow circles with the soap on Déodat's bright dripping skin. But with the first stroke (oh, what eloquence was this!) Déodat began to close his eyes, allowed the lids to droop, to sink, then squeezed them shut while Monsieur Pidou, happily ignoring the expression on the wet and reddening face, continued to wash and rinse, and pause, and admire the bright tincture of soapy skin, and wash again and rinse, with no thought at all, I was convinced, for those who watched.

"Ladies," said Monsieur Malmort suddenly, from the darkness surrounding the rosy scene that engrossed us all, and speaking so as to startle everyone, though no heads turned, "once I found myself in a Sex Arcade. . . ."

What? I thought. Interrupting Monsieur Pidou? Intruding into our pleasant time with one of his peculiar stories? Yet I, like everyone, began listening to Monsieur Malmort while watching the motions of that other kindly man and the rapturous boy.

"Yes, ladies," continued Monsieur Malmort in slow cadences filled with his age, his self-absorption, "yes, it was on a night like this one, ladies. This cold. I lost my way, as the saying goes, somewhere between what used to be the rue de l'Hôpital and the rue du Tombeau. Dark, ladies, lots of cats, which always signifies a poor and dangerous district. Everywhere the cats, and all of them frozen on their little feet. All of them. So there I was. Alone. No companion. Collar up and hands in pockets, walking, walking. A labyrinth, you might say, and not a light. No one to ask the way. Cobbled alleys with dead grass between the cobbles. Even the stars were lying. I hurried, I slowed down, the further I went the worse it got. A bad night for Monsieur Malmort. But what's that? Two light bulbs as dim as my breath? The last of the current? But light's light, even the faintest, and by the pale halos of two little bulbs still lit I saw the sign: Sex Arcade. Well, ladies, I wasn't thrilled. Desolation is the last place you want a Sex Arcade. But the door was open, there was more light that was blue and better than darkness. What else could I do? So I found myself inside.

"Voices, ladies. People at last. Maybe the place was once a stable, I didn't know. A cavern anyway, the bottom of an abandoned factory. More stones, rusted pipes, more ice, heaps of ashes in the corners. Old machines that used to sell things I'd be ashamed to buy. But voices, without a doubt. Then a little door with another sign: Galerie d'Amour. So I pulled down my hat, hugged myself, held out my arms, groped, stumbled. My fingers told me we were going now left, now right, now straight again, but at least the darkness was deliberate (in a Galerie d' Amour what else?) and the voices I heard belonged to women, I was glad to recognize. Then came an island of light, a little scene, a tableau propped in a stone niche and lit by another bulb as small as a bird and still glowing, the last gasp of dusty light in a tunnel that was taking me to an ossuary, for all I knew. But the little scene? The Kiss, according to what someone had written in a fancy script on a piece of cardboard. I stopped. I wanted to see the fingers I was trying to warm in my cold breath. And who could be offended by The Kiss? But wait: some artificial flowers, some paper vines, a bower, though cheaply made. A piece of tin for moon. Cobwebs, as you'd expect. And a top hat on the head of the man and a great red hat on the woman. Romantic, you could say. Sentimental, harmless. But, ladies, they were skeletons, that kissing pair, as tall as me, life-sized, and naked, but who cares for hats, and pants, shirt, long gown, and so forth all in piles at the feet of people who were only strings and bunches of wired bones? Elegant? Formal? Decorous?

Her knee was cocked, he had a hand (if you could call it that) on the flat bone where her hip should have been, and his other arm draped over his lady's shoulder. The fingers of her right hand were wired to his rib cage, there was a white rose in her dangling left. The gentleman and his mistress were hanging in the darkness straight and tall, that pair, sedate, immortal, naked instead of nude, and even the kiss was only a joke because the large skull was tilted toward the smaller one, and the smaller one was raised, but those rows of teeth, the big jawbone and the little: they weren't pressed together, ladies; they didn't touch; there was no breathing in the black porous triangles of the missing noses and the bones that were all they had for mouths didn't meet, couldn't ever meet, so the lovers weren't even dummies and there was no kiss at all! But when I heard a creaking sound, a clicking sound, and the fleshless hand dropped the paper rose, I turned and started running, ladies, who wouldn't?

"So, I told myself, stumbling and running in a tunnel of darkness, which isn't easy, so this is the reward of virtue? The boy blushes and gets sweaty on his brow and in the palms of his hands and becomes, with admirable resolve, the grown man who goes his own way without wife, girl friend, not a word for the woman who calls him by name (God knows how) from an open doorway, and this is what he gets for being as snow white as the man in black? Mocked by skeletons that can't even give each other stolen kisses? So much for abstinence. Flesh is better than bones, said the little bird on my shoulder, and I nodded.

"Shortly I was out of breath. I leaned against the walls I couldn't see. I panted. Pushed back my hat and wiped my forehead with a bare hand. Started off again. The scenes got livelier: The Lady's Pig; The Princess and the Swarm of Bees; The Double Bed. But they were skeletons and still big as life, even the animals, the bird that sat on the arm of A Woman Among Her Pages, and I didn't stop, though I thought I was beginning to get intrigued. Still blackness between the lighted islands. Still the cold. Rubble underfoot and bits of wire dangling like hairs in the face. How long? How long?

"Now I couldn't hear the voices. Panting, holding my chest, despairing. But then? Then there was another scene, another tableau cut into the stone and earthen wall like the rest of them, and lighted, just light enough to make you want to approach and stare. But this one's different, not like the rest, and I went closer, inquisitive again, forgetting bruises, breathlessness, fear of the dark. Circus, said the script still flourishing on the moldy card. And that's what it was, ladies, a circus. But small, the whole performance on display in a niche no bigger than the space of a coffin cut horizontally into the rough wall. I couldn't resist. Who could? The tallest acrobat was no taller than my own hand stretched in terror. Such tiny skeletons. What a relief after the monsters I'd already passed. This small, this intricate, I could even admire the workmanship, though inside me I knew that a grinning skull no larger than a thumbnail (with its little hollow eyes) was worse than a full-scale death's head on a rusty wire. And oh, those acrobatics, ladies, you wouldn't believe! What the juggler juggled, what the sword swallower was about to swallow (a bigger one, proportionally, I haven't seen), and the trainer and the hump-backed bear, and two little skeletons embracing, ladies, and hanging face to face in midflight from one trapeze: this was a clever conglomeration of acrobatics, I had to admit. So I smiled and put my face as close as I could to a bareback rider who was a dainty composition of tiny bones and tutu on the rump of her horse. Why so close? I still ask myself. After everything else, why now seduced? How many paper roses does it take?

"Because she popped, ladies! Popped! Right in my face! A hand fell off before my eyes. The other. She was losing herself. Her head lolled, the horse's head dropped off. Then the dancing rider's rib cage popped apart (like this: pop!) and all the bones showered right at me in the face! But by then the whole circus was popping to pieces, flying apart, thigh bones and finger bones like sand and skulls the size of marbles coming at me from everywhere, all at once, and stinging the cheeks, ears, getting down my collar, whizzing. I had to spit them out, ladies. Terrible.

"But I got my senses quickly enough and ran. Ran off again when I shouldn't have stopped in the first place. The tunnel ended; I saw light; I found myself in a room as big as a warehouse: cold, no windows, no-where to sit, loud voices, but still no people except a concessionaire who was standing behind her counter on the other side of that empty room with a ceiling so high I couldn't see it. Well, ladies, I took my time, catching breath, feeling my soul for injuries, you might say. But there, behind the counter, a real woman was standing with folded arms, and an apron, and a smiling face and a head of red hair that would smell good to my poor nose, even if the hair was just a wig, as I thought. She was a big woman and gave me confidence. The only person I met in the Sex Arcade, and a woman.

"Above her head, on a sagging banner, someone had painted 'Mars and Venus,' and I saw that the dusty gun on the counter belonged to Mars, since everything else was dedicated to the goddess. So I approached. The lucky man. Who wants to offend the goddess? No shooting gallery ever had more prizes, ladies: boxes of old rings, gold, silver, gems as well; boxes of old bouquets; most of all, boxes of dusty I-Love-You cards with hearts, arrows, paper doilies curling up at the edges. And what was hanging from a thick wire running the length of the counter and low enough for the concessionaire to reach? Underwear, ladies, you never saw such a flock of bloomers and panties for the young, the old, girdles and whatnot, stockings too, and garters, and still significant, ladies, so that I only glanced, so that my cold hands shook when I took up the gun.

"But I was doing the right thing, as I could tell from the redheaded woman's smile. I squinted down the barrel at the flame of a candle stuck into a bottle dressed and padded in the melted wax. Took aim, ladies, waited, pulled the trigger, shut my eyes at the same moment since I don't like guns and from a boy have been overly sensitive to noise, and held my breath, cringed and shook in the bang and boom of the gun. But no bullets? Broken? Venus playing tricks with Mars? There was not a sound, no matter how miserably I was crouched at the counter, elbows planted on the wood, tightening every muscle against concussion, seeing my own bright lights and wanting to stuff my ears, I can tell you, against the sound of the blast I had just set off, I was sure of it, and stuff my nose against the smell of the smoke that would be sailing from the end of the gun when I opened my eyes. But nothing, ladies, nothing, long after that silent shot had come and gone.

"I waited, thinking it might still go off and was only delayed, and then relaxed my finger, put down the gun, opened my eyes and looked. The woman was smiling and the flame was out. So that's how I found love, ladies, and won the enchanted corset. But the voices you want an explanation of? Your own! Yours! None other! As I recognized the first time I heard you at the foot of the stairs and started up. . . ."

So he ended his oddest story yet, did our Monsieur Malmort, as I determined by the slowing down of his thick and watery speech, and the sudden lift of it, as though he had waved to us in the darkness, before he had even arrived at his final period. But silence there was, and more silence. No one grouped around the conscientious Monsieur Pidou and little Déodat had moved. All was as it was before our attention had been so seized by the old man still sitting, as we knew, in the darkness: Sylvie's small hand was on the edge of the tub; Clarisse and Yvonne and Minouche were kneeling side by side to shield the bather and his attendant from the eyes of Monsieur Malmort, if not his voice; and Madame Pidou was staring with new and avid attention at her awkward husband who, in turn, smiled down at little Déodat half floating on his rosy tide. How he basked, that Déodat, in the reverence of Monsieur Pidou! His child's eyes were still tightly shut, and still his belly was half lifted above the water so that all attention would be fixed on the exact spot where some invisible deity had with the tip of a finger thrust into that little mound the navel. A bubble of soap sat unbroken there, bubble as blissful as the rest of Déodat, who might have thought himself the cause of so much silence, though he was not.

"Enchanted corset!" exclaimed Madame Pidou, the first to speak, while continuing to look full face and queerly at her husband. "How fortunate for both of us, Monsieur Malmort, that you chose that very corset when you had the chance!"

"Well," exclaimed Bocage into the silence and from behind my back, "at least we now have a name for Bocage's establishment! I drink to it," he exclaimed, and did so, as from the darkness in the vicinity of Monsieur Malmort two pairs of hands clapped briefly, since Lulu and Monsieur Moreau had entered quietly, it now appeared, and in time to hear the end of Monsieur Malmort's adventure.

"Clarisse!" cried a voice that could be none other than Lulu's. "Come and kiss Monsieur Moreau and me! But you mustn't fly apart in our faces, Clarisse! No ugliness like that!"

Why Clarisse? I wondered, noting that no one laughed, while the silence grew and calm Clarisse stood up, made an almost imperceptible gesture with eyes and hand, gave a brief tug on her violet cache-sexe, and entered the gloom to sit on Lulu's lap or Monsieur Moreau's. But why Clarisse and not Minouche? Yet perhaps it was for the better that I now entertained a fresh perception: namely, that in our charades the partners were interchangeable. Could it be so? From the other side of the salon came a burst of laughter, though Clarisse said nothing, made not a sound, and again the moody silence was upon us. I felt the rhythm of the tall flames; outside, the iced-over world of night was as silent as our warm night within.

"Well, Henri," said Madame Pidou at last, and in a much softer voice, "will you not look at me?"

"But, Madame," cried Sylvie. "Monsieur already looks at you! See how he smiles! And who would not, at such an attractive wife?"

"Or does he smile," responded Madame Pidou, "at his old wife's little friend?"

"At me, Madame? Oh, Monsieur has not a thought for Sylvie. I wish he had!"

Whereupon Sylvie, who had been kneeling the while and lightly gripping the edge of the tub and trying admirably, I thought, but so far unsuccessfully to engage the shy man's attention, abruptly thrust her little arm straight into the water as deeply as she could, and laughed. In feigned sleep, or feigning a dream, Déodat began to squirm so that Monsieur Pidou was made to readjust his grip, lest Déodat's head sink under. At the same time, as Monsieur Pidou attempted to maintain propriety with a frown, his long forehead turned from dry to moist; and do what he could, he blushed, poor person, helplessly coloring in a hot stain more purple than red that climbed in spasms, in sudden blotches, from the base of his long neck upwards, bit by bit, until it lodged deep and livid in the hollow cheeks.

"There!" exclaimed Madame Pidou. "There is my proof! You see? He blushes! I have only to suggest that he bathes the child but smiles for you, Sylvie, and he blushes!"

"Mathilde," murmured her husband, so suffering his blush that even his soft voice was not exempt from the pain. "Spare me, Mathilde. . . ."

"Madame," cried Sylvie without a moment's pause, "I agree with Monsieur! How naughty she is, Monsieur. I understand."

"Mathilde," appealed her husband, struggling to control his voice but barely able to mouth the words and shifting uneasily on his knees. "Now what have you done? I have lost the soap."

"No, Monsieur! No! Here it is!"

On Sylvie's face sat helpfulness itself and of course on her upturned little palm sat the cake of soap. Her arm was extended. Hand and arm were dripping. Her head was tilted, her chin raised, her eyes and smile bespoke a small triumph Monsieur Pidou was meant not to fear. But never had there been such soap! Never had mere soap assumed such properties! Mere soap it was, but what a forbidden glossy egg on Sylvie's palm! How could she so ingenuously offer him the soap, knowing as she must that once he trusted his awkward fingers to close on the slippery cake, which might well slip away once more in his agitation, he would enter into a bargain with Sylvie defined not by what the soap actually was but by what it meant? So much was undeniable. The two of them might have been in a bath together!

"Take the soap, Monsieur," came the voice, still more disarming. "Madame will not mind!"

The long face was contorted in its blushing. His voice was gone. But he had no choice and gathered strength, glanced down at the child's head he still kept safe, and then reached for the soap, looking as he did so into Sylvie's eyes. Promptly it leapt from his grasp, that soap in the service of a woman, or two women as I was soon to see, and up it went in a fine arc and down it fell, causing hardly a ripple, and sank from sight.

"Bravo!" cried Madame Pidou. "Well done, Henri!"

"But, Monsieur, you play!" cried Sylvie, on cue I thought, and mimed an endearing little tempest of feeling. "But Sylvie wants to play, if that's what you like!"

So saying, she swept her hand in a mock bold stroke through the water and raised her hand, an expression of sudden daring in her eyes, and not once but twice flicked the pearly droplets into her poor adversary's startled face. He blinked. He made himself taller on knees that ached. Retaliation was not for him, I knew, but already his blushing had begun to fade and a rueful smile to dispel the tension that had gone hand in glove with the blushing that had all but devoured the face ordinarily marred, if marred at all, by innocence.

"Mathilde," he murmured, in a better spirit, "will you allow her such familiarity?"

"How he talks!" was all she said for answer and joined in the splashing.

"But, Mathilde," he exclaimed when at last he could, "the child! The child!"

The constraint on his face was genuine, I saw, but now the long sunken face was changing. The muscles in the neck began to pulse, the eyes to water (fear, suspicion, the mantle of false dignity melting in a single moistening), and the white eyebrows rose, the bone of the brow shone through the tightened skin, comets of wrinkles broke out everywhere at the edges of nose and eyes, the teeth appeared (unashamed of stains and crookedness), and the lips began to peel, to quiver and crack upward at the corners, as dry and crudely shaped as any pair of lips I ever saw. And the expression that was the clearly heretofore untasted result of so much exertion? Mirth, of course! Mirth! For the first time in all his married life, Monsieur Pidou knew mirth, as the long face now revealed.

Both women splashed him. Both tittered and spoke his name. They moved closer, circled on their knees, used the fingers of both pairs of hands to wet his shirt, his face, his ears, the hair that was parted down the middle, while he, with increasing forgetfulness of Déodat, I thought, attempted with increasing uselessness to employ free hand and frail arm to ward off what was now unmistakably a rain of love.

"Monsieur," I whispered, having crept to his side, "allow me to take Déodat."

I knelt beside him at the tub's edge, sharing briefly the gusts and showers intended for him and not at all for me, and raised my sleeves, reached for the child, took into my own hands the child's head which the assaulted Monsieur Pidou relinquished without a thought, a word, a glance in my direction.

"Come, Déodat, open your eyes!"

He slipped away, I caught him. Again he eluded my grip, then opened wide his eyes, displeased to find mere Virginie in charge of his welfare. But I took him by the shoulders and made him sit. The bath was tepid, as I had known, the soap gone, his golden hair lying close and wet to pinkish skin in duckling curls which made more appealing his nude grandeur.

"Stand up, Déodat," I hissed, though not unkindly.

"Hear? Hear?" exclaimed Madame Pidou through the tumult of pursuit and laughter. "He calls you Sylvie! Do you hear? He does!"

"But Sylvie reciprocates, Madame!" came the merry reply of the little strident voice. "Henri! I say back to him, Madame. Henri! Henri! Henri!"

"But, Sylvie," said Madame Pidou, in a loud whisper, "shall we take him to the couch?"

"Capital, Madame! To the couch with this Henri of ours, who allows himself familiar names. . . ."

Whereupon there was tussling, more laughter, a struggle to seize and pull against the not unwilling arms, until the three of them lay at last asprawl the old and waiting couch where they could take their ease, be safe, sink together, comport themselves however they wished in dusty investigation, dusty surprise.

But what now? Will they wish the pot of steam? Lie down? Caress him? Poke him and tease him more? Shall Monsieur Pidou cry out in Lulu's joy? Growl in Monsieur Malmort's? I asked myself all this because the known and unknown went side by side, and I valued both: all our charades shared similarities, yet no two were identical, as I had learned, and I took my pleasure in the familiar road but also in anticipating the new turns that were sure to appear in it.

"Now, Déodat," I said, "I shall lift you out," and placed my hands on his slippery waist, not easily found in the plumpness of his form, and felt his wet hands take my shoulders, and breathed in the sweetness of his compliance, noted the tremor he bore without a word in the chill of exposure, despite the fire, and strained to raise him while he quite clearly attempted to achieve weightlessness by expelling breath, using his little toes, hunching his shoulders toward the ceiling. He looked up at me in dour expectation, as again I leveled my curiosity toward the couch, then swiftly smiled down at him and pulled. But no child or cherub was ever more like bronze, and I was forced to heft his head higher than mine, hold his heavy wetness to my dry length, swing him once mightily, as in a game, so that the small feet should clear the tub. I swung him free, grasped the towel, wrapped him close, hugged him against me so that the smell of his partially wet hair filled my nose.

"How good he smells!" said Sylvie from the couch.

"I shall sniff him too!" replied the wife, as her husband, in an odd sound, betrayed to me the eagerness of his partners to make him laugh. But I did not turn my head to look.

Quietly I worked the long scrap of towel against Déodat, though it served already as his cocoon, and with an edge here, a fold there, rubbed him and dried him. The head wobbled to my touch, the sleepy eyes were open, the fat body was at last so depleted of volition that only chubbiness remained. I realized the joy that the torso's curve was prompting in my divided attention, and looked longer and, on impulse, pressed my lips to the tiny navel, which produced in all of Déodat a sudden chuckling.

"How easily this Henri of ours enjoys himself!" came Sylvie's declaration, accompanied by another rupturing sound of pleasure prompted, I thought, by the mousy sensation of Sylvie's fingers stroking the entire length of Monsieur Pidou's cold ears and naked neck. I pressed my face into the fragrance of the little drum, and listened.

"We please him, Sylvie!" said Madame Pidou. "We make him laugh!"

"But what is this, Madame? Keys in the pocket?"

"Still the useless keys, Henri?" said Madame Pidou in tones of poignancy. "How sentimental you are!"

"But I shall have the silly keys!" Sylvie exclaimed, and pounced on the pocket, as I could tell, and began her pinching.

"Take them! Take them!" cried Madame Pidou, returning to the exultation which I now well knew was but the means to tenderness.

Still I did not look, still applied myself to Déodat, undraped him further, and satisfied myself that he was unmoved, one way or the other, by my inspection of his zizi, which soon I concealed again behind its ragged flap of towel. But when it occurred to me to dry his buttocks with a bare and probing hand, I did so, no matter how unnecessarily, knowing with the first exploratory touch that his little pillows engaged my attention as his zizi had not. He whimpered; I pressed him in my sisterly embrace; he planted a tiny foot on my clothed and angled thigh, near to the knee. He waited, fattened himself, left leg and right, chest and belly, and in a reciprocity I had not expected laid his cheek to my breast. But we heard the jingling together, together became more interested in the tinkling keys than in each other, though actually our embrace grew all the tighter as we listened to the flaunted keys.

"There, Madame!" came the bright voice, even the more amusing for its pride, and taking its inflection from an obviously stronger shake of the keys. "Your husband is no match for me! But what shall Sylvie do with her prize?"

"Ah," was the swift and sonorous reply, "I have the answer to that question! But it is better shown than said!"

"Wait," exclaimed Monsieur Pidou, in the voice he had somehow found again, though it was not his own. "Wait, Mathilde! You go too far. . . ."

I clung to Déodat, and he to me. Yet exactly when I knew that I had no need to deny my curiosity and, more than that, must see and watch the spectacle being enacted on the couch, and could not be denied, child in my arms or not, Déodat himself propelled me on, since then I felt beneath my hand the efforts of his head to turn to the ribaldry of the jangling keys.

"Down the front of his shirt, Madame? Oh, drop them, drop them!"

Déodat had not my understanding of this clever ruse, yet I too, and equally, was its captive witness, the only difference between us being that his watching was an intensity of fear, while mine was of amusement as I imagined the icy cold of the keys on my own skin, inside my dress, and felt them slipping and sliding down and shook and laughed to myself without a sound.

"But where have they gone?" cried Madame Pidou.

"Oh, yes, Madame! We must retrieve our keys!"

At once they were upon him: Sylvie kneeling beside him on the couch, all her near-nudity fraught with childish up-and-down motions, so bent was she on prolonging their game, and not only for the sake of Madame Pidou but for her own; and Madame Pidou leaning across and plucking with slow fingers at the shirt front down which she herself had but just now dropped the keys.

"Ah, don't, Mathilde!"

But Monsieur Pidou increased the volume and frequency of his peculiar laugh. He made minute defensive gestures. From her decorous distance Madame Pidou unbuttoned first the top shirt button, then the next. She paused, hand yet to his chest. Sylvie, in her turn, used both swift hands to slap (but gently!) and squeeze and feel all the hard and narrow area of the white chest beneath the slightly soiled shirt front— little probing accomplice to the tender but determined wife. Sylvie searched the armpits, shook her head of hair in her victim's face, and began to pinch and prod him lower down; Madame Pidou had bared half the hairless chest, and still she smiled. But the victim's long right arm had been so maneuvered that now, this moment, it fell surreptitiously into place, curving up and around Sylvie's bare body so that the hand that had lost the soap lay in the small of the gleaming back: stealthy, tentative, unmoving, it still avoided the little upraised pair of buttocks, but would not for long, I thought.

"Henri," then whispered Madame Pidou, as if her mouth were against his ear. "Be reassured. Sylvie is yours. Sylvie is my gift to you, my dear. . . ."

In this tranquil interlude he heard what she said, because I saw his body stiffen, taut as it already was. As for Sylvie, the soft and generous words of the older woman caused her only to lift her pert face toward the stilled face of Monsieur Pidou, who did not see her, and to grin once at him with lips as animated as her eyes.

"I shall find the keys, Madame! The keys . . ."

Useless though they were for doors and locks, the stolen keys now served their function, as Sylvie thrust her hand into the trouser tops, where apparently the lost keys had lodged, while Madame Pidou changed her position so that she sat as closely as possible to the outstretched body of the man she had for so long ignored. Sylvie scowled and studied belt and buckle longer than she needed to, and then with a snap of her fingers loosed the belt, pulled up the wet bottom of the shirt (exposing whiteness and a scant patch of hair), reached into the trousers and, with a toss of her head, drew forth the keys and dangled them like the proud fisherwoman she had become. But a quick glance at Madame Pidou told her that now a different mood was called for. I saw it all; Déodat saw it all. What Sylvie had left to do, what she wanted to do, would now be quite independent of whatever Madame Pidou might choose to do for her husband's sake.

Sylvie was quick to action, as I expected, and without a pause propped herself with one small firm hand on Monsieur Pidou's bony knee and the other against his chest, and wiggled her buttocks, substituted head for hands, face for fingers, and occupied with her face I could no longer see the damp space where her hands had struggled. For her part, Madame Pidou was kissing her husband behind the ear. I saw him staring upwards into the dark of our salon. I heard his laughter catch in his throat, burst forth, die on his lips. I saw his hand, all but forgotten, suddenly take one of Sylvie's pillows into its clasp, and I nodded.

But by the tightness of his little fists clutching my skirt, and the way he worked the side of his head against my chest, I knew that Déodat was frightened at the sight, his first, of Sylvie "worrying the bone," as Bocage called it, and I looked down, slightly disengaged his head, and spoke to him.

"She is not hurting him, Déodat," I whispered. "She is only 'worrying the bone' and you are meant to laugh."

He could not laugh. I knew he could not. However, once more he comforted himself against me, and did not interrupt me again.

Back I looked to the couch, and just in time, for now, exactly when I expected the black-shoed foot to kick, the laugh to become a howl, the noose to knot, Sylvie raised her head, into which the blood had run, and licked her lips, which were wet enough, I saw, and loosed her cheeks and took a shallow breath and looked upwards, abandoning to my utter surprise the zizi where it swayed, and smiling wanly at Madame Pidou, said: "I shall wait, Madame. Quickly, he is for you!"

Without a word Madame Pidou obliged the zealous Sylvie. They exchanged places, traded heads, rearranged themselves with ease and speed. The foot kicked. I heard a howl. No noose was ever jerked so tight!

So I gave Déodat a last brisk rub, and climbed to my feet, seized his hand, and, towel dragging, led him from the hushed salon. No sooner had we left than I heard familiar laughter, the crash of a bottle, and above it all the voice of Madame Pidou: "I have not forgotten you, Monsieur Malmort!" she called, as outside our windows the icy skins of night began to crack.

That night I took into my bed my little pig, as Déodat had become for me. And I loved my pig.

[1740] The art of the nun; the priest's revenge

The carriage in which we rode to our traditional rendezvous with the white bird was small, black, and in the shape of a perfect cube. It was dwarfed by its own high wheels, yet in turn dwarfed the two ponies, not half the size of my own Cupidon, and more like dogs than ponies, by which it was drawn at a swift pace. Inside were two facing seats, narrow and cushioned in leather, with so little space between them that only a pair of passengers, no more, could comfortably occupy that close and cold interior, as Seigneur and I now did, side by side in our identical black robes and hoods, and facing forward. On the otherwise empty seat before us, the edge of which Seigneur's knees grazed from time to time, lay Seigneur's heavy weapon, filling the small width of the carriage with its ponderous length. Outside, on the brief hard seat affixed to the front of the carriage, sat Père La Tour, whose legs hung near to the ground since he was too large for the seat that was intended, it seemed, for a driver no more than the size of a child.

The season of ice was always upon us when we sought the rare white bird, and the increased hardness of road and ruts caused our boxlike carriage to crack and sway in an ever more angry fashion between its four great rattling wheels. But in my mind I saw the entire exterior of the vehicle in which we rode made still brighter than it was by the skin of ice that bound us in a transparency that could be seen. The wheels and pointed hooves broke ice in a staccato continuum of the palest colors, which delighted me, so that we were borne along like a small boat black and furious in its own joyous spray. Beyond the immediate external sights and sounds of the disruption we created and carried along with us in passing, there stretched gently flattening hills, fair fields, a stand of timber like a leafless shrub, and the occasional cottage and a farm, and another, clusters of rude buildings so constructed as to provide protection as well as serve the earth, and soft valleys, a pure stream stopped in its course, shadows surviving in the universal glare: and all of it encased in ice, no matter how small or delicate the object, how thin the ice, so that the vast glare itself was reflected back upwards into the very blue from which it came.

The road turned; the ponies made themselves heard in snorts and whinnies appropriate to much larger beasts; Père La Tour cracked his whip, which leapt far afront of the frantic ponies; a glassy tree trunk passed us perilously close; fields disappeared as well as woodlands, farms, the huts of shepherds. The road began a long descent, gentle enough had Père La Tour checked the ponies, instead of which he again cracked the whip and drove them faster. The longer and more gently meandering the road and the softer its slope, the faster we went until, quite suddenly, we came to a jolting halt on a flat patch of icy earth surrounded closely by walls of gleaming reeds.

We climbed from the listing carriage. We skirted the ponies which were canted at a vicious angle from the empty carriage and were stopped in midflight only by the long black reins gripped and pulled taut relentlessly by Père La Tour.

The narrow and icy path into the frozen marsh was known only to Seigneur, was not revealed even to Père La Tour, and now Seigneur found its concealed mouth, gave me one backward and wordless glance, and entered it. He walked ahead, I followed. Aslant his chest he carried his weapon, the long and monstrous machine of brass and iron with something like a wooden thigh which fit against his shoulder when he raised up this marvelous thing and aimed it, and a long barrel as broad in diameter as the palm of my hand, through which the missile roared when he set it off. The way was so narrow that the protruding ends of the mammoth piece disturbed the tall and golden rushes, like fingers in hair, as Seigneur moved at his consistent pace deeper, deeper still, into the vastness of water, air, rush walls. We could see little for the closeness and height of the walls, which were papery and as dense as gold. Now we walked through tunnels, now crossed causeways, long, curving, barely wide enough to provide for footing, that connected small tufted islands like the tawny haunches of a submerged beast.

We stopped. We stood together, side by side and breathing heavily, in a sparse opening in a perfectly circular wall of rushes which enclosed a round unblemished circle of thick ice as transparent as the thinnest film I had seen throughout our journey: so transparent, despite its thickness, that I could see blue rocks, algae, a firmament of sculpted mud, a frieze of bones all timelessly visible within or beneath the ice. The silence around us was frozen too; the light was so intense that even Seigneur made a gesture to shield his eyes with the edge of the black hood. I shook more from pleasure than from the cold, my nostrils burned, with each painful breath I took I smelled the still breath of ice, and smiled, pinched though I was.

We heard a tinkling sound, then one clear note of some different bell, then the softest sound of parting rushes that made me think of curtains thrust open from the vertical center by two hands one moment together, the next drawn slowly wide so that their owner might stare at us fully, silently, from across the round space of ice.

Another bell note, a long expulsion of majestic breath, a secret unsettling behind the tall curved golden wall at which we stared. Seigneur in silence shook off his hood. I did the same. With all the strength and grace I loved to see, he raised his weapon to his shoulder, held it there, apparently unaware of the weight of its brass, its iron, its wood like iron, and with body sideways, one foot before the other, bare head lowered with eye to sight, waited. He could not have been more composed, my Seigneur, and having used this much time to ready himself and weapon, time obviously given to him by the very creature he sought, he was now prepared to destroy, in but an instant, time, silence, readiness, and the creature still invisibly attending him. He was rigid, said nothing, gave no signal that I could see. Yet into the stillness his signal went.

The bird rose. Directly opposite from Seigneur and me, on the other side of the icy mirror which I could cross in a few steps, from what golden nest I did not know behind the rushes, slowly she rose and appeared to us: white, soundless, black feet contracted yet no distance at all from the tops of the rushes, wings each the length of my body and spread wide, slender neck somewhat longer than the oval body and bearing the billed and sloping head in which the honeyed eyes were clearly set, and from which they were just as clearly fixed upon us. The rare bird drifted slightly higher; hovered above the wall of rushes; made no sound, no movement of the broad wings ribbed and sheathed in sensuality. Down she stared at us, rare bird known only to Seigneur. I had seen her silent duplicate on past occasions, had seen the floating creature become visibly invested with her own white doom in the air before us, had felt myself struck with the same awe that struck me now. Yet this bird was larger, whiter, more serene, and my awe impossibly greater. On the ankle of the left leg there glinted a gold band though there was no one who could have attached the golden ring around the thin blackness of the creature's leg.

She moved, lifted again, revealing tints of blueness in the white, and with a single sweep of the wings, propelled herself to a position directly above the center of the circle of ice, and looked down, moved no more, would make no further exertions for the sake of her hunter or the doom she pursued. Over all the surfaces of wings and body a whiteness of the smallest feathers was being ruffled, though the air did not stir. She waited. I looked up, wondering at the pink bill, the honeyed eyes, the glint of gold in the white.

The blast! The blast! Without a sound it came! I had not expected it, yet clapped hands to ears and shut myself into the darkness of eyes squeezed shut before the instant of the silent roar. Near and far ice cracked. The clear reeds moaned. I opened my eyes and saw the bird's head explode at the end of the long and stately neck. No matter my surprise, my huddling, my slight gesture of self-defense, still I kept my eyes on the headless bird and watched as finally, released by an invisible hand, the wings folded, the body collapsed, the banded ankle swung down crookedly, and in a tumbling rush she plummeted. But she did not have far to fall and before my eyes went down, fell heavily, became a tangled heap of white feathers and dead flight there in the very center of the ice. The shape of blood that appeared on the cold transparency was a ruby-colored tincture brighter than any light we saw that day.

Seigneur lowered the weapon, that looked not at all different for what it had done. Only now did he show the effort of holding it. I no longer felt the cold, though my head was bare, and I noted that I had already begun what I knew would be a swift recovery from the bird's destruction. In fact, with hardly another thought for what I had seen, I took my cautious steps across the ice, reached the bird's remnants and, as usual, managed to lift its sprawling formlessness, and holding its thick awkward length against my own, carefully rejoined Seigneur for our return.

Again he preceded me in silence, machine weighing in his arms and against his breast. Again I followed, struggling to carry our prize. Through all our serpentine way back to the carriage, accommodating myself as best I could to my burden, I felt and listened to the heart still living deep in the headless mass, the thick beats slowing, growing fainter, and stopping altogether only when Seigneur took the immensity of feathers from me and pushed it onto the otherwise empty seat against the weapon that had brought it down.

Off we started, clanging and racing as before, jolting and jouncing, while I found myself reflecting more on the bright blood than on the stately flight.

"Virginie," said Seigneur suddenly, and despite the difficulty of talking, "Virginie," he said close to my ear, "once I considered giving up my art."

What a profound and troubling remark to make at such an incongruous moment!

"Seigneur," I answered at last, "to say what you have just said is dreadful," though riding as we were inside the noise our journey made, he may not have heard.

"Yes, Virginie," he continued, all but touching his cold lips to my naked ear, as the windows clamored in their frames and we were flung together, torn apart. "Were it not for you I should have stopped. I am convinced of it."

"But why, Seigneur?" I cried, suddenly alarmed in my fatigue, "and why me?" But he did not hear.

"Oh, yes," he reflected, hooded figure clasping his knee and musing as if to the heap of white feathers. "It was on a far distant day, but it comes to me now as I lived it then. At the end of that day, another of failure with some Volupté or Bel Esprit I hardly remember, the thought of stopping lodged in my mind as it never had before and has never since. Why not? Would a creator of women be so sorely missed if he gave up his art? The constant effort of invention; the occasional intractability of my materials; the disapproval of most of those in rude huts or elegant châteaux in the vicinity of the mysterious Dédale, all of whom had only rumored knowledge of what I was doing; and my hours of wakefulness, uncertainty (yes, uncertainty!), patience uselessly expended on impatient women, celibacy arduously maintained in the heat of their more insistent moments of desire for the man they detested: Why? I asked myself. Why bear all this? And of course there were those I most despised: those few for whom objectively I labored, to whom I had no choice but to entrust the precious products of my art, and who never, not the best of them, understood what I was doing or appreciated the gifts I gave! *How, Virginie? How* work for men who insisted that my women were women and not works of art! Ah, but the answer was easy; the answer was simple; and of course I had known it from the first and know it yet: the created woman is reason enough for her creation. I thought of you, Virginie, and it came to me, at the end of that day, and I revived. I resolved to withhold from you my doubts, and soon I was absorbed in the thought of a garment I immediately wished to invent as the sweet reversal of an old and cruel device (treacherously intended to lock the entrance to a woman's labyrinth) which suddenly I wished to mock and make sublime. But of course, I thought to myself . . . such a task was not so difficult . . . I had but to make . . . had but to venture . . . but to exert my will . . . to select with care. . . ."

In a brightening mood he entertained me, in the relief of the day's task completed, until in failing light, as the ponies vied to be first in the race, our curious equipage stopped safely in the courtyard of Dédale, and forgetting weapon and dead bird both, and laughing, Seigneur took me into his arms and lifted me down. Thus for the first time he touched me.

Another dawn. More ice. New light. Our second dawn in the season of ice. Again our sparkling carriage was in midflight and risking accident for speed in the same flashing sprays, same ruts, drawn by the same ponies still struggling to catch their bits in their teeth. But now we traveled in a direction opposite from our path of yesterday, and now on the seat across from Seigneur and me there lay no ugly machine, no feathered carcass, but rather the enormous yellow sack, flamboyant despite the dead bird inside it. And there, across from us and beside the sack, sat Bel Esprit.

"Where are we going," she declared rather than asked, and clutched at a handstrap, lurched suddenly as if a brute had pushed her. "This is no hour for traveling. Bel Esprit is cold and sleepy!"

"My child," said our Seigneur, using a term of endearment he rarely used, and deliberately employing archaic diction, "the hour is early because the way is long. As for our destination, Bel Esprit," he added, reverting to the voice we were familiar with and the good humor which I, if not Bel Esprit, particularly welcomed, "we are going to the Couvent Sainte Angèle, a place long abandoned except for the aged Mother Superior and her small collection of young nuns. It shall be a day well spent. You shall be the center of attention, and greatly admired, and shall enjoy yourself, Bel Esprit, I am sure of it."

"Nuns!" exclaimed the predictably ill-tempered voice, as its owner was pitched suddenly against the handsome sack, and righted herself. "Fit company for you, Seigneur, as we all know. But not for me!"

She tossed her head, gasped at another loss of balance, lifted chin and torso in a semblance of dignity which I was happy to see preserved with only the greatest effort, as along we sped on the fractious road toward the ruined convent which was still a place of industry I much enjoyed. The nuns of the Couvent Sainte Angèle, which we visited but infrequently, Seigneur and I, and always accompanied by her who had reached this crossroad in becoming the woman Seigneur envisioned, these nuns were extremely youthful (though where the Mother Superior found such girls and how she bound them to her devotional days and what became of the nun who betrayed the first sign of age and was hence replaced by another, I did not know), and by one occupation only did these sweet young nuns support the Mother Superior's convent: by sewing! They were seamstresses, all of them, and sewed delicacies ordered and then proudly worn in secrecy beneath their dresses by women of the world, as Seigneur called them. I loved to sew, as well as work my loom. I loved the nuns and their needles, and the anomaly of what they sewed for piety. I could be one of them, I knew, and laughed at the thought, but never would Seigneur abandon me to the small and aged woman with her flock of girls and silver crosses, though both he and I knew she coveted his Virginie.

"Oh, you will like the Couvent Sainte Angèle," said Seigneur, ignoring Bel Esprit's injurious retort. "The young nuns are seamstresses, and a happy lot. And you shall have a gift, Bel Esprit, which shall quite compensate for this ride which I see you do not enjoy. Trust me a little. Trust me. . . ."

Then, looking him full in the face as best she could: "Never," she said. "You have my submission but never shall you have my trust or inclination."

"So hardhearted to the end, Bel Esprit? But I shall hunt down your little heart and hold it in my hands as I would my own severed head. You shall see."

She did not reply, though her silence and unfriendly words failed to dim Seigneur's good mood.

But my own sense of this morning did not depend merely on infallible sun, Seigneur's zest, the occasion I looked forward to, the difficulties of the previous day behind us, but most on Bel Esprit and the way she was dressed. When one of Seigneur's women was to be exposed to the ordinary life beyond Dédale, she was not allowed by clothing or in any other way to betray the idealistic regimen of Dédale, which those in ordinary life would wish to destroy, if they but knew of it. So Seigneur himself had deprived Bel Esprit of her familiar white gown, straight of cut and unadorned, had himself removed it from her body and then assisted Adèle and me in dressing Bel Esprit in a garment of the liveliest fashion and gay splendor.

There she sat across from me, the dove turned tulip, and never had I seen a tighter bodice, tighter skirt to the ankles, more frills and flounces meant to draw the eye to the diminutive anatomy concealed yet proudly announced. But most important, the entirety of this silken masterwork was of the wettest red, the purplest red, the sunniest red in fact that I had ever seen. Against her will she wore a broad hat to match. No more provocative young woman could be brought so brazenly into the Couvent Sainte Angèle. Surely the young nuns would share my taste for red!

The extensive ruins of the convent appeared at last in a serene valley below us, a once massive and handsome retreat now partially fallen, generally abandoned, vine-covered and with rows of windows smashed by time and darkly glinting. Once the color of gold and old bones, it was growing darker with the years, as stones remained where they had fallen and rust devoured a tall cross of iron. Only the cupola atop the central building appeared unaged, as pure as the day constructed, a soft white columned offering to Sainte Angèle which housed a bell, was blue-roofed, and could be seen by the most distant rider.

Through the fallen and icy gates we rushed: without warning came to a full stop; alighted; left Père La Tour to cuff the ponies and blow on his hands. In silence, Bel Esprit having placed her fingertips grudgingly on Seigneur's proffered arm, I with the sack and trailing, thus we walked to the central hall, only a small portion of which was used. The door and windows were thrown wide, despite the cold and ice, and suddenly, as if Seigneur had called aloud in announcement of our arrival, the bell in the cupola emitted one silver stroke and from the door came the Mother Superior, arms wide in greeting, and from the windows the laughter of young girls which neither rose nor fell, stopped nor started, though it had become audible but now. Oh, how I loved the sacred seamstresses! They, the youngest of girls, who sewed and laughed all the day, were so expert with their needles that they pricked themselves to produce delicious droplets bright and red only when they wished to, deliberately, for their own amusement!

"Welcome, Seigneur," exclaimed the aged woman not as tall as I, and bent, the white face bound in its wimple and the figure all but lost in black folds.

"Ma Mère!" replied Seigneur in distant but agreeable tones.

"So you come to us again, Seigneur. We are prepared."

"Again, ma Mère. And shall we have Soeur Doucette as usual? Is she still here?"

"Still here. And you shall have her."

"I am partial to Soeur Doucette, ma Mère."

"As I am too," quavered the voice I could hardly hear, no matter its fierceness in its dusty source. I listened, I saw the swift dart of the eyes, I had a brief glimpse of the soft hairs matting the tiny chin and the hollows of ever-shrinking cheeks. But not a word for Bel Esprit? Not an appraising glance? The tulip might have been invisible, so abruptly did the ancient religieuse turn to lead our way inside. Bel Esprit's cheeks were colored at the slight, but Seigneur was smiling.

A stone cubicle in a far-off wing reached through moldy corridors and containing no more than a platform, a mossy trough as for watering horses, a narrow bench and, affixed to the wall, a rack containing spools of bright thread, rows of vicious needles of increasing length (some hooked, some large enough for leather), and an array of shears and scissors as formidable in size and function as the needles: here we were led. But the window was high and wide open, and through it flooded the full sun, filling the cubicle with a richness of light nowhere else to be found, I thought, but in a convent.

"They are here," said our guide to the person awaiting us and suddenly what I could see of the old woman's face grew bright, contained no longer shrewd eyes but warm, no longer dry lips but an uncertain smile: what was it now, the expression on this small fragment of an ancient face, if not the look of adoration? But without transition the expression fled and the religieuse herself was gone. The figure inside the cubicle, who had looked upon the little face quite unmoved, now used her dark eyes in such a way that we three involuntarily stepped forward.

"So it is really you, Soeur Doucette, and not some other," said Seigneur. "I am relieved. . . ." Then in an aside to Bel Esprit: "Do not be alarmed at her failure to reply. She refuses to speak, at least in my presence. But I have heard her voice when I could not see her, and have heard none other like it. We hear in the young voice of Soeur Doucette what we see in the eye of the hunter who knows his forest."

Was she smiling, this Soeur Doucette, though there was nothing of a smile to be seen on the palest and yet most sensual face of any nun who ever took vows or knelt alone at dawn? She was my elder by a few years, yet appeared never to have been a child, whereas I would never be more; nothing showed of the head except the barest amount of face, yet it was a face to lure to itself in one swift rush even my own lips, had I dared; within the folds of her habit there was as little to be detected of the young body as of the Mother Superior's old body in its own black drapery, yet at once I was convinced that beneath the habit this young nun was nude, as the aged woman was surely not. But the eyes were the most compelling of all, and made me weak to see them, bold as they were yet unperturbed by what I could only think of as the forbidden sights they saw wherever their gaze fell. A single strand of dark hair had escaped the wimple, and why was it (as Seigneur had so often said) that one strand stirred the viewer as an entire head of hair could not?

"Soeur Doucette is the most skilled seamstress in the Couvent Sainte Angèle," said Seigneur to Bel Esprit. "In fact, she holds her shears as steadily as might an executioner his ax. But now she wishes to work, as I can see."

Soeur Doucette reached for the yellow sack, which I gave to her. She pulled from it the headless bird become, in its first decay, a treasury of white feathers of all shapes and sizes, and placed the mass of feathers on a table especially readied beside the odd platform whose round surface was only large enough for one person to stand upon. She glanced at Bel Esprit, then went purposefully to her rack and made a swift selection which she arranged in a row on the table serving as altar, I thought, for the dead bird.

"Climb onto your pedestal," said Seigneur to Bel Esprit, still watching Soeur Doucette.

"How can I do that?" asked Bel Esprit, her flaming hat imitating the motion of her little chin. "And why? Will she take up my hem? But Seigneur is mocking Bel Esprit, who shall not submit to your nun."

A long moment passed in our icy cell. Then quietly, without a word, Seigneur seized Bel Esprit about the waist and placed her gently on the platform, from which she could not descend without aid, except by risking an ungracious and unpleasant fall.

"I do not mock you, Bel Esprit. To the contrary. But now I must ask you to raise your dress."

Silence. The sun's serenity. The far-off silvery stroke of the mysterious bell in its cupola. The obvious spiritual strength of the waiting nun.

"Dress? Raise my dress? For what reason? But this is an indignity I had not expected to be made to suffer, even by you, Seigneur."

The nun waited. I watched. If the small woman on the pedestal had been capable of shedding tears, as I knew she was not, it was now that the eyes would have been moist and the cheeks glistening.

"Raise your dress, Bel Esprit," said Seigneur quietly, knowing that the mounted beribboned creature had no choice. She defied us hopelessly with the tilt of her face. In the sunlight the poor tulip she was glowed as redly as the blood still impossibly wet at the severed end of the bird's neck. But her small hands took hold of the shiny cloth and tugged.

"Higher," said Seigneur, and the wrinkling red sheath rose above the little knees.

"Higher," said Seigneur.

"What!" she exclaimed, looking down at him abruptly, hat crying out for balance. "What indecency is this! What depth of indecency must I perform? But I shall not!"

"Higher," said Seigneur.

"Never!"

"Bel Esprit, gather the skirt of your gown into your waist and hold it there."

She controlled her lips. She squeezed shut her eyes. She tugged and pulled until around her waist and in her arms she held upraised the entirety of the shiny skirt in angry folds and bunches. She stood before us naked from waist to shoes, and no sooner was her lower abdomen exposed to the light of the sun and temperature determined by the open window than all the whiteness of hips, thighs, and calves betrayed the cold in tiny bumps, and schools of silvery fish began to swim under the skin.

Swiftly Soeur Doucette commenced her work. Bel Esprit was poised so high that hips, loins, and buttocks were at the level of the nun's chest, and easily reachable, as intended. In an instant Soeur Doucette had circled her subject, appraised her, taken measurements on a long strip of demarcated cloth, with quick and clearly speaking shears had cut but the briefest double triangle from a square of white satin, which she now meant to affix to the private portion, front and back, of the bare body on its stand.

"What!" Bel Esprit could not help but exclaim when she understood the nun's intention. "What! She wishes to cover me where I must not be covered? She stops me up? What then of my functions? Your nun is ludicrous, Seigneur. Ludicrous."

"Bel Esprit," came the quiet voice, "there is not a moment when you are not slapping gnats, as the peasants say. Will you never learn? Never attempt to understand? The garment you are ridiculing, and which you shall soon be wearing, is of my own invention. Countless have been made before this one; countless have worn it ahead of you. It girdles lovingly the mouth of the labyrinth, and that other mouth that is the rosebud furled; contains all of the woman's peach in a teasing tightness; for the lover who raises high the dress it becomes an additional enticement, an additional artifice to be admired in sight, in touch, and slowly removed, thus prolonging the anticipation sought by both. It is, in short, a sumptuous surprise where the lover expected nothing more than bare flesh. This garment provides a pleasing secret to the woman who knows its snugness beneath the dress that hides it, and is warm in the season of ice, absorbent when the air is warm. It is a remarkable invention, Bel Esprit, of which I am justly proud. And it is removable, Bel Esprit, removable!''

Bel Esprit was self-girdled in nudity, and now she relaxed her girdle. How could she not? Yet even as she loosened her upper thighs, allowed space to show between them at the top of the fork, it was at once clear that she was doing so more in response to the hands and fingers of Soeur Doucette than to Seigneur's words. The nun did not use her hands and fingers to pry, to probe, to convey impatience or insistence through a touch indelicate, too strong, too clear in meaning. Not at all. But Soeur Doucette's hands and fingers might have been Bel Esprit's own, so familiar did they seem with that fleshy puff, this nude roundness, that darkness where the cloth must fit: hands and fingers that belonged where they were, conveyed mute tenderness for what they touched, so that the most ordinary placing of the nun's hand to inner thigh or mound of abdomen became a caress. Occasionally she glanced up at Bel Esprit with her dark eyes. Yet even in this context of Seigneur's words and the nun's touch, still Bel Esprit could not restrain a final complaint, though it was softly spoken and not serious.

''Feathers!'' she said. ''Your Soeur Doucette sews feathers to the flesh of Bel Esprit? But is your nun so cruel, Seigneur? She is! She is!''

On worked Soeur Doucette (while Seigneur and I sat together on our bench and beheld her artistry), plucking the feathers, choosing this feather over that to follow a curve, sewing and trimming the white feathers to conform in pillowy softness to Bel Esprit, who herself stroked the feathers newly cleaving to her small shape. The light of the sun remained unvaried. Bel Esprit's seat of passion swelled, grew white, was padded with layer upon feathery layer; and the more Bel Esprit resembled a bird in her seat of passion the more womanly she became.

So the bell rang distantly and the day passed, until suddenly there was a change in Soeur Doucette. She paused. She touched her strand of hair. Her dark eyes looked at each of us in turn. Then the nun took up again her shears, seized one of the bird's black claws, and with the sound of a single stroke that filled our cell, severed the claw from its long black leg. Holding the rigid claw talons downward, moving the needle in bold sweeps, tugging with new sharpness on the strongest thread she could select from her rack: thus Soeur Doucette affixed the claw in place and stepped back and directed us to Bel Esprit's white fork, where was embedded the black claw that fiercely gripped the mouth of the labyrinth inside its snow.

"Bravo!" said Seigneur. "Again you have done well, Soeur Doucette," and so saying, he nodded to Bel Esprit and quickly lifted her down from her confining perch.

Our guide was waiting. Back we went the way we had come, to the open air. Beside the waiting carriage Seigneur and the Mother Superior exchanged their parting words.

"You shall not have her," said the old woman simply, flashing her eyes and cocking her little cowled head to the side.

"And *you* shall not have *her!*" replied Seigneur, not looking in my direction, though it was of me he spoke.

In our rattling carriage, in the middle of our homeward journey, Bel Esprit lifted her red flounces, thrust a hand beneath her skirt, and with warm hand cupped the claw.

"Bel Esprit," said Seigneur, noting her slow possessive gesture, "the woman whose loins are girded in the whiteness of the rare bird is soon to experience the Morning of the Noblesse. I promise you that."

She did not change her position until at last we alighted in the shadowy courtyard of Dédale, but with her red hat on the seat beside her sat face to glass and hand to claw as we rocked and swayed and the light surrounded us in showers.

Dawn. Ice. Light. Third dawn in the season of ice. For the third time we submitted ourselves to the cold and cramped interior of the black carriage, and in most respects this ride, though shorter, was like the last: Bel Esprit was again dressed in red and wore her hat; Seigneur and I were hooded; beyond us the world garbed invisibly in ice was blinding. Our driver was a hatless and coatless fellow from the stables, Père La Tour being otherwise disposed, and Seigneur's mood was by turns pensive and ominous.

"Bel Esprit," he said, his eyes cold, his long face framed in its cowl, "I have all but assured you that soon you are to be Noblesse. It will not be long, I think, before we return to the Couvent Sainte Angèle, where Soeur Doucette shall fashion the rust-colored costume in which you shall ride away from us astride your mount. Astride. Perform your part this day as I have taught you, and it shall be yours to command flowers and an entire universe of love. But you must not fail, Bel Esprit. You shall have no second chance. Be your most sensual self this day, demonstrate to the full your talents, and Noblesse you soon shall be, the embodiment of all my art, and leave us in the ritual of honor the Noblesse demands. But anything less than perfection, Bel Esprit, and by tomorrow dawn you shall be sent from Dédale in haste and ignominy, to pursue only the ill fortune of plainest womanhood. So I warn you, Bel Esprit. Beware!"

I thought that these few threatening words were quite enough in themselves to destroy the confidence of many a stalwart woman, and for an instant I saw the invisible spiders hurrying over the features of the white face. Then Bel Esprit, with a toss of her head, put on once more her familiar mantle of self-sufficiency and, pressing herself more deliberately and dramatically into her corner, though she was alone on her seat, spent the rest of the journey in remote study of the twin mirrors of the land and sky.

The village, a nameless place belonging to Seigneur, appeared to the left of us. The squat and blackened spire sat atop its grim church, bedecked with iron thorns and fetters. We entered the village, stopped at the gaping portals of the church, from which fled a starving dog. We alighted. We entered the church. In midday night was upon us, and the smell of dust, wax, and incense, and no tomb could have been more cold. Through a pink heart high in the colored glass came a ray of hope, and in the shadows I saw a little Eros, and on the altar a few flowers. Again with a slight jump of spirit I recognized this church for its perfection: what setting could be more inimical to love? more obnoxious to flesh and sense? Any passion kindled here, I thought, was true passion.

Two waxy thumbs were flickering on a stand of iron spikes beside the confessional, a tilting boxlike affair which emitted a strong and sour smell. Bel Esprit knelt as she had been instructed and put her mouth to the hole; from inside the dusty cabinet and from behind its closed door there came a cough; Seigneur and I took our places, kneeling at prie-dieux not a body's length from where Bel Esprit began her confession. We could hear all, since we were close and the confessional stood in a small and clearly echoing vault. The candles cast their humble light on the back of kneeling Bel Esprit, and though dimly, we could see her well. By the deepness and regularity of Seigneur's breathing, I knew that he was concentrating on Bel Esprit's least consequential gesture, her every sound and word, and wore his frowning visage of severest judgment.

"Mon Père," said Bel Esprit in a voice that so betrayed the cold that I thought she must fail, and felt myself shrink desperately at failure's door. "Mon Père," she repeated, "no girl has ever sinned as I. Oh, I am disreputable, mon Père, for I have caused a priest to sin and then betrayed him! Oh, how I have doubly sinned, because my priest, whose serving maid I am, is good and devoted and temperate in middle age, and until his first night with me, when neither of us could deny ourselves, had for a noble lifetime honored his vows and so preserved his celibacy: which I would return to him this moment, were it in my power. . . ."

Her clear voice was stronger, she was vigorously applying her mouth to the wooden hole soiled by centuries of wet lips and ugly words, as undaunted by that wooden hole as by the ear pressed to its other side. Next to me, clasping both hands in reverence, Seigneur was lowering his guard, abandoning his fears, relaxing into the pleasures of the pupil's flute that does not falter, and in all this I could not have been more cheered, despite the mordancy of this cold church.

"So much for my first sin, mon Père," continued Bel Esprit in a voice so tonally contrived as to deny her own in winsome subterfuge. "Yet even now as I remember when I first raised his skirts and freed what divinity could no longer bind, even now I long to insert my hand beneath my own raised skirts: but I shall not, mon Père, I shall not. But there is worse. . . ."

From within the frozen darkness of the confessional came a groan, as

Bel Esprit let fall her hat, which she had been dangling, and leaned closer to her invisible auditor and made her high girlish voice still smokier.

"Yes, worse," she continued, shifting so as to free her skirts beneath her knees, "for there came the day when my poor priest was ordered by his bishop to deliver that sermon ordinarily intoned at the Pentecôte by the bishop himself when visiting my poor priest's church, and what could the good man do except spend an hour voicing aloud his bishop's words while the bishop himself was in my kitchen doubling dishonor and steaming alive the good priest's maid. . . . But I must, mon Père, I cannot help myself! Who would deny my hand, my fingers, this desperate need? Oh, how I throb, mon Père, no matter how I grasp and squeeze. . . ."

From within the confessional came a sudden sharp sliding sound, as of shoe leather on the small worn floor of the listener's station, and within the great folds of his cowl Seigneur was smiling.

"Oh, mon Père," cried the small voice in its sumptuous modulations, "I make no efforts to deny it! I sinned that day, I am sinning now, I have thrust my arm beneath my skirt, have spread my knees in penitential kneeling, have allowed my hot hand its hungry leap between the wet thighs, to the top of the fork, and now my hand and fingers cannot stop, won't stop, contaminating even now my beloved confessor with sounds more vile than the vilest words, and filling this sweet darkness with the smell which no sacred perfume may drown. This is how I am, mon Père, and what I am doing, so that I have hardly the strength or courage to speak, yet speak I must. . . . For no sooner had my good priest taken his bishop's place and begun to sound the bishop's words, than the burly old man found me in my kitchen, as I knew he would, for even I understood from my poor priest's first sad word, when he told me how he had been so strangely charged, though perhaps honored, that the bishop was practicing on my priest a ruse, though my priest, an honest godly man, never quite comprehended what had happened, and to spare him pain I made no mention of the matter, from that day to now. But I pause, I stroke what cries out for succor. It is not enough, mon Père! Not enough!

"So into my kitchen leapt the bishop! Before I could move or defend myself, mon Père, though I was expecting him! There he was, and while I groped behind me for the broom of faggots, the evil man seized his dusty red skirts in both his fists and pulled them high, shook them in my very face while I could not help but ogle what he had exposed. Never had I seen such a chunky hogshead, mon Père, as fat, as long and harder than his forearm, and as raw and red as any slab of wet meat chopped by the ax.

"I was not spared. Even before I had dropped the turnip and dismissed the broom, the bishop in one swipe had torn off my gown, then kissed my neck, and clapped a hand to my right breast, a hand to my hip, a hand to my thigh, a hand to my buttock, a hand to my labyrinth that was enlarging like an owl's eye to his fierce grip. Without knowing what I did, through steam so thick I could not see, floundering as the bishop bounced me to the floor and onto my back, to this side and that, to my bare stomach so as to pull me to my knees, thrust down my head, part my moons, mouthing my tight witch's eye and forcing my witch's eye to accept his barrel as had thrice already my labyrinth. But no, mon Père! Yes! No! I shall! You hear my determination in my helpless voice!"

So saying, her kneeling figure still agitated by her fevered hand, and shuffling backwards on knees we could not see, Bel Esprit so extended and used her free hand as to turn the brass device of the priest's flimsy door, and open it. I saw the whiteness of his thin bare legs exposed, white ankles rising from the tops of the pathetic shoes like stalks in the night. For a moment Bel Esprit fell gasping at the feet of her father confessor, then gathered herself, once more attained her knees, then worked her way between the priest's spread legs, spread and extended, until she was where she wished to be, with her bent figure obliterating all our vision of the priest in his confessional except for shoes and legs protruding to Bel Esprit's either side.

"Mon Père!" cried she. "My absolution shall be your relief!"

A convulsion seized the confessional. The backs of the heels of the poor shoes began to tap, then rapidly, faster and faster, hammering out their dreadful or elated noise into the cold and gloomy vault as if it would never cease, that noise, and priest and penitent never again be freed from their agony. I thought that the confessional would fall, that the pounding feet would set the bells to vibrating above our heads, that so near to victory Bel Esprit might yet fail. I knew, still listening to staccato blows, that the purpose of this entire episode was to elicit from the priest his cry. But if he could find in himself no cry to give, could offer her at last no more than moaning, what then? Moaning was not enough, as Seigneur had said repeatedly, and I understood that the cry was wanted, that the capacity to produce this cry depended finally on the priest himself and not Bel Esprit. She could bring him to the verge, as she was doing, but she could not sound herself his cry. Thus the fate of our Bel Esprit depended on the power of the priest to find his voice.

I leaned forward. How well I wished her! I listened. No one could exceed the determination of our Bel Esprit. Without a doubt he was beginning: the first and barest resonance of palate; a squeaking as of mice in the dry throat; a whimpering which was soon displaced by clearer notes, though of uncertain pitch. Then more firm, the first color of the vocal rainbow, and the cry's shadow, the summoning of the lungs to the trumpet's mouth, the shattering of all the poor visceral system that would produce the sound. Then, oh, then, there came the cry! Freed from its strangulation, up it soared, out it came, its rainbow lighting the entire church, the priest's pure voice echoing from vault to vault, stone to stone. It rose, it fell, it faded, until on the wall the little Eros flew and the pink heart glowed.

Done! Magnificent! I felt myself weaker than Bel Esprit appeared to be as she climbed to her feet, paused once before the prostrate figure she was now abandoning, then turned and made her way alone, as planned, from the dead church. We waited, Seigneur and I, peering at what little we could see of the priest, then in silence we followed after Bel Esprit.

Our last ride was our fastest, and Seigneur, in obviously enlivened spirits, once thrust head and shoulders from the lowered window into the blast our little carriage made, and in full tones pressed the driver to curse the ponies and employ the cruel whip. That done, and cowl thrown back, Seigneur produced from beneath our seat a blood-red leather case containing, as we soon saw, three plums, three glasses, a bottle of white wine brook-cold and green. Bel Esprit was sunk in her corner, hatless, with hair and red gown in disarray. Indolent, more fiery than ever in exhaustion, indifferent to the abuse inflicted upon her by road and carriage, thus she was so dispassionately nursing memories of what had but now befallen her that she accepted Seigneur's glass without a glance, a word, and drank it down, spilled a second into her lap, drank down a third, refused the plum.

"Faster!" cried Seigneur and cast upon Bel Esprit his admiring countenance, which she ignored, as was her right and even to be expected, while I, struggling to balance my glass and suck my plum, took to myself one ray, another, of the golden light intended for Bel Esprit.

We arrived. Dédale was empty in the silence of midday. Swiftly, and as she had been instructed, Bel Esprit took the lead in climbing to Seigneur's chamber, and swiftly entered it and surveyed the one curtained wall, the great bed with canopies tied back, the great fire rolling and hissing on the hearth. Seigneur locked the door behind him.

"Now!" exclaimed Bel Esprit, wheeling upon him. "Now you shall send the child from the room!"

But Seigneur made no move, made no reply. Yet did Bel Esprit not know that the key had turned and I was not to be evicted? Slowly the thought came to her:

"But why do you wait?" she cried. "For whom, for what person do you make me wait?"

He did not reply. Then with an arm's infinitely expanding gesture, slowly he pointed toward the wall hung in velvet cloth, and smiled, whereupon from behind the blue hangings stepped the silent priest, in every way as familiar to Bel Esprit as she had seen him in black skirts and hat inside the church, except that now he wore a black mask that added sinister vigor to the slender and dusty skirts. There he stood, in his treacherous disguise, and Bel Esprit gasped, faltered, stepped away.

"What!" she cried. "Here? Now? He who withheld himself so long that I thought my task thwarted by a mere village priest? The same?"

"See for yourself," said Seigneur mildly and nodded.

She frowned. Suspicion and returning courage brightened her face. She crossed the blueness of the majestic rug and placed herself within reach of the long arms hanging at the priest's sides. Suddenly with a flick of her raised arm she snatched away the mask, stepped back, and gasped upwards into the unsmiling face of Père La Tour, for it was he.

"You!" she cried. "You!" Then returning to Seigneur: "But it was he in the church? Or is he now pretending? Is Seigneur practicing his ruse on Bel Esprit?"

"Try him," replied Seigneur, "and know for yourself."

"Enough!" she cried, the tears starting at last from her eyes. "Do not play with Bel Esprit any longer! What is Bel Esprit's ill temper if not the little mask through which she squints always at Seigneur, whom she loves. . . ."

"Bel Esprit," he interrupted. "Take care. I have warned you, I warn you now. In our final moment, with the prize in sight, do not throw all away for the sake of frail feelings!"

"But look at you!" she cried and dropped to her knees. "Look there! Will you deny it? Seigneur strains! And for once I shall have Seigneur's scepter and not Père La Tour's!"

It was a noble but hopeless declaration, though for a moment I half wished that Seigneur would relent, which he would not, even as I told myself that Seigneur's curt nod was intended to save Bel Esprit from her own disaster, and not to slight her sentiments. But Père La Tour had been watching for Seigneur's signal and now strode forward, pulled Bel Esprit to her feet, and with one tug from top to bottom tore open the two halves of the tulip, which dropped away. She quivered, put palms to naked breasts, then desolately let fall her hands and waited as the still unsmiling Père La Tour removed his hat, knelt down, and with his angry face drawn close to Bel Esprit's feathery seat of passion, studied through cold eyes the black claw. At once Père La Tour became again him who comforted the horse and carried the child, and he smiled and looked up at Bel Esprit and plucked away the claw.

When the last feathers had settled, the impostor priest seized Bel Esprit about the hips and drew her down, lowered her, smothered her in his black robes.

"Well?" Seigneur asked Bel Esprit, after the departure of Père La Tour. "Can you identify our priest?"

"I cannot, Seigneur."

"And will it ever matter whether there was one actual, one false, or one false on two occasions?"

"It will not, Seigneur."

That night, through the silence, again I heard the singing and sewing of young nuns. At dawn I added the white bird's golden band, which Seigneur had given me, to my collection.

⟦1945⟧ The peacock pin

The beams are falling in our salon. Maman is on her hands and knees; Monsieur Malmort lies in Sylvie's chamber, having lost his way, and sunk to the stones, and succumbed to airlessness at last. At last the fire is at its peak: there is no light. My eleventh year, the year of Maman's muteness, has reached its end.

For those below, all, all is lost. . . .

"There is something different about Lulu!" shouted Lulu himself, and heads turned, eyes looked up, Clarisse and Madame Pidou advanced with outspread arms to the newly arrived Lulu who, wrapped in the green breeze from the open casements, awaited the inspection and approval of our ménage.

"He has shaved," said Clarisse.

"He has used his scented soap," said Madame Pidou.

"But it's his hair!" exclaimed Minouche. "It's pomaded! It's been cut!"

"No," said Yvonne. "Somebody has run a heavy iron over his sailor pants and scrubbed his shirt. He's fresh. He shines."

"The foot! The foot!" cried Sylvie, pointing to what all of them had seen from the start. "He is without crutches. His cast is gone!"

"Yes!" shouted Lulu. "His cast is gone! And see what he has brought you: cream!"

Bocage came forward, taxi cap aslant on his head and long apron tied around his waist, and gently shouldered his way among Lulu's admirers, winked at the boxer, and took from his arms, as we were soon to see, four cardboard canisters taller and fatter than Bocage's wine bottle and filled with cream as thick as soft cheese. Into the kitchen we trooped, and around the table we crowded ourselves, while Bocage poured out the cognac and scooped the heavy cream into bowls and saucers, and turned on the electric bulb though the kitchen was sweet with the warm green breeze of the day that had already turned to night.

"What luxury!" said Madame Pidou, and thrust the cream-heaped spoon into her wide mouth and shut her eyes, licked a white pearl from her lip and, on the tip of her tongue, showed it a moment, and then savored the droplet for as long as she savored the next spoonful, and the next. As for me, I was seated on the lap of Monsieur Malmort and shared both his spoon and his dish, preferring, however, my finger to his tarnished spoon. It was then that Clarisse began to speak.

"As we all know," she who never spoke now said, "once there was life beyond the Sex Arcade. . . ."

Spoons hung in midair. On every face astonishment was tempered with tenderness. Who could deny that for such a person as Clarisse, whose slimness emphasized each curving rib, whose narrow shoulders did not allow the least caress, whose bareness was the plainest fact, whose thin face was one of silent clarity and nothing more: that for such a person, whose feelings were at best concealed, at worst simulated, to speak to us at last was an event inspiring in all of us surprise and attention as clear as the voice in which Clarisse was speaking?

"Before the Sex Arcade," she said, "my life of passion was confined to a single day so distant it only now comes back to me. But now I can speak of that lost life of mine. Once," she continued, holding her empty spoon and straightening absentmindedly her bare shoulders, "once I was a couturière. I am young now and was younger then. I was no more demonstrative than I am now, but a woman's clothing gave me pleasure. It pleased me to unroll a bolt of silk, to sit and work an old sewing machine I had, to arrange scanty undergarments with a violet ostrich feather in the empty window of my boutique. I liked to dress myself as well as others. My favorite costume had belonged to my mother, whom I

154

had never seen and whose name I did not know: a dove-gray satin sheath with a fringed skirt above the knee, and her bejeweled peacock pin which I wore in my hair. What a costume for someone like me, who lived alone, worked alone, and was without feelings! But I wore it every day. Every day I sat at my old machine in my tight gray skirt and peacock pin and sewed. The pin was so long that it swooped down the side of my head to the jaw. What a woman my mother must have been, whoever she was! Perhaps I had become my mother, except for love.

"One day I had a customer. She was a mere girl but wanted a bridal gown, and quickly. Would I make it? I would make it. She undressed. I liked the sight of her. When I took her measurements she put her fingers on my preening peacock. I had never made a wedding dress and for two days and nights I stayed in the boutique: hunching at the machine, working the pedals, creating the whiteness that would soon hold the shape of the girl's body. Nothing I ever made was like it. The veil was three meters long. Now you know why I am round-shouldered and self-conscious.

"On the afternoon it was done I found a box and a white ribbon. Off I went: cold, unsuspecting, elated in a way I didn't show. My sheath was tight and made walking difficult. But the box dangled and I was breathing quickly. At last I came to the address and rang. Who was rich enough to have a stone Eros above the door?

"'But there's a mistake,' I said when a tall man answered. 'I expected mademoiselle and not monsieur.' He replied that she would soon return and took me in.

"I blinked. I was uncomfortable. I didn't know what to do when I heard the door close and saw him studying my pin.

"'Mademoiselle should have a last fitting,' I said, thinking that by my words and the box I carried he would know that I was the couturière. He replied again that she would soon return and proposed that I wait. There was no time for a decision, yet I who had never been accosted, touched, admired, and had matured in self-sufficiency or indifference, whichever it was, knew suddenly, without any previus experience at all, that a decision was unavoidable and mine to make. I understood that I had a choice; that the man I was facing was aware of it; and that I could either shrug and leave or stay. I raised a hand to remove my splendid peacock and felt inside me a peculiar smile at the choice I had made.

"'Oh, no,' he said, 'leave it on,' and as simply as the way he spoke he drew away my hand and from the other took the box and set it down on the floor. There was nothing in the room where we stood except a divan of gray leather. The room was large and had white walls and a bare floor of pink tiles, and it took only a glance to feel embarrassed at the sight of the divan, positioned in the middle of the room instead of against a wall, and to recognize in room and divan my own colors (since the peacock's long green tail curving toward my jaw was studded with pink jewels). I had never known such a coincidence. But never had I stood alone with such a man.

"He was tall, yet for his size as thin as I was, and dressed in nondescript trousers and a dark blue sweater-shirt that buttoned up his left shoulder and had holes in the sleeves. He wasn't strong; he wasn't trying to impress me; he wasn't offering me a glass of wine or calculating how to get me to the divan. Why did I stay? I can tell you: that nameless man had a long thin face that might have been a saint's face carved in blond wood, and the expression on his narrow face was of an innocent urgency I didn't know could exist. In all his consciousness there was only me; such innocent concentration was irresistible. The bulge in his pants was obvious. I had seen bulges before, but never one as large as this and orphaned, as I wryly thought.

"'Come,' he said. 'We'll sit down and wait.'

"His words were ingenuous. His voice was ingenuous. When he took my hand the gesture itself was ingenuous. But my mouth was dry at what was happening. I agreed with myself that the outcome was inevitable: my groom-to-be did not know what he was doing, and yet he had already as good as loved me on the gray divan. It was inevitable, though I could not help but think of the girl who soon would wear the gown I had made, and because of her, and for her sake, I kept trying to convince myself that no honest man could love someone this abruptly and that I would not submit to him.

"We sat on the edge of the divan and I allowed my hands to stroke the grayness of the shiny leather. When I felt his lips nibbling my neck and kissing my shoulder, I was surprised and gave him a little push, though it was exactly for the sensation of his mouth on my neck and shoulder that I had been waiting.

"'Monsieur,' I said. 'Think of my situation. . . .'

"He kissed me more gently, more firmly, with a moistness that did not dry on my skin. He laughed as he seized my arm and kissed its length. Inwardly I was thinking that there was something still more strange about this man, but could not define it.

"'Monsieur,' I said, twisting away and hearing a tremulous quality inflecting my cool voice. 'She'll return . . . she'll find us!'

"'We have an hour,' he murmured happily, and put his hand on my knee.

"'But you said yourself that she'll soon be back . . . there's no time . . . she'll find us . . .'

"'We have an hour.'

"I could not help but hold my legs together, yet raised my chin to tighten the cords in my neck, which I had never done before in my life, and arched my feet so tensely that only the toes were touching the floor. I closed my eyes; I felt his hand on the crown of my head; I felt his fingertips touching my mother's peacock. It was a long and dazzling pin that set off attractively my pale face and short brown hair. Then I opened my eyes and twisted away my body but not my face.

"His own face was close and peering at me as at the page of a book. I tried to tug down the hem of my skirt and pushed off his hand. His eyes were hazel, his teeth tobacco-stained, his forehead serene and dry, his smile wide and childlike.

"He was not young, which was his final strangeness. I had seen him as young, had thought him young, had decided to risk to him my untested flesh because of what I had perceived as his colors of youth. But he was not young. He was beyond the middle of life, my groom-to-be, and had found again and had preserved his child self, which a younger man might have long ago destroyed. Whiteness gave his hair its blond color; without his age he could not have had his complete and urgent desire that was like a child's. Thus his betrayal of the girl who had stood nearly naked in my boutique was not a betrayal; thus I forgave him in advance for giving me no more than an hour. I allowed my forearm to fall across his thigh, wishing I could dispel my worry that the girl would return in time to humiliate me and interrupt my hour.

"'This is impossible,' I said. 'You must stop . . . I must leave. . . .'

"He responded at once by breathing on my parted lips and sliding my tight skirt upwards toward my hidden lap. I wore gray stockings and a pink garter belt. That's all. Bending over and shaking his head in admiration, as if he had never before seen any like them, he studied the tops of my stockings and fondled the devices by which they were attached to the pale pink straps that traveled down the tops of my legs from the elastic belt. He sighed. He shook his head. Then he raised his face to mine and kissed my mouth.

"We fell apart. For the first time in my life I knew what it was like to lose my breath inside a kiss. He closed his eyes and leaned against the back of the divan, while I sank away from him until I half lay, half sat, on the slippery cushions. He had only to touch my leg nearest him for me to understand his signal, and to raise my leg and stretch it out across his lap, so that my stockinged legs could not have been more widely spread (the one across his lap, the other angled to the tiles). I knew what he wanted. He wanted my hand-sized sphinx exposed. Now it was.

"When I felt his fingers, automatically I tilted my hips to lift myself to his hand, feeling on the softness of his fingers my own wetness, as I saw that on the ceiling above us was sculpted a large round circlet of white flowers. I caught my breath.

"'Don't, monsieur, you mustn't,' I said, remembering from a book of my girlhood this prohibition with which I sought to amuse him.

"He covered my entire sphinx with his hand, and worked his thick fingers in circles like the one on the ceiling. Then he put his mouth where his hand had been.

"I bore the sensations of his mouth as long as I could, suffering the pleasure of not being able to distinguish lips from tongue, or the inside of his mouth from the outside. Finally I struggled upright and put both feet flat on the floor. All his lower face was wet, and I reached up with my mouth and kissed him.

"With a timid hand I cupped his bulge. He shifted himself gently and spread his trousered thighs.

"My breath was short. Never in my life had I touched a man's pants, or wanted to, and now I hardly knew how to begin, what to do, and even after I had coped with the buttons, which took all my concentration, still there was the confusion of his brief white undergarment refusing to yield up what it contained, and the distortion of the thing inside so great as to prevent its extrication. So I stood up.

"He did the same, with his pants half open, his bulge half visible, his face flushing at the sight of me. We were both perspiring.

"He removed my dress and underclothes. I left the pin in my hair, though I told myself that it was me he wanted and not my mother's pin. He stripped away his trousers, his white briefs, his sweater-shirt; totally unconscious of his own nakedness, he stared at mine.

"'Myrtille is not more willowy,' he said, and drew me again to the cushions.

"Again we sat on the edge of the divan. His stomach, like his face, looked blond and made of wood. I knew that his mouth tasted of tobacco. He had demonstrated already what I should do, but first I gave myself the satisfaction of studying what I had never seen, just as this man had studied me. What had been only a bulge before had now become the shapeliest of sights, with a head as large as a ripened apricot and of that color, though darker. I wondered how he could bear the pain of it.

"I bent over and took it inside my mouth, my thin lips giving way and stretching, my mouth so choked that I thought I might not even be able to move my tongue. But I did. Again I felt him caressing the crown of my head and the peacock's jewels.

"He raised my face and wiped my lips with a finger. When he kissed my breasts, which were flatter than a young girl's, I was not embarrassed. To the contrary, I felt between my legs the exhilaration of his holding to my flat chest his generous head.

"I lay back, following him as I might a dancer, and moved myself so as to rub thighs, flanks, and buttocks against the cold leather. He came down on me, touching all his nakedness to mine, so that I could smell his breath: yet for as long as we clung together on the dove-gray divan, he never imprisoned me, though he gave me his weight, which I wanted.

"He was motionless, and suddenly I knew that nothing more would happen unless his couturière became alert and acted on what he had in mind. But what he wanted was obvious: I reached down for his apricot and found it and pulled it into me, all the rest following as smoothly as if it had been unattached to his body, and had belonged to me alone, and had been lubricated in a bowl of oil. But I knew what was his and what was mine, and that we balanced.

"He cupped the back of my head as I had cupped his bulge, and gentle or not, joyous or not, he covered me in a vigorous rhythm and filled me not with a single fruit but with a whole garden. Despite his muscles, which I felt all over me, there was about him a certain awkwardness, no matter how he thrust into me, and rocked me, and cupped my buttocks as well as my head, and suddenly I found for him a sinuousness and rapidity of motion that surprised me as much as anything, wriggling and even bucking in circles, so that I was still more like a dancer, flat on my back.

"I could hear his appreciation in his wordless voice. He could hear mine. The circlet of flowers was jerking in zigzags around the ceiling.

"Then came the sound. Not even an hour for the couturière. No bliss for me. The sound I knew I should have to hear, I heard. My luck was never good. She was home. I waited for the cry of anger, the slamming door. But betraying the bride-to-be was no worse, I thought, feeling myself slowing down and cooling, than interrupting the couturière at such a time. What I was losing, I longed for. Perhaps I longed for it more than she longed for the return of monsieur's innocence.

"No crying? No shouting? Monsieur had slowed down too. We were treading water. Inside me he was as hard as ever, and I admired him for not wrenching away and starting on his explanations. Then I turned my head and felt a rush of embarrassment stronger and sweeter than the confidence of monsieur's embrace: a reprieve lighter than air.

"Not an arm's length away she was kneeling beside the divan, smiling and naked except for the flowered bridal wreath which she wore on her pretty head with the long veil winding down her bare back and across the tiles. The box I had brought was opened. The gown, which I had made, lay carelessly on the pink tiles. I knew that my lover had turned his face as I had mine, and was looking at his nude near-bride with a pleasure that equaled mine, though it lacked my surprise. Then I understood that the young kneeling woman had been in the house when I arrived.

"She came to us on her hands and knees. She was younger than I and slight. She put her face to mine, her lips to mine, she touched a buzzing tongue to mine. The bony hand that had cupped my buttocks now lay on her shoulder. Was she wearing her flowered veil in honor of my peacock pin?

"Then I felt a heave, and heard the girl gasp as if it were her body that the aged groom-to-be was holding instead of mine, and her nudity that was nestling his instead of mine, until my clearheadedness was gone and nothing was left to me but ribs and loins, and, at last, the hot concentric floating of my circles. One of them spiraled off, and then another. Another. I saw that the bride-to-be had climbed onto the back of our aged man and was astride him and riding him, smearing on his back her wetness with every lunge, all the while leaning over his shoulder and laughing down at my upturned face. The wreath was crooked and had fallen low on her forehead; her face was wet; I felt her breath on my eyes and heard her voice.

"Like a child she dismounted, quickly, and as she did so he withdrew. Smoother than ever, harder, the color of the apricot becoming plum: their hands were on my neck, my shoulders, my flat chest, behind my ears, as without another word or sign from either one of them I bent down again and molded him inside my murmur. I felt it mounting, felt more circles starting up within me, and would have cried out had I been able to. Before I knew what was happening the girl was tugging my blind face to hers and holding me more tightly than had he. When we came unstuck, each of us could see her bright and sticky mouth in the other's, her dripping chin in the other's, her own face swelling with new desire in the other's. We embraced, her firm and ruddy breasts pressed to my flatness, my hard hand clasped to her soft waist.

"Down we went, pulling each other to the pink tiles, and there we sprawled, and tangled the long veil between us, and sucked and fingered, gleamed and dazzled, setting each other off at the slightest touch, pausing for the sight of each other's eyes. All that time, while we groped and disregarded the hardness of the tiles, our sainted man sat as naked as ever on the divan and smoked a meerschaum pipe whose white bowl was carved into the head of a wise old patriarch replete with long silken hair and a beard. So at his feet we lay, wreathed in his smoke.

"How could they have given me so much and nothing? When I tried to find them again the next day there was no such place, no such address or street, no stone Eros above a polished door. Never again did anyone want me to make a wedding gown. Myrtille's was the only one. After Myrtille there were no more brides."

The timbre of Clarisse's voice had undergone no change from the beginning of her narrative to its end, and now her boyish voice was still audible, though she had ceased to talk. The plates and cups were filled with cream, the silence with loving deference to Clarisse, who had picked up her spoon and begun to eat. Monsieur Malmort shifted his knees beneath me.

"I tell you," said Bocage, the first to speak, "I would give a week of charades to have that pair in the Arcade."

"I would give more than that," murmured Clarisse.

"What, Bocage," said Madame Pidou, "we ladies aren't enough?"

"Nor the men?" said Lulu. "Tomorrow Lulu brings his meerschaum pipe!"

"But speaking of youth and age," said Minouche from her end of the table, "I shall now ask Monsieur Moreau some questions. Are you ready, Monsieur Moreau?"

He nodded, that little misshapen and self-effacing man, who was seated beside Minouche and tipping his anxious face and staring into his dish of cream, unable either to speak or to eat. Lulu reached for the cognac; Madame Pidou put a hand to her hair; Yvonne turned so as to face Clarisse, beside whom she sat, and licked her lips, pumped up her chest, and by the glowing of her broad face made clear her gathering purpose, which was to kiss Clarisse. I felt Monsieur Malmort taking hold of my waist, and once more leaned my head against him. Through half-shut lids I saw Yvonne caressing Clarisse's cheek; through the green night I listened to Minouche and Monsieur Moreau, thinking that it was not merely Lulu's mended foot that made this night unlike any I had ever known. What was it, then? Why was I so sad, so languorous? Had I too some story I could not tell? When I heard Minouche's voice my attention drifted in her direction, as I waited for Monsieur Malmort to stroke my head and watched Yvonne, for whom there was now nothing in the world except Clarisse. Never would I be so consumed in someone else's concentration. Still I waited.

"Tell me, Monsieur Moreau," said Minouche, "Do you know the name of your daughter?"

He nodded.

"But did you ever forget her name, as you once said you did? Was it true that you found your daughter boring, as you once claimed you did?"

His silent answer was in the negative.

"But why did you say such things about your daughter?"

He hung his head. He was a cat with his cream. We could hardly hear his voice when he spoke. He was not purring, that much I knew, as I remarked the strangeness of hearing about someone's daughter when I myself was a daughter about whom no one would ever speak or wish to.

"Well, Monsieur Moreau?" said Minouche, though not unkindly. "What is your answer?"

"I was ashamed," he said at last, and licked one corner of his mouth. "I was so ashamed that I pretended boredom."

"Tell us her name, Monsieur Moreau."

"Félicité."

"A sweet name for a little girl."

He nodded.

"But tell us why you were ashamed . . ."

"Wait!" cried Bocage, interrupting.

"What's all this, Minouche?" cried Lulu in the same breath. "Leave him alone!"

"Yes, Minouche," said Monsieur Pidou, his brow furrowed and his voice considerably soft. "Aren't your questions ill-advised?"

"Let her talk!" cried Sylvie. "You shall not shout her down!"

"But look!" said Madame Pidou, raising her hand for silence. "Monsieur Moreau wishes to speak. . . ."

"To be honest," said that now perspiring person, "I myself suggested that she ask her question. I have pressed my face to Minouche's bosom; she has restored my manhood and hence my fatherhood. I myself want to speak about my Félicité."

"Mon Dieu, Moreau!" muttered Lulu. "Get on with it."

Through fallen lids I watched Yvonne's mouth approaching Clarisse's, saw the large hand of the one on the slender neck of the other, and through my green silence I listened to the halting yet fervid voice of Monsieur Moreau. Slumberous yet partially awake, I would have thought that Monsieur Malmort was sleeping, except that he had begun to stroke my head, and I could feel his fingers straying off my bright helmet of hair, occasionally, to touch the soft heart that was my face, now sunk, as he thought, in the sleep of a child. But I was listening to Monsieur Moreau.

"My betrayal of my little Félicité," he said, "came naturally enough. Everyone understands a father's fears for his daughter. I too worried about my daughter, which was natural and no fault of mine. But her illnesses, her gloomy days, what made her sad or angry, though she was so small and young: these preoccupied me less and less, until I was left with a single worry, which was that she would one day be molested in an empty street. Each morning I watched her from the window until her little figure became invisible; each afternoon I stood at the window hours before she could possibly come into sight, my Félicité with her skirt to her ankles and her satchel as large as she herself. My worry increased: I contrived to keep her at home, accompanied her down to the doorway, hatless and coatless began to meet her on the nearby intersection of our shabby street and the rue des Fleurs, despairing when she left me and dashing across the street with insane pleasure at my first distant glimpse of her, the frantic father catching up his child and carrying her the last of the way home, despite her surprise and gentle protestations. I had no wife and Félicité no mother; my desperate fears were understandable. Yet never did I think to allay my worries and do the obvious: simply walk with her to school and back, holding her hand as any ordinary father might.

"The torture of waiting for Félicité increased, and each day when I snatched her up at last I clutched the small and lively body beneath its homely garments, attempting to detect with my hands the harm that I was convinced had befallen her. I began to suspect that she would not tell me if she had in fact been harmed, and my helplessness caused me to stop dead in the street and frown and sweat. At each greeting I hugged her harder to my chest, and in each wave of relief detected a larger seed of distraction. Worry had become distrust.

"How my betrayal of Félicité at last became shameful is already evident. I no longer feared that harm would come to her, but that she herself was seeking harm in secret. Yes, I began to suspect the very daughter I longed to protect; on her I turned the dread and anger I had felt previously for the shadowy figures waiting motionless in doorways. She met me so brightly, suffered my hugging with such patience, put her face to mine with so much cheerfulness, talked so quickly into my suspicious ear about a book, a drawing, a little game, was in every way the opposite from the injured creature I was sure she was, that suddenly I knew I was being deceived not by men in doorways but by my child herself. When I carried her home on the day of this discovery, I was unable to speak, and so caused my little daughter to worry for my welfare as I had for hers.

"In such a situation there was only one thing to do: I followed her. I could not restrain myself. I could not stop. I followed her until the sounds of children's voices drove me back, and among hordes of working women and at great distances kept her in my view with a skillfulness that became vindictive. I found the doorways deep enough to conceal me, managed to walk and stoop for unrewarded detection. Then, curiously, I gave up pursuing her. I hardly greeted her when, at the end of the afternoon, she called my name and entered the room where I had spent the day. Her sad puzzlement increased.

"Still my distrust lingered. The scale grew smaller, the picture more confined. I suspected Félicité of less while the intensity of my suspicions began to grow. I searched her orderly collection of books and papers for florid notes destined for men I would never meet. I searched her room: its closet where the dresses hung and two small pairs of shoes stood side by side on the floor; the bed with its coverings as smooth as she could pull them, and mattress too heavy for her to raise; the drawer containing her underclothes arranged in as orderly a fashion as her books and papers. I looked behind the floral print I myself had hung on the wall, and into a lacquered box where she kept her pencils, and beneath the small and faded rug on the floor. For all my troubles I discovered nothing: no secret letter, no inappropriate book or magazine, no hidden photograph of a handsome male head and face she might have pressed to her lips. Nothing. There was nothing in the little world of my Félicité that could not have belonged to any child, and nothing that anyone should not have seen. No sign of what I suspected, nothing personal, not even a photograph of her mother on the bureau. Yet these things which I touched and studied made me wish to weep.

"Then the moment came when I noticed that behind the closed door of the salle de bains, where Félicité was readying herself for bed as usual, there was silence. Why silence? Why not the sound of water? The tinkling of glass? As quietly as I could I approached the door. I listened. I waited. At last, and in midphrase, or so it seemed to me, clearly I heard the prettiness of my child humming.

"I retreated. But night after night I did no more than listen. The strain of listening was the worst. My most savagely selfless efforts on behalf of worry could not compare to the final desperation I was subjected to: the strain of listening. Inwardly I saw the narrow sink, the cracked bidet with one faucet loose, the tin container into which I dropped dulled razor blades and bloodied tissues, the mirror too high for the eyes of Félicité, unless she stood on the chair. Was the door locked? Had she in fact climbed onto the chair? Had she somehow filled, without my hearing the fall of water, the deep and nearly square white bathtub barely large enough to hold me seated and with my knees under my chin? Was she now similarly immersed to her narrow shoulders in the clear water? What was she doing? Was she listening?

"Each night when finally I heard her talking to herself or humming, I frowned, shook my head, and retreated once more into my puzzlement. Sometimes I saw her through the closed door, my dripping child, and the silence and vivid images caused me to stand longer and longer every night with my breath held and the side of my head pressed against the door.

"The inevitable occurred. One night, midway in my vigil, I realized that I was unable to move. I had no volition. I could not move, I did not wish to move, but in my stealth would stand pressed to the door until I should have no longer the need to listen, the need to look. I would discover what my obsession had promised me from the start.

"The door opened. It opened slowly, away from me, and I felt it peeling away as if one half of myself had peeled away from the other, leaving me at last exposed in silhouetted profile in the empty doorway. Finally I was able to turn my head and look down at her. There was no steam in the room. Only the strong odor of my cologne.

"She was looking up at me. Her little perfectly proportioned form was naked. Her thick dark hair hung midway down her back, though I could not see it. She was holding her folded nightdress across one arm. Her large and upturned eyes were the color of her thick hair.

"'Poor Papa,' she said at last. 'Poor Papa. . . .'

"That was the night Bocage found me smoking on the bridge. That was the very night I sat with Minouche. And now? Now I am a loving father, though since my Félicité lives with her mother's sister, and I alone, it is too late."

Even before Monsieur Moreau ceased speaking, his story, I knew in my half sleep, would not be followed by silence. No silence would be allowed to gather around his words, where he sat on the edge of his chair with hands clasped between his legs.

"Poor Monsieur Moreau," Madame Pidou whispered immediately. "Poor man...."

"Moreau," said Lulu, "you don't belong in the Arcade. The confessional is the place for you."

"My story," said Yvonne, as she and Clarisse, who had been kissing each other like birds feeding their young, now drew apart and faced the table, "my story is also about a child, but a boy instead of a girl: my little brother...."

I envied Félicité, and as I was savoring my envy, and waiting for Yvonne to continue, and leaning in the crook of the faithful arm, and letting my legs dangle, it was then that I felt and heard Monsieur Malmort whispering another story into my ear: "Once there was a little girl who became a flower...."

But he was not allowed to finish.

⟦1740⟧ A woman spurned;
a woman marked

That morning I lingered about the cloister. Everywhere I smelled the air at its fullest bloom of serenity. The air was still but our pennant flew; from within the cloister came the murmur of low voices and the occasional irritated sounds of the cock forced suddenly to avoid the strollers speaking on their endless path around the perimeter of his domain. If he had not been startled in time and given way, they in their preoccupation would have stepped on him, small majestic creature of dark rusty red and blackness as bright as coal.

The day was different. The same, yet different. Sky and earth reflected between them the sweet air's clear light, like a pair of mirrors; Seigneur's cows were on the horizon; a single bird of pale blue was circling Dédale; a lute in a chamber opened to the sun was conspiring with the sound of mowers in a green field. Yet all was not well, and I could not help but hover where the trouble was. I listened, frowned, strolled outside the cloister in imitation of those within, and crept closer, insinuated myself into the shadows of cool stones. All was not well.

La Comtesse, for it was she, had arrived early, was staying late, and in the majesty of her errand loomed larger beside Seigneur than ever, from where I spied them between the columns. Loomed larger, was more determined in whatever it was she pursued, and louder of voice, more strident, prone to sudden swells of supplication such as I had never heard. Her mood was both light and dark; Seigneur's was dark. But the person of La Comtesse, how it had changed! If she was causing our trouble, and indeed she was, her vestments were in all their qualities its opposite. Never had she come to us except in her own color: black. How could a woman so tall, so heavy, so merciless as the overbearing person that she was come to us in any other color than that of the night? And now, when pleading and haranguing in a garden too small and soft for her aggressive ways, surely now her five black ravens were more than ever appropriate to the storm she was setting aswirl in a small cloister created for the sake of peace and purity. But not at all! The opposite obtained! For what was La Comtesse's color on this occasion? Yellow!

There she shone between the vines, between the columns, burst into view and subsided in her course around the path of white pebbles: yellow! a cloud of yellow sucking to it light and air and fragrance, as I approached and laid my cheek against the stone and watched. Her hat was one vast flimsy petal of a monstrous daffodil and drifted above her massive face and violent argument like a summer hat on the head of a girl; and so too the gown, a gauzy yellow like a film of light on a golden head, and flowing, capturing the eye in its buttery net, a gentle breeze of yellow that bespoke modesty and budding youth instead of the brute weight of her tyrant's body which, at this moment, was bolder than ever, as if she were whipping her horse instead of whispering in fury to Seigneur.

"Madame," came the shreds of his voice, "it cannot be . . . it shall not be . . ."

"Do not deny . . . do not presume . . ."

So went the yellow cloud wrapped about the heart of its black storm, the poor color of innocence in a new season now made a mockery by its wearer's flesh and the mind which weighed as much as all her flesh heaped on the balance. Yet today she must have meant herself to be not black but yellow, not matronly but girlish, not bloated on mannish wrath but as slim in spirit as the green twig. But how she had failed!

"No, no, Madame, it affronts the glory of your nature . . . the higher laws . . . we are constrained from further fruits of incest . . ."

". . . no argument confounds . . . what I demand . . ."

What cause was she pleading? What thin shoot was she attacking with her ax of iron? And was not so much contradiction merely ridiculous?

What was I witnessing if not the substance of my own imagery? And was not this substance worthy of compassion rather than ironic musings and impatience? This big woman contained inside herself something delicate: it was not her fault if, in attempting to show it forth, she shook the frail leaf, mowed the field to pluck the flower, made yellow ludicrous in a power she could not restrain and which would not abate. Still, why must I scoff? Why not an ounce of tenderness for the woman who wanted only to be tender, and could not? But her yellow costume inspired fear, and I could do no more than muse ironically within earshot of her fulsome will.

"Madame . . . Madame . . ."

". . . shall wait no longer! . . . shall brook no pious negative!"

". . . we must submit . . ."

". . . I crave . . . the course of craving . . ."

". . . sinister desires! . . . consequences not to be endured . . ."

". . . would bear five more to have my way!"

"For shame, Madame, for shame! . . . She has no right to life . . . should not exist . . . to risk a repetition is but to mock the sacred irregularity that she is . . ."

They stopped and faced each other. The black cock scampered and then walked regally away. The suppliant in yellow, as I thought of her, or militant woman who made of the fair color a travesty, obscured my view of Seigneur, and their voices had fallen. Still I knew that here was the partial exposure of a truth I did not wish to meet in the light of this day, some discord struggling to burst its bonds and which, once loosed, might gather even myself to its hurtful breast and crush me. But I lingered. The volume of the voices again increased.

". . . I do not forget . . . could not forget, Madame . . ."

". . . spurn the very source of who you are? . . . refuse my declaration? . . . reject my petition? . . . stand fast?"

And after a silence: "Stand fast . . ."

I hid myself. I watched. They said no more. When La Comtesse exited alone from the cloister, passing to within a whisper of my secret self, the way she moved and the way she looked made me believe that in the courtyard, where her horse frothed, she would tear the yellow clothes from her body, hat and all, revealing beneath them the familiar gown of bulky black, and the black hat on wing. In her fury she would destroy what was a mere disguise, while Père La Tour turned aside his gaze.

Rending and trampling underfoot her clothes, even she would know that yellow, in all its sweet significance, was not for her. The vision so made me quiver that for an instant I thought of intruding on Seigneur where he stood alone, speechless and expressionless, with the little cock comfortably at his feet and the air still. But I could not and could only wish that La Comtesse had not come to us this day. The universe had been tipped from its axis imperceptibly for Seigneur: nothing could right it. So I left him and gloomily preceded him to the hall of dead boars.

We waited, I at the one table beside the empty chair, the women of Dédale at the other, in a silent row. By my presence they anticipated the mood Seigneur would bring to us with his arrival, and, accordingly, prepared themselves for sober comportment. But looking at the women across from me, a single thought stirred before I was able to dismiss it: might I be wrong? Might I incorrectly assume love and allegiance where there were none? Unthinkable! I silently exclaimed, and set myself to admiring the wet flowers in their vases. I wished the flowers had been of another color, but took consolation in their freshness and green stems.

"Mesdames!" Seigneur cried happily, and to me surprisingly, as he came at last among us and took his place at my table. "Mesdames, she who loves well punishes well!" With this jocular admonition, which might have been a dangerous mockery, it seemed to me, voiced as it was by a man who had himself but now borne the misery of a woman's punishment, he raised his glass and saluted the small company across from him and laughed. Immediately all glasses rose; quickly the women across from us proposed his health; their laughter leapt after him, and they sighed, chatted, tinkled their glasses, kept themselves ready to show Seigneur their eyes, at his slightest provocation, and in their eyes the attention and appreciation fired by him alone, and for him alone. I too was relieved. His rare benignity continued throughout our meal; in fact his pleasure, feigned or actual, erupted instructively with every course.

"Give an egg to get a beef!" he cried, when he saw the hard white silky flesh on the first of our blue plates.

"For lack of hummingbirds," he suddenly exclaimed, as Adèle served each of us from a steaming crock of tiny birds in a sauce of herbs, "one sups on the crow!" His lips glistened with the taste he licked. The new asparagus was of the palest green.

"Mesdames!" he cried, watching with unrestrained approval the appearance of our plates of lamb, each portion resembling a tempting square of pink butter: "All tastes are natural!" He swept his ladies with a beaming countenance, and then savored his meal. But while the spices lingered and the mouths grew sweet, he told them that the desire to restrain one's appetite reflected the quality of the fare and not the chary eater's strength of heart; that the more one eats, the more one loves; that as the eyes are the mirrors of the meal, so too the distance between the cup and lip is as vast as the vineyard. He said that hunger augments the appetite and dulls the taste, while the meal that is merely wholesome remains a hidden treasure because no one seeks to find it. He said that the powers of the sensitive palate improve with age, and more, much more, while his audience nodded and applauded, debated the ingredients of sauces and grew thoughtful over the driest wine. Each of Seigneur's words was as delicate of flavor, yet robust too, as the morsels of Adèle's cuisine adorning our plates. He talked, we ate; he ate, we listened. No other Noontide feast was richer.

"Now," he said at last, crossing his knees and restoring rapt silence to our hall with but the single word, while the boars on their blue plaques looked down and we looked at Seigneur: "Now, who is to read? Is it you, Finesse?"

"It is I, Seigneur."

"I hope you have improved your style of writing, Finesse."

"We shall see," she answered in her cool fashion which concealed no effrontery, and raised her book. "My story is about Arnaud and Celestine and, though short, takes for its theme fidelity, which concerns us all. I shall read you my story without pause or comment, since my meaning and my music are inseparable. May I begin?"

"Begin, Finesse."

She rested a frail elbow and slender forearm on the table, opened her journal in its binding of violet silk, and without once glancing down at her written page, recited her narrative in a clear and pleasing voice. She attempted to look at the rest of us while she spoke, yet for the most part sought and received with her violet eyes the steady look of Seigneur's bolder and larger eyes. She began:

"The men return from distant places, and Arnaud is mounted on the first horse. His company rides past the château of Celestine, who sits in her window. Arnaud does not raise his eyes.

"'Ah! my friend Arnaud.'

"Celestine sits in her window, in the light, holding across her knees a cloth of clear color. She calls aloud: 'Ah! my friend Arnaud. Once you would have suffered had you passed my father's château and said nothing to me.'

"Arnaud draws aside and the riders pass. He says, with his eyes averted: 'In my absence you have forgotten what we shared in love. So I have heard.'

"Celestine speaks softly: 'By the relics of our saints and before a tribunal of pure maidens and ladies of honor, I will swear that I have never loved another. Ah! my friend Arnaud.'

"In haste he climbs the tower. When she sees him again, Celestine begins to moan: 'Ah! my friend Arnaud.'

"He seats himself on the bed painted with flowers. Celestine sits too.

"'Ah! my friend Arnaud.'"

The story ended, the light deepened, and still Finesse and Seigneur looked into each other's eyes, and for so long and in such a way as to arouse in her sisters, as Seigneur sometimes called them, the pleasure that can be prompted only by what silence promises, and in me discomfort. Why were they staring at each other with such deliberateness? Their expressions were neither friendly, challenging, hostile, nor bemused. Never had I seen empty faces and empty eyes so prolonged in their engagement or so eloquent as in this blank exchange.

"Finesse," said Seigneur at last. "It seems to me that you have been reading Colère's journal. What I once said about her work applies to yours. But I believe I understand what you have read to us. The lover does not require the lady's oath. Is that what you mean?"

For answer she merely returned the book to her lap.

"I myself may illustrate your concept more concretely," continued Seigneur, whose seriousness and disregard for the rest of our assembly now caused an uneasy fluttering as of birds in a trap. "Once a former Noblesse abandoned the chevalier for whom I had fashioned her, which was in itself a violation of our understanding, but did so in order to marry, which is opposed to the spirit of my enterprise and to all the qualities and attributes of the true Noblesse. But she wished to marry, and wished to marry the new man of her choice for the sake of his honor, as she thought of it, and did so. Once married, she refused the chevalier the happiness to which he had become accustomed, thus incurring three violations in all, this dishonest woman. But the chevalier appealed to my judgment and requested that I put before the ladies then living in Dédale this problem. The edict of these ladies fortunately agreed with mine: the marital tie does not exclude the right of the first lover, unless the lady abandons love entirely and withholds herself from husband and lover both. Thus we see that what the religieux call adultery is in fact a necessity of love, if a still-loved mistress marries. Yet, paradoxically, marriage is antithetical to love, since duty is the fundament of marriage, and duty, by definition, destroys the free reciprocity which is the heart of love. Fidelity in marriage is duty in a false cloak; between lovers fidelity is the yearning of the freely generous spirit. Thus on two counts I implore you, mesdames, to avoid marriage.

"Yet I need not urge you in this direction. You, at least, shall not find yourselves tempted to marry. But so that I might leave you on a livelier note," said he, rising suddenly and looking away from Finesse at last and smiling round the hall, "and also leave you with a thought more important than anything you have heard in Finesse's story or my own anecdote, let me tell you that our concern is love. Love in all its colors and disguises. So here is what you must keep in mind forever: that the grace of novelty is to love as is the skin to the fruit: it provides a luster easily removed but never replaced!"

With that, Seigneur laughed and strode from the hall, Le noir and La jaune close on his heels as always.

"Volupté!" he shouted from an angry mouth, an angry face. "Will you never learn? Never? You are worse than Bel Esprit! No one tortures her horse as much as that smallest woman in Dédale, except for you, the largest!"

Those words brought more dismay to me than any others, and once again the serenity of a bright day faded, and against my will I felt myself flooded with pique at the naïve good humor of that big woman bouncing on her white horse: why must the bland and happy Volupté mistreat her horse, and hence anger Seigneur, and hence dim my day? I knew what must now occur, as she did not, and did not respect my role in it, so I could only feel piqued that Volupté could pain her horse and force me into this disagreeable role. Would she never learn?

"Dismount, Volupté," said Seigneur. "Dismount at once. . . ."

The high sun, green field, circle created by Seigneur at its hub and huge white horse cantering around and around on the end of Seigneur's white line: the sum of the scene was that harmony of mind and naturalness that best characterized Seigneur and most inspired the tranquillity I knew in the sight of him. But now, even as Seigneur was stopping the equestrian lesson, Volupté still sawed with her reins and pulled as powerfully and thoughtlessly as she could on the mouth of her white horse. The face of the rider was broad, soft, uncomprehending; the head of the horse, with its yawning jaws, bloodied mouth, bursting eyes, was a twisted parody of the fair rider's jouncing head. The pain of the horse was there for Volupté to see, but she did not, and merely gave her largeness to the horse's stumbling rhythm, leaned back, pulled, with her thick and thoughtless arms exerted all the strength she could against the tender mouth, while smiling happily at the stationary sky and revolving field.

"Dismount! Dismount, Volupté! At once!"

Shirt ballooning though the air was still, and beribboned hair reflecting his dark energy, and thick legs turned actively to muscle in the tight stockings and knee britches, hand over hand Seigneur drew in the long white rein, thus slowing the horse's canter and diminishing its circle, until at last he clutched the bridle and held the poor beast at a standstill. The man was as agitated as was the horse. He stroked its nose. The horse submitted to his touch. Volupté relaxed the rein. There she sat, sidesaddle on the creature's back, her thick blond hair braided as was the horse's tail, the long red skirt of her riding costume spread like an inverted fan against the whiteness of the horse's body, and as she looked down on Seigneur it was all too evident that, in the utmost innocence, she yet considered the white mare on which she rode to be no more than the appropriate counterpart to her own large size, and nothing more. Volupté was as kind as she was naïve. Yet she had hurt the horse, the largest and gentlest in our stable.

"Get down as best you can," said Seigneur quietly. "I cannot bear to touch you."

The severity of this remark was more understandable to Volupté than Seigneur's shouted anger, and the benevolence of the big face disappeared in puffy shades of blight. The enormous mouth gave up its smile; the light of injury swam in her eyes; the smooth forehead acquired creases. Her soul was as sweet as the scent she wore, and as detectable, and now the whole of it was thickening in her cloud of error. She wanted only to do her best, to please, to comply with Seigneur's every wish, from whim to ultimate command. Now in her red and golden slowness she set herself in motion, kicked free her foot from the stirrup, managed to turn herself face downward on the beast's broad back, then all but tumbled to the earth, from which she gathered herself up and stood waiting for she knew not what. Seigneur led the horse to a nearby tree, fleeced in leaves the color of ripe plums, and made it fast on a long tether. In a slow, deliberate, methodical fashion, Seigneur unfastened the straps of the shiny bridle, slipped the bridle from the white head, loosed the bit from the bleeding mouth. At once the white mare lowered her head and began to crop the grass. I regretted that Volupté's honest heart and bounteous beauty were not accompanied by the third and most necessary partner in the quadrille: good sense.

"Down, Volupté," said Seigneur, approaching. "Get down on all fours!"

Never had she heard such menacing tones, and could not account for them, or comprehend what she had been told to do. She could not understand what vast sinister quality had so discolored the ordinarily clear and happy picture of her equestrian hour. I watched her puzzlement, thinking that she needed cleverness or a lighter touch or both, but was possessed of neither, and now the sight of the still standing Volupté was changing the object of my own sympathies from injured horse to hapless rider.

"You do not understand what you have done, Volupté?"

"No, Seigneur."

"You pulled too tightly on the reins."

"And that is a frightful culpability, Seigneur?"

"It is."

"I don't see how."

"You shall. Now do what I have told you to do. Kneel down. Position yourself on all fours. You have exhausted my patience, Volupté. I am going to teach you a clear and unforgettable lesson. Down with you!"

176

She could not help but obey, and gathering her heavy skirts in her hands knelt on the grass, then swung herself forward and supported herself on hidden thighs, hidden knees, and on broad palms and sturdy arms, the woman thus transformed into an animal, the white horse transformed to red. The air and light grew softer; the white mount enjoyed the grass; Seigneur pursued his ruthless demonstration.

He stooped above Volupté's head. He seized her jaws. He shook her head. She murmured, grew flushed, revealed little flashes of fear in her placid eyes. Still gripping the jaws he again shook the head, then inserted thumb and first finger into the corners of her wide mouth and forced it open, her poor agreeable mouth, though she would have opened her mouth willingly had he but asked her to.

The bridle was of heavy and shiny leather decorated with plates of gold, and was still damp with the odor and perspiration of the mistreated horse. The enormous bit was still warm, still dripping its reddish froth, its greenish slime, and in its brutal size made even Volupté's wide mouth small and feminine. Seigneur shoved the bit into the open mouth, flung reins and bridle over the hanging head and onto the red and swaying back, stepped away and surveyed his handiwork, which pleased him, as I could see.

"To saddle, Virginie! Your mount is ready!"

I was at Seigneur's disposal and had to obey. True that in the past I had "ridden" other riders guilty of Volupté's same sin; true that I had witnessed repeatedly the effectiveness of this lesson. Still I deplored it and considered it the most repellent ritual in all of Seigneur's regimen, and would have refused my part if I had dared, and could neither understand nor condone this aspect of Seigneur's character revealed in the present instance of his inventiveness. But I obeyed.

I raised my gray skirts, since I was always favored to ride astride, and gathered up the reins and with a little hop flung my thin legs across Volupté's soft back and mounted her. I sat as straight and well-seated as on Cupidon, and lifted my head, breathed deeply, felt the woman's warmth beneath my flesh. My feet dragged on the green grass, but I was comfortable.

"Use your spurs, Virginie! Let me see a good gallop!"

I did not actually apply my heels to Volupté's body. But I squeezed her waist with my thighs and leaned toward her hanging head of blond hair, and in the way I used myself imparted to her clearly enough her rider's will, which, following upon Seigneur's brisk words, caused her to embark on a slow-paced awkward journey around a cumbersome circle. The reins were heavy in my hands; even in the guise of an animal Volupté was strong and sizable.

"Now pull!" shouted Seigneur, and pull I did, having anticipated this avid cry and being ready to execute his order with verve and mastery. I leaned back, I tugged, tugged sharply, sawed the reins, languorously enjoyed the sky as I did so.

"Pull again! Pull harder!" shouted Seigneur, and for the second time I threw myself into the spirit of this desperate game and in wrists and fingers and extended arms felt the bit become unyielding in the open mouth, and heard Volupté gagging under my tight rein.

"Pull! Pull! Pull!"

I redoubled my efforts but Volupté could no longer move. Still and heavy and unflinching she remained, though I jerked her head at will and though she moaned.

"Now you may dismount, Virginie, and leave us."

I did so, I sped away. Behind a small and thorny bush I knelt in nausea. How long I submitted to its spasms I do not know. But eventually I became aware of the gently thudding music of a cantering horse.

The almond trees in blossom had become an alley of passion. It was this scent, or so said Seigneur, that drove the animals to the height of passion, especially in the final effulgence of daylight or on the edge of dusk. Down the alley of flowering trees we went, behind Seigneur, and the trees were all but crying out in the full burgeoning of their whiteness, while the light through which our small flock walked was at its peak of a color so intense that it appealed as strongly to the tongue as to the eye. A thick color, a sweet color, making of the air itself a substance to be smelled, then tasted, then devoured. I could well understand how this same scent, which was peppery as well as sweet, could arouse the very animals to silent feats of amorous desire.

The light turned crystalline. The uncupped aroma of the trees was thickening. Nothing could have contributed a more idyllic flavor to this landscape already drenched in ripening. And yet there before us suddenly appeared a sight still more suited to the pastoral eye.

"Mesdames," said Seigneur softly, "let us for a moment study ravishment."

It was a curious remark, and as soon as it was uttered it introduced into our mood of sultry expectancy a trickle of the clearest fear. At their most relaxed, Colère, Bel Esprit, Finesse, Magie, and Volupté were on their guard, so that if the master of Dédale was never entirely to be trusted, simultaneously gentle and intractable as they knew him to be, so the ladies of Dédale were just as paradoxical, having learned never to close the inner eye and always to anticipate the waiting wasp on the other side of the pear. Once more the spirit of our troop was a guardedness against assault in whichever of its many forms: large, small, slightly injurious, beyond the toleration of the strongest. A mere word or two from Seigneur and invisible barbs began to fly, and the body's conformity to light and aromatic stimulation became only the softness into which the blow must fall. Who of them was safe? Did she wish to be? No one more exemplified than did Seigneur security informed by risk, seduction all the more stimulating for its threat of pain.

"Oh," whispered Bel Esprit, "what thing is that hanging from the limb of the tree?"

Well might she ask, I thought, as our troop faltered, since there, not twenty paces beyond where we stood, something was hanging from the lowest limb of the largest almond tree, a carcass or body in the unnatural light. Beside it waited Père La Tour, knife in hand.

"Mesdames," said Seigneur, "you see before you no horror, nothing to fear, contrary to what may be your expectations, but only a dead doe so recently brought down in my forest that the eyes still reflect the image of its hunger while the body still contains the warmth of its life, which you shall touch and feel. I think that you have not yet understood the dead doe. Now you shall. Let us approach her where she waits."

The tree was a white mass of seduction. The doe's suspended body was as long as mine was tall, and of a sandy color or the color of a lady's saddle, with a white tuft for a tail and clear eyes starting from the head. It was hung from the tree by a tasseled rose-colored silken cord bound about the slender neck and tied above to the limb. The legs were hanging, the small black hooves were pendant, the head was twisted unavoidably against the straight vertical of the rosy cord, and the body, no matter how briefly dead, hung in the limpness engendered of desolation, or in that utter loss of will no living animal could ever feign.

"This is ravishment," said Seigneur softly. "Come, touch her flanks. Touch her breast. Each one of you, follow my example and put your hands against the body of the dead doe."

They did so, cautiously, without comment, and even Bel Esprit restrained her usual uncooperative behavior and rebellious remarks. The impressions of the cool hands remained visible in the sandy coat.

"You see," said Seigneur, "the body is as warm as the eyes are clear. The heart beats, though the blood is still. She is ravishment itself, beyond repair, never again to soar, to stand alert, to fade into the greenery of my forest. There she hangs, and could not more lend herself to gravity, to solemnity, to this silence so different from the very silence of life. But in the dead doe we see the living creature as we never could, were we to glimpse her closely in the green glen, see her as fiercely as did the hunter, watch her feed from our own extended hands. The dead doe is fleeter than the living; in her sunken body we see the rising and falling of her breath; in her deadness we learn that in her life she was not timid, as we had thought, but only of the pure grace we associate with timidity. You do not see before you merely the carcass of a small, young, female deer. To the contrary. You see the doe herself, in a circumstance that could never be more auspicious for our purposes. Ravishment is contemptible only because it reveals its slain victim as lovely life cannot. But now, Père La Tour," said Seigneur, half turning, "now we should like to have the first stroke of the knife."

Upon hearing those words, which of our women did not suddenly recoil, as did I, yet at the same time lean closer to a spectacle that would have been nothing less than a precious sacrifice, had the doe been struggling on the end of its cord instead of still. But was not the spectacle more precious precisely because its victim was already dead? That, I understood, was the essential filigree of Seigneur's thought.

Up went the hand of Père La Tour. We held our breaths. The clear blade flashed. Then the tip of the blade punctured the doe's throat and cut it in a straight line, and then at a constant depth and unvarying slow rate of speed traveled the gentle curve descending from the throat to the velvet parting place of the haunches. I watched and, like the other members of our silent flock, felt the bloodless incision in the soft parts of my thumb and fingers, and did not wince.

The body of the doe fell open. Two horizontal strokes of the knife, at the base of the slender neck, and the soft hide and initial tissue of the doe's underbelly fell away the entire length of the incision, and in two ever-widening folds curled back, like waves, and exposed the community of organs compacted and glistening within the body as in a golden sack. No sooner had the body opened in its bloodless wound than there came a soft sound, a final exhalation of inner breath, and suddenly, and strongly, the smell of the entrails filled the air. But the character of this burst of smell was not at all what the women of Dédale had expected: not the rancid, sickening stench of lifelessness. Oh, not at all! The smell that swept us in one strong puff was sweet and unlike anything that they had ever smelled.

"Breathe deeply," said Seigneur, holding open the carcass with a careful hand. "Inhale the interior of the dead doe. Take to the depths of your lungs the smell of the tubes and bulbs and pipes by which she lived. What do we smell? What is the nature of this jumbled secrecy? She smells of grass; she smells of the sweet fields; her fleshy masses smell of the sun and water in a mossy bowl. Who amongst you could have believed that the animal's insides, which you do not like to see and should refuse to touch, are defined, by our sense of smell, as pure fragrance? Here is what the hunter ravaged! Here is the field he destroyed! And at my bidding. At my bidding."

Even as Seigneur spoke, and while we stared at everything the wound contained, and smelled its aroma fast fading, even as we were thusly occupied, the interior of the violated creature began to slip. It loosened, as it seemed to me, and developed shadows between this glistening mound and that, and then, in the slowest motion, began to slide away, slide down, flow from the cavity like a stream of cold honey from the lip of a crock. Père La Tour had placed a large and heavy copper vat beneath the little carcass and now it collected what descended in warm coils from the slippery darkness. All that had been solid was now loose and soft. Intricacy lay at our feet in disarrangement. The doe was empty.

"Père La Tour," said Seigneur, "show them your eyes."

He who had been commanded to do so turned to us: his eyes were wet.

"And yours?" asked Seigneur, and gently seized Colère's jaws and raised her face, looked at her eyes. "And yours? And yours?" he said, until he had satisfied himself that all were wet. "Very well," he said at last, and turned again to Père La Tour. "Now you may take down this carcass, and prepare it, and carry flesh and entrails to Adèle."

I would have remained for the dismemberment, but went away silently behind the rest.

"Finesse," he said softly, "regard this child. There is much to be learned from Virginie, who shall now perform for us and demonstrate an ability you must acquire."

Only on the rarest occasions was I anything more than a privileged witness to the acts and processes of Seigneur's art, though I argued with myself that in his eyes I was his phantom accomplice and valued utterly as such, though I could not say why or even how I served him. Never did I fail to have my quickening, my pleasure; without my passive presence, as I deemed it in my moments of severest self-judgment, he would not have been able to repeat himself with such perfection, while I awaited every word and flow of form, or to create still more ingenious ways of bringing into life the women he but had in mind. Yet I aspired for more than presence, longed to do more than merely watch. I welcomed my opportunity to "ride" the incompetent equestrienne, no matter how it sickened me or destroyed the tranquillity for which I lived. Still more did I enjoy displaying the sound of my small voice in song, within our empty chapel and unsupported by any musical instrument, since according to Seigneur my singing voice possessed the clarity of air forced swiftly through a dry bone and was the only fit accompaniment to the lesson of the first kiss, as he called it, in which Père La Tour was the actor and I the singer but never the person embraced and kissed. Then too I was pleased to hold forth on my two upturned palms Seigneur's supple riding crop: the whipping of the butterfly, as it was termed, was for another artistic purpose and was not in any mere consequence of ineptitude, however large or small, and hence entailed no aftermath of nausea. But I was happiest when called upon to demonstrate what Seigneur termed my prowess (how I loved the word!) with bees, as now I was.

A full hour was at our disposal, before the Rite of Noontide, and an entire world lay within the sunny confines of Le petit jardin, which now, on its small central carpet of grass, contained not the stately chair so often situated on that soft green, but instead a marble bench bearing but a single object: the thick hive in which dwelt the bees. The crypts were near, on the air was a freshness that was the scent of dust. Every surface of this small and solemn place pressed back to us a warmth that was like no other; within it light became lucidity itself. And there, on the marble bench, was my hive of bees.

"Proceed, Virginie. The gate is locked. We shall not be disturbed. You have only Finesse and me for witnesses."

The removal of clothes was my mystery! What was Dédale if not a château for dressing and disrobing? disrobing and dressing? the putting on and taking off of garments grand and complicated, or pure and simple? Did I not watch finery flowering? and sit patiently through all the comings and goings of nakedness? Surely cloth and skin were the staples of Seigneur's art. Yet I was dressed in gray and was never presented with the occasion to remove my dress. And I wished to shed it, put it back on, throw it off again, to expose my small and reedy stature to the eyes of our women, and to Seigneur's eyes as well. The beauty of immodesty was Seigneur's goal, and this was denied me by definition. Nonetheless, bareness was a form of inspiration, and I longed for it, and wished to cast my bareness with that of the women, but was not allowed to. Except for now. Now nakedness was a necessity, even for me.

"What the woman loses," murmured Seigneur, "the child retains. . . ."

I raised my hem and raised my arms, and in the instant disposed of my dress and apron too, which fell to the grass like rags, and once more kept to myself my pride of nakedness, valuing not exposure but completion, and knowing that only naked did the true self exist.

"How small she is!" murmured Seigneur. "How thin and balanced! It is the child herself that the woman must regain. There can be no womanhood without the inner child. . . ."

But the bees were waiting, and in their still hidden colony were themselves the sole purpose of my unclothed state: I felt my skin but was

183

thinking of the honey-hearted bees. So I turned to them, approached the marble bench, wondering as always at the largeness of the hive, its apparent solidity, its grayness that was the color of my dress and ashes, its somewhat oval shape and its texture of thick wrinkles in which I saw nature's mystery. There were no openings that I could see in the hive, no little portals for the emission of its inhabitants. But they would come to me, as I well know, and placing a bare hand on the top of the hive I felt for myself the heavy throbbing. I picked it up.

Oh, how sinister and misshapen was my hive of bees!

"What folly is this?" whispered the ordinarily undemonstrative Finesse. "She shall be stung!"

In my two hands I held it, so light for its size, and gripped it to my face and against my ear, feeling and hearing the engines of its darkness, and smelling antiquity in its thick crusty walls, and thinking to myself that it was an airy mausoleum for the bringing forth of life. I weighed it, as if to test the deep and frightening chaos of its sound, which I much enjoyed, and held it against my receptive chest as I did so, smiling over its top at Finesse, whose clear face reflected an understandable reproach. She could not know that it smelled of dusty stone, that weightless hive, and of some distant flowering, nor know how sensuously I touched its dead surface, nor how unafraid I was. But the bees were not new to me and I was confident.

Now there was nothing more to do but fit the hive into the crook of my left arm, and hold it against my hip, and wait. Once I ceased fondling the hive the bees would emerge. I waited. I thought myself a statue of a young and naked girl on her way for water, as if I were an essential member of a functioning household and the hive a ceramic jar awaiting the fountain's spout.

Then blindly and slowly the first emerged. I felt him! So he had found the secret portal after all, and had ventured out of the darkness and onto the shiny elevation of my sparse hip! He seemed to be wearing tiny feathers, to walk on hairs, to be touching me with angry exploratory tendrils. But I felt him insert himself tightly into my navel's hollow, which was just his size, taking it to be his chamber and I a flower. He was fat, and gold, and in the rear seemed to be covered with black stripes, like the bold chevalier in silk pantaloons.

"Look," murmured Seigneur. "The bee comes to us not from inside his hive, but from within the child. . . ."

"And if he stings her there?" whispered Finesse. "She'll die of the pain. . . ."

But the first bee did not remain for long alone. He moved, he climbed, he circled my head in sudden solitary flight and was soon followed by the entire colony. Out they came, my golden sleepwalkers with their dangerous noise. A blind mass unintelligibly aroused, inexplicably summoned from dark to light, they swarmed on me, clamored in thick layers upon themselves as on my tender flesh, spreading and shifting like a sea, like a blind carpet, imparting their tickling weightlessness to my thigh, my bare and narrow saddle, my hunching shoulders. Still they came. They stumbled through their secret gate, pushing and quarrelsome, and stuck to me and fell away, in great clumps took flight to the area about my head, so that everything I saw I saw through a dense and moving screen. I was not afraid, and could only smile to myself when an envoy, larger than the rest, detached himself from the squadron and flew aimlessly yet unmistakably toward Finesse, who stepped away and raised one thin white protective hand to her face.

"Finesse," murmured Seigneur happily, unaware of her discomfort, "Eros has changed his sex! How the bees blanket our Virginie! How they love her! She herself has become the source of sweetness! Her arrows have been changed to bees, and how they pour from the lips of the little fount and dart to the world!"

"I loathe them," said the young woman softly. "I am afraid of bees. . . ."

What tickling! What crowding! What eagerness to explore my bare terrain! The noise had so increased that, inundated with sound, my other senses could no more than succumb to it. I heard the bees as strongly as I felt them, and the auditory vision reverberated within Le petit jardin as if the colony had swelled until it occupied the entire garden instead of a child's body. I loved the sound, I heard it in my chest and head, which I threw back to accommodate all the more the bees. They forced me to close my eyes; they found my ears and followed their roar inside them; in my armpits they formed little pulsing clumps of grapes which I was careful not to squeeze or crush. I had learned that by bunching my tongue so as to seal off the back of my mouth, I could receive them into my open mouth, and this I did. What was my navel or my armpit to my moist mouth, small as it was? Was there another accomplishment to compare with holding inside one's poetic orifice a mouthful of bees? What had the bees become if not my voice?

"Enough, Virginie," murmured Seigneur anxiously through the roaring sound, and no doubt watching the fat bees on my eyelids and on my parted lips. "That is enough, Virginie. Put down the hive."

I was happily as blind as the bees, yet knew my way to the bench, and turned to it, and with the gentlest of motions replaced the empty hive on the marble bench. Out of my mouth, my nose, my ears, flew the golden bees. In slow and heavy columns they left me, by what instinct I would never know, and slowly and in due time returned to the hive. I laughed and donned again my dress and apron. Had the swarm of bees detracted from my nakedness, or clothed me in a second nakedness like music spread across a vale? I did not care.

"Now, Finesse," said Seigneur in a louder, more authoritative voice, "now you must undress yourself and do exactly as did Virginie."

I wished I could have stopped my ears to her cries of pain.

"Stifle its motion and love, like fire, dies. . . . So shun stillness! Never cease your swaying!"

"I have not seen a woman who does not dare all, no matter how timid she appears to be. The smallest and sickliest of women is robust with desire. If she is accused of wantonness, she becomes the more wanton. The number and variety of her amours increase disproportionately to passing time; with each amour she accrues in her hive a memory more vivid than the last; each new memory of kiss or nakedness makes her the more willing to throw wide the door. Thus the old woman is not stupid. Far from having lost the flame and withered, as many think, she has become the fire. The old woman is the walking hive: her grin, which we consider silly, is the full and joyous sign of her invitation. From such understanding was I able to conceive my first Noblesse. . . ."

"The art of pleasing is only one of creativity's voices, and not its mind. But of all the voices of creativity, that one known as the art of pleasing is the strongest, the richest, the most splendid, the most unpredictable and ever new. So exalt the labyrinth! Let your clear calls swell the labyrinth!''

High on the broad balcony with access only through Seigneur's locked chamber, and providing vistas of Dédale's courtyard, slender turret, and fields beyond, there in the morning sunshine we four were assembled: Seigneur and Père La Tour, Finesse and me. The massive waist-high balustrade was sculpted with military shields and scallop shells, while at our backs the vines, through which the wide doors opened, obscured the château's white wall beneath their tangle of tortured stalks and thicknesses of waxen leaves so dense as to accommodate with ease all the birds of our season: small creatures flitting, singing, and feeding their young invisibly but audibly enough in that dark and vertical forest. As for its floor, Seigneur's immense and peaceful balcony was tiled in blue and white squares and diamonds, a bright pattern highly glazed and polished, across which fell the shadow of one of several chimneys, which in itself was in the shape of a many-roofed château. But the furniture! The furniture of this secluded and suspended place intrigued me most: two pieces appropriate to a throne room and nothing more. The first, and by far the more interesting, occupied the center of the balcony and was like a couch, except that it had no back, and resembled an immense chaise longue, except that where it should have been constructed at one end to hold the recliner in a half-sitting position, it was merely flat. Long then, narrow, a curious but innocuous bed of sorts consisting of a gilded frame and a thick mattress sheathed in crimson velvet which, even at the distance at which I stood, smelled of the warm sun. What then made this piece of furniture so marvelous? Its hump! Its great deformity! For precisely at its center the couch rose to the peak of a tall rounded hump, which sloped gently away to either side and then, at the ends, curled suddenly upwards again in small crimson waves. A bed, a couch, but not for sleeping, not for sitting! What then? I knew the answer, though Finesse did not.

The other stolid, ingenious piece of furniture consisted of two gilded lions, winged and seated, yet standing almost as tall as my chest and between them supporting a marble shelf. This remarkable contrivance was positioned parallel to the couch and near enough for someone standing between the two to reach shelf or couch with equal ease. There they stood together, empty and waiting. As usual I thought that the unpredictability of the disfigured couch was far more pleasing than two lions carrying on their noses a heavy shelf.

"Your gown, Finesse," said Seigneur mildly.. "Your case of instruments, Père La Tour."

Without the slightest show of emotion Finesse pulled up her gown of pale violet, drew it over her head of short-cropped hair, and shook free of it, and seeing my two arms outstretched to her, draped the discarded gown across them, without a word. Similarly, in silence and with blank expression, Père La Tour deposited on the marble shelf his large leather case and, lifting its heavy lid on ornate hinges, removed from it dusty vials and four bone-handled stylets, which he arranged in two rows conveniently, along with swabs of soft white cloth and a jar containing a clear liquid that made the eyes water and the nose burn.

"Look at this compact creature, Père La Tour. Have you ever seen one more willowy? Thinness is indeed a woman's virtue, since it causes the figure to cleave to the spirit and draws attention to the breasts. But look closely, Père La Tour: on that white skin do you find a single blemish? a single mark? Turn her around, study her white slenderness. Touch it. Test the flesh for firmness. There. Am I not correct? No body could be harder, though not a muscle shows, nor any woman's skin more white, more clear, more free of the smallest disfiguration under the scrutiny of the relentless eye. Who would believe that this same white skin so recently revealed the anger of a thousand bees! And now nothing, not a sign of it! But enough! To your task, Père La Tour, and take your time. As for you, Finesse, you may assume your place on that bed of crimson velvet, belly down so as to conform most easily and comfortably to its unusual shape."

Père La Tour rolled up the sleeves of his soft gray shirt, and unstoppered his vials, tested the long and sharply honed points of the blades of his stylets, which were like thick needles. Was there a flicker of scorn in the glance with which Finesse surveyed the monstrous narrow couch and the silent man on whose lined face age and indifference fought a nearly equal match with concentration? I thought so, as I hugged her gown to my gray chest and noted that the smallest flame of scorn in Finesse's complacency aroused a corresponding color in the cheeks of Seigneur.

Finesse's nakedness, the unselfconsciousness of her naked stance, the silence in which she so clearly hid the self that was hers, as the tree hides within itself the treasure of its smallest circles: these, I saw, gave Seigneur signal pleasure, and I shared it.

With easy strides and supple slowness Finesse approached the couch, rested a light hand on the velvet, then mounted the couch in the only way she could: by kneeling at one of the low ends and crawling upwards until her buttocks were at the crest and her slim body was bent in two, legs descending one slope and head and torso the other. Her face was turned not toward the balustrade but toward Père La Tour, who, still showing her his back, continued to test and rearrange his shiny blades and bright vials. I positioned myself between couch and balustrade so as to have an unobstructed view of this operation. I hoped that Finesse would prove herself braver than with the bees, and my hope, as it turned out, was amply fulfilled.

"You have not lost your skill, Père La Tour? The image has not blurred? Your touch is as sensitive as ever, yet ruthless too? If all is ready you may proceed, but slowly, at your slowest pace: take all the time required for exactitude, prolong the ordeal for the sake of splendor. . . ."

The neutral atmosphere. The sun in which Finesse's nakedness was only natural and neither warm nor cool. The sudden silence of the birds in the vines. My shifting of Finesse's gown and the surreptitious way I touched my hand to her hair, which she did not feel. The white buttocks lifted as on an altar. The supervising grandeur of Seigneur, who dominated our picture with his closeness, his attentive face, his hands clasped casually behind him. It was a picture I had often seen, though with other bodies than Finesse's at its center, and well did I know that Père La Tour would begin with gold, as indeed he did.

He turned. He placed one hand in the small of Finesse's back and with the other seized the buttock nearest him, as he might a mammoth sausage or white loaf of bread, and fiercely and silently squeezed the white flesh until it reached its deepest shade of pink. Then he reached for the first vial and the first stylet. He dipped in the blade, withdrew it, studied the pendent tear of gold on its tip, then leaned forward and, with the exactitude demanded by Seigneur, thrust his needle into the very spot for which he aimed, and stepped away. With that first puncture ap-

peared not only the first drop of blood, hardly larger than the point that
drew it, but the entire mass of droplets necessary for the completion of
Père La Tour's design: there, already imprinted on the white flesh in
drops of blood, was the pattern of a butterfly as large in diameter as a
ripened plum. The veins of its flat wings were indicated; droplets of
bright blood outlined the whole; the entire figure might have been lying
invisible just beneath the skin's surface, awaiting only the first deft jab to
make it rise and show itself in a diagram as of bloody bites of infinitely
small size. But into each droplet Père La Tour had yet to thrust his point,
apply his color, and no cautioning for slowness had been needed: the
process was laborious, hence slow, and throughout it all Finesse held
back her tears, made not a sound.

Père La Tour used his hand and knife as if the one had been the
much-magnified head of a hummingbird and the other its beak: in rapid
thrusts and dartings he applied the gold, pausing now and then to daub
the flesh with the cloth soaked in the violent liquid, and thus to sweep
away the blood, for an instant, in order to appraise the film of gold
suffusing more and more the wings. His blade darted, slowed down, he
changed stylets and vials, moving on to emerald for the body and vermil-
ion for the tracery across the golden wings. Slowest and thickest of all
was the deep blue with which, at last, he bound the perimeter of the
dazzling creature lying like a livid welt on the flesh that had lent itself to
the applications of Père La Tour. Pursing his lips, peering at his work
with a cold eye, indifferent to the icy smell that drugged our day: here,
surely, was the artisan's disinterest in anything but what he made. How
frail my needlepoint appeared beside his craft!

"Finesse," murmured Seigneur, as Père La Tour tossed the last stylet
into the disarray on the marble shelf and wiped his hands on the bloodied cloth, "we are done, and now you bear upon your person Seigneur's
symbol, as does Bel Esprit, while Colère and Magie and Volupté have yet
to be marked and thus are that much farther than yourself from the rank
of Noblesse. No one can become Noblesse without her butterfly! It sits
on you, it clings to you, nourished by your own life fluids, its colors
having substance only on the substance that is your flesh. Forever shall
this thickly colored creature move when you move, fly when you run,
turn silky beneath the hand that strokes you, hover about you and above

you in the chamber where you are engaged in the art of pleasing. Love's soul, Finesse! It lives as long as you, as part of you, inseparable from the skin it colors, inseparable from the clear mind in which it lies. . . . The pain will fade, Finesse, but the butterfly is yours forever."

He ceased to speak. He and Père La Tour and I looked down at the brilliance that had just been wrought in the shapeliest cushion of Finesse's anatomy. We waited. We watched. Then, as we knew it would, slowly the butterfly began to quiver. It quivered, it wrinkled, it trembled as if to tear itself from the tenderness to which it adhered: Bit by bit it loosened, came free like a leaf from a wet stone, and with the briefest fluttering began to rise, and gathered strength and climbed a hand's width above Finesse's body. It hovered, shifting and stationary in gauzy flight, a blind splash of color struggling to hold itself aloft. And then it sank. Back down it drifted to the very place it had only just now quitted before our eyes, and settled, quivered again, grew still. The birds returned again to life and song.

Père La Tour created the butterfly. But it was Seigneur who endowed it with the will to fly.

From its ashen niche I draw forth my journal, which no one allows or encourages me to read aloud, nor ever shall. I carry my journal to the bare table. I open my journal. I turn to its most precious entry, and read again that entry in silence and to myself: "I see them tall and glorious, and bright of eye, lips moving in speech that I alone can hear but know as well as I do Adèle's or Père La Tour's. Marvels come to me and crowd me round, of wind and bees and animals and women and a single man, and heat my face and make me clasp my quill in ecstasy! Few would believe that from sources purely imaginary such happiness can be derived, nor such scenes as I witness and write down. Thought is a treasure, reverie a privilege. I am thankful I have the power of solacing myself with dreams of creations which neither I nor anyone shall ever see. May I never lose that power."

[1945] The peacock pin continued; the end of the Sex Arcade

". . . And one day, when this little girl who had become a flower lay with the other flowers on her mother's cart, she was so much lovelier than all the rest that the poor woman noticed her and picked her up and sold her to a nice old man who put her in a silver vase. . . ."

But he was not allowed to finish, though I listened attentively, and put my cheek against his chest, and smiled at the way he mocked me with his story intended for a much younger child, and would have been glad to listen through all the shifting hours of this green night, though even then I knew that the night had tilted from its axis and that in my partial sleep I was sliding swiftly and feet first toward the edge of some blinding wakefulness. I did not remember how our scene had changed, or who had changed it, or for how long Yvonne and Clarisse had been embracing each other on the couch while Sylvie and Minouche and Madame Pidou and Bocage and Lulu and even Monsieur Moreau all knelt or sat around them to watch and listen. But this was what I saw through lids that I allowed to flutter. I had no way of knowing that soon the green night would be a night of fire, yet so it would; nothing called me to come wide awake, yet awakening I was. Monsieur Malmort was holding me as lovingly as ever, yet he would soon give me up, as I knew just then with a delighted shiver though it was a sourceless premonition that supplied its message with hints of neither sense nor consequence. But I was alerted.

"Yvonne," said Clarisse in a voice clear and loud enough for all to hear, and freeing herself from the other woman's soft embrace, "you must not begin your story until I return."

The cream was gone, Lulu was drinking cognac from a china cup, the first fly of the season was circling above our heads.

Bocage lit the candles atop the mantelpiece, and cocked his cap, resumed his seat beside the impatient Lulu. The light of the candles only intensified the greenness of this night which, had I but known, would be long in beginning and swift to die.

"Now you can see for yourselves," said Clarisse, returning into our midst and standing still and yet slowly revolving with her hands on her hips, like a naked mannequin on a motor-driven pedestal. Then while she revolved she raised her hands to her hair. The fringe of her violet cache-sexe became a metallic green; her slender boyish muscles were green and silvery; I too might have aspired to such modest breasts.

"My peacock pin," she said, and removed it, and to each of us displayed her treasure in the palm of her hand. She stopped, leaned down, looked at the pin as if she too were seeing it for the first time, and I could not keep myself from opening my eyes and leaning forward. What a grand and glittering peacock he was! Shaped like a knife held handle upwards, he curved from his black head to the point of the long and folded tail. He was a crescent, a sweeping bird encrusted with pink stones and green, a bejeweled simulation of the softest feathers and most regal mien. His head was a black bead with clear gems for eyes; the curving tail, which comprised the greater part of the pin, was tight and sharp. Suddenly I yearned for the peacock, wanted to be given the peacock, would have begged Clarisse to fix her dusty, dazzling trinket in my brown hair, had I not restrained myself. Instead, Clarisse carried it to Yvonne and fastened it to the great yellow head of hair.

"Now, Yvonne," she said softly, "tell your story."

Again Clarisse sat beside Yvonne, the slender, naked, upright torso appealing to the bulky bareness of the other. Yvonne exuded oblivion from her fleshy weight; Clarisse sat so as to retain the independence of her nakedness. They were side by side; their bodies were not touching; they were not holding hands. But they were bound together by the peacock pin and the story we were about to hear.

"Le Pigeonnier," said Yvonne in her warm, soft, heavy voice that reminded me, as always, of a beast's tongue stuffed into a jar of honey, "was the small hotel where I tried to make a tidy home for my little brother Jean-Christophe and me. It had no more than seven rooms, Le Pigeonnier, and from the outside looked as if it had been burned in a fire. Yet the girls who worked there liked it well enough, including me, because it was warm, even on the iciest of days, and clean. The patron selected his clients well, and never hesitated to throw into the street those burly fellows who wanted women only to abuse them in any way they could. Every morning the smell of baking bread rose among the stale fumes of wine, beer, and anisette, a motherly aroma suffusing the smells of pleasure. The patron's rosy wife, who patted our fougasses, as she called them, after the country loaves she baked, and who inspected us for good health, labored long and hard each morning at her ovens. Actually, I liked Le Pigeonnier more than well enough, and for four reasons: the room I shared with little Jean-Christophe was on the troisième étage and faced into a court where someone kept a lonely cock, so that, except for the cock, it was a quiet room high and undisturbed under the eaves of our "roost"; then too, the patron's wife had seen her own child struck down dead in the narrow street on which their shabby establishment had long before been built, and she was happy to feed bonbons to Jean-Christophe when I was occupied with my client; but my client himself was the main reason for my pleasure in Le Pigeonnier.

"He was old and portly and soft, my client. Old enough to be my grandfather, yet sound of mind, and gentle, and good-humored, and well-groomed though obviously he had survived for years his fall from some fancier estate. His face was rimmed with a fringe of silken whiskers. He had a plump nose and little feet, like Monsieur Moreau's. He wore a blue cravat, a formal fedora, a patched overcoat with a velvet collar. Rarely did he catch a glimpse of Jean-Christophe, yet he never failed to bring my little brother a book or pack of cards or pencils and a pad of paper, all of which he pilfered from the shops he passed. He never failed to bring me three wet flowers or to press upon me, surreptitiously, ten extra francs. Oh, but most important were my old client's inclinations! His desire was the simplest of any, the most easily satisfied, and gave that old man more pleasure than the sum of all the nude encounters that might fill an entire night at Le Pigeonnier. He liked my fougasse. He told the patron's wife that I had the finest fougasse of any woman in her hotel, and that he adored it.

"Wait," said Yvonne, interrupting herself, and licking her lips and holding up a powdered hand. "I know you're thinking that poor Yvonne was more stupid then than now and didn't understand that that's the worst desire and the hardest and least agreeable for any girl to accommodate, despite her pliancy and except for a specialist, as we might say. But let me explain: his adoration of my fougasse was platonic, or nearly so!

"Every night he would climb our stairs, tap at my door, timidly enter my small hot room (its extra heat was another of its advantages), then kiss my hand, seat himself on the carelessly mended chair, and pretend that his ardor was not already aroused to the very brim by the images of me with which his poor mind had been filled all day. I would take his hat, bend over on a flimsy pretext, and he would sit with legs together and hands clasped on his trembling knees. His eyes were like a bird's, his nostrils flared, and in the corner of his mouth was often a droplet of saliva which he would eventually remember to dispose of, with a little flick of the tongue. No man ever waited for a meal more expectantly than he awaited my uncovering. Yet never once did he presume to reveal to me what was in his mind or to touch me or to ask me for what he so ardently desired. It was not a game; I was not cruel. I knew that he wanted to be decorously treated and that it was my lot to be the arbiter of his pain. If he wanted to impress me with his courage, his respectability, the homage he wished to pay to my own sensibilities, he did so a thousand times, and my admiration for my old client never waned.

"Finally, and as always, I would say to him: 'Monsieur, I have an inexplicable inclination to kneel on my bed, just there. Would you mind?' As always he would nod, for by this time he would be incapable of speech, and when my back was turned I would hear his hands fumbling with the blue cravat and hear his unbearable breathing relieving itself into sound at last through the plump nose. I would fluff my pillow, arrange it comfortably on the pink quilt, which I did not remove, and slowly assume a leisurely, inviting pose with my arms bent, my head on the pillow, my knees apart, my fougasse lifted high in what must have been, for him, the most stately offering he had ever seen. Sometimes I thought of affixing a mirror to the wall so that I too might admire the curves and undulations that he admired. But like my old client, I preferred an ordinary life in a plain and ordinary room.

"'Monsieur,' I would whisper then, 'would you be so kind as to raise the hem of my kimono? Can you believe it, Monsieur? I would like you to see me partially in the nude.'

"Hearing his pleasure aroused my own, and it might well have been that my enjoyment of the warm and lighted lamp on the table drawn close to the bed, and of the sour smell that lived in the walls, and of the size of my very self which I could feel as I lay in waiting, was greater than his own. I had not even to fold down the bedclothes to please this man, and far below us little Jean-Christophe was eating bonbons.

"I would hear the mincing of my old client's tiny feet. I would hear his breathing. Then I would feel his fingers trembling at the edge of my red kimono, and then a little tug, which always amused me, and then I would share with him the reverence with which he drew up the shabby silk and exposed at last my spread thighs and uplifted buttocks, which I felt immediately turn pink, though I could not see them.

"'I am all for you, Monsieur,' I would whisper. 'Do what you will.'

"But there was no danger. There was no incipient pain or indignity for me to fear. I tried to imply some monstrousness in his nature, tried to hint at the possible diversity of his desires before which I quailed, all to add piquancy to what he sought of me. But there was no bestiality or inventiveness in my old client.

"Patience was all that he required of me, for he savored and prolonged each night as if there were to be no more. So I made of my fougasse a cushion for his quivering face. At the first sensation of his breath I sighed; at the first tickling of his whiskers I sighed still louder; as soon as I felt the full planting of his bewhiskered face I returned his pressure with a gentle pressure of my own, and into my pillow whispered a few words of endearment which he could hear. After a time he would become more avid, so that I would find it more difficult to hold still, and then his kissing would attain a firmness of purpose I could not deny, and I would forget myself until I felt the steadying reminders of his emboldened hands on my hips, and once more ceased my moving. That's all he wanted. That's all he did. What could have been easier for me? I was the envy of Le Pigeonnier, and not without reason, since I had nothing to do, no preparations to make, and ran no risk of catching the old man's toothache in my fougasse, as the patron's wife told me every day.

"I will confess that finally I was so stirred by the solemnity of his pleasure, and so curious, that one night I coquettishly proposed that we exchange positions, allowing each of us to know the joys of the other. But he declined, in a sad and gentle voice, saying that he was much too old for a gratification so intense.

"By now," said Yvonne, taking a heavy breath and resting a large hand on Clarisse's knee, "by now you probably think that I have forgotten my brother as well as the fourth reason why I accepted so readily the life of Le Pigeonnier. But I have not.

"My fourth reason for finding contentment in Le Pigeonnier was small and yet significant. There were two toilettes in that hotel, and these were not the usual pits of stench in which one was forced to squat above a greasy hole. Such was not the case at all. The toilettes in our hotel were narrow whitewashed cells containing black cast-iron bowls adorned with wooden seats. The smell was minimal, the pink paper was of adequate supply and came in rolls, air and light entered by small openings through the stone near the ceiling, and there were locks on the doors. One could sit in comfort and take one's time. I was not a person to ignore the privilege. My incident with Jean-Christophe, of which I wish now to speak, occurred in the toilette on the deuxième étage.

"This toilette was occupied, I knew at once, yet its door was ajar. I approached. I listened. I clutched my kimono closer and, naturally, put my face to the crack in the door. There, in a thin shaft of light, with his trousers dropped and bunched around his ankles, there stood little Jean-Christophe in what I recognized at once as the rigidity of childish despair. His back was to the door and hence to me, yet nonetheless I saw the fluttering pages of the well-worn book he held in one hand, and in the merest glance knew exactly his childish employment of the other. He was short, his thin legs were white, he was hobbled in his fallen pants. The story in photographs had long ago lost its cover; its pages were few, and of cheap paper; he held it awkwardly in one hand like a little choirboy his score. Oh, I understood at once the pain that was gripping my brother and all its circumstances! One of the other women in Le Pigeonnier must have amused herself by giving the child the floppy book he held, because he could not have obtained such a rare yet ordinary volume from another boy; he had looked, and for the first time in his life had felt what he had never felt before, the surging in his little twig. But the twig would not flower, as I could see, and here was my own brother trapped in his dream. Poor Jean-Christophe!

"I slipped into the toilette and, as unobtrusively as I was able, locked the door. The prisoner grew yet more rigid and caught his breath and awaited the punishment his sister would surely inflict. But gently I touched his shoulder and turned him aside. He hung his head and bit his lip, holding the unruly pages in one hand and his twig in the other, wishing only that he were seated with the patron's wife, and that he had never seen what was staring at us from one of the pages, and that he could obtain relief.

"I turned him aside and seated myself on the wooden ring and through the thinness of my kimono felt the cold breathing of the beast below. I smiled, though Jean-Christophe still refused to meet my glance, and slowly lifted Jean-Christophe to my warm lap. His legs dangled, his buttocks were hot, his twig, when I gently pried loose his fingers, was as small and stiff and unappeasable as ever. I put my arm around his shoulder, leaned my cheek to his hair, shifted slightly to call his attention to the broad and nearly naked lap on which he sat.

"'Turn the pages, Jean-Christophe,' I whispered.

"Slowly he began to do so, while the light came down upon us and the wooden pull-handle gently swung on its chain that descended from the tank above. In mere moments my attention was as firmly engaged as Jean-Christophe's. A woman's head, with a hat pulled tightly onto it, filled one page as fully as her invisible partner's zizi filled her mouth. Her photograph was black and grainy; her eyes and indrawn cheeks were shadowed; her eyes met mine mutely but without appeal. The next page was filled with the brim of the hat, her dark eyes, her laughing lips, and the homeless head of the zizi which momentarily she had dislodged. This pocked and pitted photograph showed a scar on her cheek; she might have come straight from waiting for an autobus to the bed of the still invisible owner of the zizi, and had not even bothered to remove her hat. On the next page her ringed and scrawny hand was planted forever on the front of the man's pants that were bulging like a pouch stuffed tight with little birds. Here one fingernail was chipped; the poor unattractive hand was strong. Then the rim of the hat, the eyes on mine, the lips in a pout, the bare hand pressing the stalwart zizi against the side of her head, as between the tips of my thumb and forefinger I rolled Jean-Christophe's thin twig, that refused to throb.

"Then framed by the rumpled edge of the upraised skirt and dark shadows like closed eyes in wood, now her coarse, unveiled sphinx filled the page, disembodied and thirsting for a mammoth thumb that pushed it. How could so thin a woman be endowed with so grand a prize? Why did the fat thumb appear merely to be squashing beneath itself a helpless bug? But on the next page the woman's own finger joined the thumb and I sighed. Then the dark sphinx gave way to the woman's open blouse and a protruding breast. How I admired it! Stealthily disturbing my brother but a little, I used my free hand to imitate the woman and pull open my kimono and expose one of my breasts. A drop of water fell from the tank above. The light became a shaft of the brightest silver.

"'Jean-Christophe,' I whispered, 'look at Yvonne.'

"He did so, wordlessly, and the sight of my bare breast now brought the color into his solemn face. Still there was not the smallest throbbing in the tortured twig. Slowly, still staring at my breast, he turned a page.

"'Jean-Christophe,' I whispered again, thinking that the boy on my lap would one day become the old client of an appreciative woman, and thinking of the first photograph that I had studied with my brother in this private place, and smiling, 'Jean-Christophe,' I repeated, 'I shall not allow you to remain unsatisfied a minute more. Stand on my lap.'

"Wordlessly and awkwardly he did so, dropping the book and kicking free his trousers and clambering upon me until his poor boots were planted on my spreading thighs and his small hands clutched my shoulders. Thus he stood before me precariously balanced, while I sighed and reached forward warmly with my waiting mouth. In an instant he shuddered and, in a spasm of recklessness, reached out a hand and yanked the pull-chain, so that far below us the beast bellowed in his lair and cold air came roaring upwards between my thighs. I waited and then threw back my head and laughed and hugged my brother. What a way for a small boy to achieve his manhood!

"Manhood was what he had in fact achieved, because from that day forward he forsook the patron's wife and spent what hours he could with this woman or that in our establishment. Then, despite my admonitions, he began to frequent a nearby café and to drink wine and return to me with the smell of tobacco on his breath. Finally he disappeared entirely, pursuing, as I thought, older women who did not remove their hats. Thus I was left alone with my old client and the tattered book I never showed to him, until the old man died and even the faithful men lost interest in Le Pigeonnier.

"As you can see, my story ends as does Clarisse's."

"Bravo!" cried Monsieur Moreau at once, though he was wrong to do so, since Yvonne's story had been both sad and beautiful and hence did not deserve such gusto, as the rest of her audience attested by the silence in which their evident appreciation matched the warmth of her voice. After such a story her listeners could well preserve their silence.

"So now I must grow whiskers," murmured Lulu, at which they laughed.

"But where is the book?" asked Bocage, and again they laughed.

"I would rather have your memory than mine," murmured Clarisse, and without embarrassment embraced Yvonne, whose body shone in the perspiration her story-telling had exacted.

"But both your stories make Sylvie think that Monsieur Pidou still owes a little debt to Sylvie. It is not so, Madame Pidou?"

"My husband shall pay his debt," said Madame Pidou. "But not tonight."

"Because tonight is Bocage's night," whispered Minouche, and it was with this soft declaration that I came awake in the arms of Monsieur Malmort, though I kept my eyes half closed, and felt myself quickening in fear and expectation, though I did not know why.

"Ladies!" cried Bocage, as if he had not heard Minouche or understood her words, and leaning toward Clarisse and Yvonne intending, it seemed, to interrupt their embrace. "Ladies, there are people who think we do not live solely by the sphinx and zizi! I despise them all! There are people who would destroy my Sex Arcade if they could, but they shall not! There is forbidden life enough for everyone! There is a charade for each of us, can we but summon it to mind!"

Bocage's outburst fell upon silence of another sort. Why was he so vehement? Why did the stories we had heard this night cause him to declare so stridently what he believed? All the world was indifferent to his charades. What then did he fear? Beyond the endlessness of his charades there was no world. What then did he fear? Or had his word related in some subtle way to what Minouche had said? In another moment I understood that this, my last intuition, was correct.

"And you, Bocage?"

"And you?"

"And you?"

"Which is your charade, Bocage?"

"What pleases you?"

Softly they questioned him, softly assaulted him, spoke to him as one and faced him, held him in the union of their partial nakedness and what they wished to know. I saw his eyes; for an instant I wished that they had not turned upon Bocage, no matter their gentleness and loving tones of voice.

"Which of us, Bocage?"

"Who is your choice, Bocage?"

"Make your choice, Bocage!"

He smiled. He licked his lips. He clasped his hands. He said nothing and did not move, though I thought there was a tightening in his arms and legs. Feigning sleep, I watched; feigning sleep, I listened; feigning sleep, I waited. His smile was crooked. His brow was wet.

"Which of us shall be yours for the night, Bocage?"

"Choose!"

"Choose!"

Then I saw that he intended to obey them. He smiled more crookedly, climbed to his feet, removed his cap and dropped it, and surveyed them all. Sylvie? I wondered. But Minouche had been the first he had found. Or might he choose Yvonne for her size or Clarisse for the quiet boldness of her mind? But perhaps his secret favorite was Madame Pidou, the wisest and most willing woman in the Arcade? I waited, and all of Lulu's tattooed women were inside my head. Then Bocage stooped and reached for me.

High in his arms, and through the silence as we paused in the doorway from our salon, there I heard the softly calling voice of Yvonne: "Where are you, little Déodat? Where are you?"

Maman is dead. Monsieur Malmort is dead. The ceiling falls. The fire is at its peak and in its nest of flames I am cool and comforted. Dear self, who now can deny my childish desires?

The field is mine.

[1740] The Tapestry of Love;
the end of us

I awoke with a start and knew before drawing my first cold breath that the fire was dead and that against my skin and in my clothes the ashes were cold, but oddly cold, strangely cold, as if they were three days frozen in the season of ice, which they were not.

What was wrong?

I listened on my cold stones and heard not a bell, not a bird, not a beast, not a distant voice, not one sound of life. Was I alone at last? abandoned without a single companion to love me and allay my fears?

What was wrong?

I dispensed with the bowl of cold water and thought not of food. Boldly before me stood my situation, and I knew it was fruitless to visit Adèle's bare cell, to search the stables, to call out in the hopes of hearing in return sweet answers. Yet I could not admit such a plight; surely I was not entirely alone; it was impossible that Seigneur had not remained behind for me, and more to discover the truth of this conviction than the reason for the general emptiness of Dédale, which I could not deny, I hastened down stone corridors, crossed the cloister bereft of its little cock and its flowers as well, and climbed circular stone stairs until at last, and breathless more in anxiety than from exertion, I stood before what proved to be the open door to Seigneur's chamber.

"Come in, Virginie," he called from where he stood outside on his balcony across the room, and with my relief at his presence there came also the pleasure of hearing in his voice no fear, surprise, dismay. Seigneur was not gone, and whatever had happened had not unsettled his composure and good humor. "Come here, Virginie," he continued softly, "and see the worst."

I joined him. I looked where he pointed. There below us in the courtyard awaited the ugliest sight I had ever seen: an empty calèche; two black horses with ears and tails freshly amputated; a silent, hatless driver with a shorn head. Thoughtlessly I reached out my hand, and Seigneur seized hold of it as he had not before.

"What does it mean?" I whispered, feeling strength in the way he held my hand. "What has happened? What is wrong?"

"Virginie," he answered, "the end comes swiftly when it comes. Now, before it is too late, I shall show you the Tapestry of Love."

So saying, and attempting to deflect my questions, as it seemed to me, he freed me and, stepping back into the room, took hold of a pull-cord which would draw apart the velvet covering the wall that faced the mammoth piece of furniture that was his bed. I had expected him to lead me away, and off, and down, and into some distant, sacred place of incense, lighted candles, burnished prie-dieux and, of course, the grandeur of the sacred tapestry housed in that mysterious chapelle or grotte. But no, I saw, at the moment Seigneur tugged on the cord, it was here in this very chamber that he kept the Tapestry of Love, here where he slept and behind the same drapes which had concealed Père La Tour when last I had seen him in this room. I should have known! How clever of Seigneur to keep his treasure here in the most obvious place of all! Now the parting of the curtains revealed the grand tapestry; there it hung, resplendent, filling the enormous wall with its colors, which were of the deepest pink and palest blue, and filling to the full the viewer's mind with the immensity of Seigneur's vision.

"Your scepter," I whispered, staring at its soaring flight and feeling all my person flushed in surprise and pleasure. "So that," I whispered, "is the secret of Dédale!"

He nodded. He stepped backwards to regain my side. Again he took my hand and together we looked long and with happiness and solemnity at what was his, sublimely and in the purest colors. The blue was so uniformly pale that it might have represented the unchanging sky or even emptiness, and flowed to all the edges of the tapestry, and hence of the wall, existing solely as the eternal realm in which might rise the central subject of the artist's skill. There in that blue it rose! the scepter as tall and big around as Seigneur himself! Upright, but at the slightest angle too, and entering the tapestry from the bottom, so that its base was not depicted, and positioned in the lower-right-hand quadrant of the blue field, so that its asymmetry made it more than ever pleasing to the captive eye: there it rose, borne aloft by two great wings, the uncontested occupant of the blue space! No other object was included; there was not the smallest detail to detract from the scepter and its domination of the field. Oh, but the marvel was its color! full, dark, throbbing; so rich that it glowed not merely on the scepter's surface, but was instead the color of the entire monument, inside and out! Now pink was no mere color, but a substance: yet mere color too!

"It is splendid," I whispered. "It is superb. It is magnificent. It is
. . . it is a magnificent mirage!"

"Exactly so," he answered, after a pause. "And exactly as are the man, the woman, the labyrinth itself. The scepter is the emblem of them all! and just as indestructible! and as much a mirage!"

"Oh, but, Seigneur," I exclaimed, turning from the tapestry, taking away my hand from his, and staring up at the features that were mine alone to see and love. "What has happened? What is wrong? Why have they forsaken us, and to what fate?"

Slowly he drew the curtains, cloaking forever his tapestry, had I but known it, and strode again onto the balcony, where he placed his hands wide on the balustrade and stared down at the waiting carriage with its sickening spectacle of shaven driver and disfigured horses. I joined him. I was not restored by the deep inhalations which I took without thinking. The sun was stationary, and it occurred to me that without the sun I was nothing, though I could not account for the thought.

"I can tell you in a few words what you wish to know," he said, as a trace of darkness crossed his features and gave way to mildness. "I have denied Maman. Yes, Virginie, Madame La Comtesse is my Maman, as well as yours, while Père La Tour is in actuality Le Comte de Cocagne, my father."

"And my father too, Seigneur?"

He shook his head.

"But, Seigneur," I repeated, rushing headlong beyond that question as though I had never asked it, "La Comtesse is my Maman? and yours as well? and I am your sister? and you are my brother? Sister and brother, Seigneur? Is that what we are?"

"Yes, Virginie," he answered in a low voice, "that's what we are. But more than that," he continued in his lowest voice, "for we are father and daughter too. I am your father. But did you not know? Did you never once suspect? Oh, but do not look so grave and white, little Virginie! You are the rarest daughter in all the world, and the most treasured, and the most honored. You are not merely my sister and my daughter too, Virginie, for you are more, much more. I am the artist and you . . . you are my soul."

To myself I then asked a single question: "And I? Do I not have a soul? Or does being another person's soul deny my own?" Then to Seigneur I asked aloud a single question: "Do you love me?"

"I do," he said at once.

"But for myself?"

"For yourself."

"But why?"

"Virginie," he answered in a voice a shade stronger in its relief, as I thought, "I love your innocence. I could not love it more."

"But what is innocence? What is love?"

"Innocence," he said, and once more clasped my hand, "innocence is the clarity with which the self shows forth the self. Love is the respect we feel for innocence."

"But still you have not answered me, Seigneur!" I exclaimed, and again pulled loose my hand, and faced him: "What has happened? What is wrong? What is to happen?"

He took a breath, looked down, then answered me briefly.

"I have denied Maman," he said, repeating his first declaration, which it was yet not entirely for me to understand. "I have thus offended Maman. She has set the women of Dédale against me. They are in revolt. Now I must die for my art, as I have long known I must."

A breeze commenced. Maimed horses and empty carriage looked as if they would move no more. But then I knew that I too possessed a soul, for to my lips came language that flowed from what source if not my soul? A girl of eleven with a heart large enough and vigorous enough to hold the swelling spring of pure, full eloquence: for such I was as I declared my love, pronounced my love, expounded upon it and gave it wings, and told him how I saw him in my mind and that no person in the world was more dedicated than he or more strong, more honest, courageous, or more filled with life. He was the colossus above the endless sea, the creator of garlands, the inventor of forests and the willing field, the figure thanks to whom I had found my voice and my soul as well, which were forever his. All this I told him in a long period of rolling crowns, as he had once defined the sentence, and without a tear.

He said nothing, and put his hand on my shoulder.

When we descended to the carriage I carried neither personal possessions nor my journal, though in a silken purse tied to my apron I bore with me my host of golden bands that Seigneur had removed from the long thin legs of the white birds: bore with me those trinkets that never again entered my mind, though I thought them charmed.

I had assumed that the shaven driver and abject horse would come suddenly alive and rush Seigneur to his doom, but they did not. Was it that the mute driver wished to prolong our final moments on the universal calendar of dreams and stars? to provide us with our last illusion of leisure in which to value the passing fields and the few clouds drifting above us? Suffice it to say that I did not enumerate Seigneur's creations, as once he had requested me to do, and that we rode entirely in silence to Le Baron's château, which proved to be our destination.

It was a low, squat, ugly pile of walls and turrets on the horizon, a place that declaimed its impregnability to anyone who might chance to see it, and breathed off a fetid air appropriate to the ceremony it would host this day. The black rooks massed above it in circling flight were as thickly congregated as were the great stones composing the château. The entire company of rooks cried out their warning at our approach, though we were hardly an enemy to that château so clearly and abominably the residence of an aggressive mind.

We entered its mighty gates and stopped beneath a gloomy arch and were met by a slight woman clothed all in black. We alighted.

"Noblesse," said Seigneur gently, and moved thoughtlessly in her direction as if he possessed her still.

"No," said the woman, though I too recognized all too well the severity of the small white face. "No," she said again, "you are mistaken. I am La Baronne de Fontfroide."

"And soon, I see, to bear a child," remarked Seigneur without further comment.

She turned, knowing we were obliged to follow, and led us into an untended cloister four times the size of the cloister at Dédale but overgrown, half wild, and given this moment to the rompings of two tawny mastiffs that sported in the ruined flower beds and even raced around the stake and faggots that occupied the gravelly center of this foul space. At the sight of the mammoth post and its still unlighted heaps of fuel I felt my first and only sensation of fear. The preparations for execution were worse than the event to come, and for that instant my eyes were contaminated, my breath choked off, and all my being scorched as to a cinder. How could it be suffered, that death? How could I watch? Then the sensation passed, my spirits revived, and I noted that the limbless tree to which the body of Seigneur would soon be bound was tall, rough, black, and as ominous and hence majestic as the man himself.

The last Noblesse, for such she was to me and thusly I would think of her from start to finish, led us across the cloister without a word and without a glance toward the waiting pyre, though it could not have loomed larger and had taken her workmen long hours to build. Broken stone serpents coiled up the cloister columns; the cold sun shone down upon the centrally positioned pyre; the brute dogs tumbled silently in that hapless place.

She opened a heavy door and passed into a vast salon whose leaded windows gave onto the decaying cloister and whose entire atmosphere was of dead smoke. We followed. In this cold room I determined to resist dejection and meet each approaching minute with good grace. The last Noblesse opened a smaller door at the far end of this dank hall, indicated to Seigneur that he was to enter, which he did, then blocked my way with her little figure and turned to me. I caught a glimpse of the rest of them in the smaller room, saw them clustering around Seigneur.

But now my view as well as my way was blocked.

"You who have seen so much shall not see this," said the last Noblesse in a cold voice, and stepped through the narrow door and shut it.

For the second time that day I was alone. But if I could not see I could still hear, and swiftly I pressed my ear to the dismal wood. The red and purple furnishings of the vast salon where I waited; the stone hearth larger and colder than any I had ever seen; the dust and cobwebs that transformed grandeur into death and ruthlessness, so that I could not tell what dreadful man or creature might now be creeping upon me from behind: for all this, and the possibilities of a different order of fear, I cared nothing, gave not a thought, as I pressed myself to ancient wood in order to receive in all of me the information which now I craved. Every sound was clear! I heard it all! Seven women were in the act of rending my Seigneur, for my eye had taken in one fragment of that female bulk belonging to no other than La Comtesse, whom at this moment I denied as mother. Yet the cold and strident voice I heard belonged not to La Comtesse but to La Baronne, so that age and rank had given way to youth.

"Bare your breasts, mesdames," cried the young voice through the door, "as I bare mine!"

Then I discovered that the last Noblesse was wrong, for not only could I plainly hear but see as well: not through any crack or keyhole, but in my mind! I heard the murmurings of all those women and their exertions, yet saw them loosening the cloth and pulling free, and letting the tops of their black gowns hang down. I heard the sounds of breathing, yet saw the naked bosoms thrust without mercy toward Seigneur. I heard the crackling of a fire, yet saw that they stood close to it for light and that it was a small fierce imitation of the immense fire in which within the hour Seigneur would burn. Close to the fire two chains hung from a ratcheted device affixed to the ceiling. By this device the chains could be tightly raised.

"Now, Madame," came the next command, "make fast his wrists in the irons . . . so . . . and pull the chains . . . so . . . haul high those bold wrists and arms. . . ."

I heard the clanking of the links, the turning of the ratcheted wheel lost in the darkness, and saw the great arms raised and from them the massive body suspended helplessly, with the poor feet supporting but half his weight on the stone floor.

"There he hangs, mesdames, our prize! See how he breathes in our scent, and how his eyes are fixed on our nakedness, and how he cannot help himself and swells in his britches! Yes, mesdames, the lust he taught us, and inspired, and which he refused to appease or even acknowledge through the slightest reciprocity in his own flesh, our lust now comes home to him full score, and shall destroy the manhood he withheld from us! He is only a man, as we have always known: a man, a beast, and not a god. Yet not a man, or less than a man, in the abominable arrogance of his chaste being. But now we shall see what we have never been allowed to see: expose what until this moment he has so well concealed. Loose the britches, Madame, and let them fall. . . ."

I squeezed shut my eyes but could not obliterate the sight. I saw it as clearly as under glass. I was overcome with Seigneur's indignity, but did not faint.

"There it is!" came the elated voice. "There stands the case between us! There sways his pride! There, mesdames, is the model for his Tapestry of Love, as I may tell you who shall never see it! The model is worthy of the weaver's art, as I may add."

"But what a waste of abstinence!"

"Oh, sad disuse!"

"How like the man . . ."

"But must we burn this man?"

"Now, mesdames," continued the last Noblesse, disregarding the speaker whose question clearly implied a change of heart, "now each of us shall take her leave of it, beginning with you, Madame . . . so . . . just so . . . and you, Madame . . . and you . . . and me . . . whom he cannot bear and struggles to refuse, as I have often imagined him, mesdames: grossly exposed, doomed, a monument of pain brought down at last, not for his pleasure but for our revenge. . . ."

He moaned. He moaned again. He moaned protractedly, though with such restraint that his poor sounds hardly reached me through the door. Still did I try fruitlessly to stop my ears against them with two hands, yet was forced to watch. My creator and protector surged in his chains, but was no match for them.

"Now, Madame! The privilege is yours! The moment is yours! Be bold! Be irresistible! . . . Just so. . . . Be rough! . . . Exactly so. . . . Be swift! . . . Just so. . . . Just so. . . . Now spare it not! . . . Bravo! Bravo, Madame! See the ignominy in which it dies! . . . What an amusing sight!"

I turned. The curtain fell. In my cold room I waited for more sounds, for the sounds of voices, or those of feet. But there were none. Even his chains were silent when they freed him, as freed him they surely did and removed him by some secret exit, for my narrow door remained unyielding, no matter how grievingly or angrily I tried it. It was then that I knew, in that cold room, how much they despised me, had in fact despised me during all our days at Dédale, for they did not come for me, had forgotten me, and what clearer sign of how they felt toward me could there have been?

When finally I made my way outside and found a column behind which I could stand and wait and watch unobserved, the entire assemblage was already in place, and still the sun was cold. There stood Seigneur, clothed again and tied to the stake; there stood seven women with bosoms once again trussed in modesty; there too, on the other side of the pyre, stood two regally attired men in plumes and ruffles. How large and fat was Le Baron! How thin and hardly recognizable was Le Comte de Cocagne, who was Père La Tour to me, as always! If I detested, as indeed I did, Le Baron, now married, I detested more Le Comte de Cocagne: he who had been displaced by his son, dismissed from his own marriage by his wife, demeaned by both, yet now accepted reinstatement with plumes flying and a beribboned decoration on his breast! Better had he remained in Seigneur's stables! But my attention turned: helplessly I studied the two dogs sitting patiently; the two ignoble men holding their torches that were aflame; the last Noblesse, who stood before Seigneur with head erect and belly bursting her black silhouette. Silence swelled the cloister and I clung to my column.

"Seigneur," cried the last Noblesse, signaling her henchmen to apply their torches to the pyre, "speak now, if speak you must. But briefly."

A single rook dipped low as if to alight in the silence and tangled growth of this fell scene of judgment, then swooped upwards and away. A face of some little servant appeared in a window and remained to watch. The plumes were undulating, though the air was still. Now the fire was making its first circle around Seigneur. There was no smoke.

"Mesdames," he called in his clear and undaunted voice, "I have helped you to discover for yourselves and within yourselves the art of pleasing, the rhetoric of pleasing, the sense of pleasing, and its music. Many have died happily for less."

Each face betrayed the eagerness of its spectator, while all of them gave way, reluctantly, before the heat.

"Seigneur," cried the last Noblesse, "at this moment when you are burning, so burns Dédale! The flames climb about your body and about Dédale! Your art is gone! Your art is dead! In days to come, nothing shall remain of it but a few blackened stones. In the years to come, even the blackened stones shall have disappeared. Your page is justly blank, Seigneur. Our condemnation ends."

The cloister filled with a still colder light. We breathed the ashes of Seigneur. The light wavered, grew more intense, and still he lived. Then, before succumbing, he cried out to me.

"Virginie!" he shouted as he burned. "Destroy your innocence!"

I looked at his clear and fading figure. I looked around the cloister and felt the cold stone. Then I ran forward to do his bidding and, unseen and unimpeded, since all eyes were on the suffering man, thus I reached the great pyre and flung myself, and hence my innocence, into its embrace of flames.

HER FINAL ENTRY

Brightness falls from the air. The day dies. I am committed to the earth at last. I am become at last what I always was for my Maman.

Remember the ghosts of dead flowers.